Claimed

A.D. Martins

New Generation Publishing

This book has been produced with assistance from
The London Borough of Barking and Dagenham
Library Service
Pen to Print Creative Writing Project 2017/18
with funding from
The Arts Council, England Grants for the Arts.

Supported using public funding by
ARTS COUNCIL
ENGLAND
LOTTERY FUNDED

London Borough of
Barking&Dagenham
lbbd.gov.uk

For all those who are battling demons, keep fighting.

1

Every muscle went stiff. His heart hammered heavily in his chest, reverberating through his ears. Palms sweaty. The sticky heat formed droplets in the nook of his back.

"Not me!" he whispered, desperately trying to regain control.

He needed to make the necessary precautions for the hours ahead, but it was past curfew. A crack of light crept through the curtains, illuminating Jacob's face.

"Eurgh, I forgot them, how did I forget them," he announced angrily to an empty room.

I could just use the sheets. That'll work.

It won't work. It didn't work for Hayden.

But Hayden left the window open for Christ's sake. She was asking to be claimed. I'll be okay, it won't get me... I'll be alright.

It's six steps, total. It's worth the risk. Go on. Move it. Now.

Okay, okay, I can do this. I have to do this I've heard the stories and I don't want to end up like them. I don't want to wake to the feeling of hot sticky blood soaking into my pyjamas. Or the cackling calls of his laughter as he glides a razor sharp nail across my wrists. I have to get the bandages.

His lungs felt heavy, a pressure built on his chest. Panting, he tried to get his breathing under control. He felt the pressure shifting, climbing up and settling just behind his left ear. He seized the panic, harnessing it. Closed his eyes, took one final breath, pulled back the covers and leapt.

His foot landed with a thud onto the unvarnished floorboards. Splinters dug sharply in between his toes causing him to wince in pain. He twisted his body trying not to let it hit the ground.

"1, 2, 3," Jacob felt his lips move and had to silence them with his hand.

His muscles tightened and his toes curled inwards desperately trying to maintain his balance.

Thud.

He landed inches away from the loose board. It had caused so many to be claimed, even before Jacob had arrived.

Another deep breath, *it's taking too long, hurry up!*

Suddenly the overwhelming fear bubbled up, his fingers and toes twitched as minuscule impulses convulsed through his body. Pressure built around his eyes and his muscles ached as though he had been smiling too much. With his face screwed up, he gulped, hoping the saliva would coat the fear and drag it down away from his mind. He needed to keep his head clear if only for the next few minutes.

This one was always the trickiest, his body was growing and he couldn't fit behind the table as easily as he had done years ago. He managed to keep his momentum going. Foot, hand, fingers all stretching out simultaneously. The thick white gauze caught against flakes of skin. The fabric scratched slightly as he tucked it deep within the folds of his shirt.

The three steps back, happened without much thought. His body took over and the first thing he remembered was slipping the covers back over his head, making sure every inch of his body was held in the comforting cocoon of his bed. Jacob reached within the folds of his shirt, feeling his fingers lightly brush against the cloth. He grasped the bandages and pulled them free, twisting and wrapping them around his right wrist in a circle of 8, only stopping to pull the fabric tight. He heard his whispers, "palm, wrist, palm, wrist, palm, wrist," it had become like a prayer for him, a mantra of hope.

A dull throb built in his fingers, quickly turning into tingling. Movement in his hand was restricted by the time he had finished. Wrapping the left wrist was always more difficult. He held the end of the bandage in his palm and wedged the remaining coil into his mouth. Dry fuzz clung to his tongue. He twisted both arm and head around in matching motions until his left wrist was engulfed in layers of cloth. His teeth rippled down his tongue, restoring the moisture to his mouth.

Jacob's stomach turned over, the feeling of butterflies twitched through his muscles as his shoulders sunk deep within the folds. The moment of triumph made him smile.

"Not me, you're not getting me."

Prickles of cold travelled down his body making every nerve stand on end. He lay on his right side. One hand pushed down into the mattress. The pillow sat squarely on top. His other arm rested close to his face, so close in fact, little balls of sweat formed on his nose as the heat radiated from his bandaged limb.

Pushing his head into position, the cold metal bar pressed against his forehead. He squinted as the light from the window streamed down the tubes, bouncing from mirror to mirror until it reached his straining eyes.

Slowly, his mind drifted. Names scrolled through his thoughts, he caught some of them and others went too fast for him to hold on to. So many had been claimed. He started to think of her, she filled his mind and he let a sad smile curl over his lips. Giggling, smiles and cuddles. Replaced. The whites of her knuckles, fists clenched, eyes wide. The noise expelled from her tinged lips, deep and anguished. Tears welled in his eyelids, trickling down his face.

A high pitched scream pulled him away from his thoughts. His lungs burnt as he held his breath, forcing all of his concentration to search for the smallest of noises, anything that would pinpoint where it had come from. The glass of the windows vibrated.

Oh shit, he's here. Help. Help. Shit. No, no, no, no, no, no!

His eyes were still bathed in darkness. His forehead pressed against the cold metal cutting into his skin.

Open your eyes.

Geez, those lights are bright.

3

Huh…

Nothing there.

His neck uncoiled from his shoulders, shuffling down against the pillows. The power fizzled in the street lamps. Jacob blinked against the momentary glare.

What!

No. Wait. Deep breaths, the power's out again. That's all, just the power.

The lights flickered on. He heard the sigh before it had left his lips. It caught and twisted into a gasp then a scream. The yellowing eye stared back at him through the crack in the curtains.

Hayden, Marie, Rob, James, Alex… oh Alex, but not me, not me!

Every muscle strained. Nails dug deep within his palms. The eye continued to stare. It seemed to be getting closer. His body repulsed and he fought to pull away. Erratic heart beats pulsed through his ears. His chest began to heave under the weight of his quickening breaths.

I can't get out. It's past curfew. They've locked the doors. Shit. What do I do?

Stay here.

No, that's stupid, I'll get claimed.

Hide then.

Stupid!

Fight? Fight!

A nail dug into the glass, etching and scraping. Jacob recoiled from the noise. He wanted to look, but knew he should find something to defend himself with. Scrambling across the room, he fumbled to pick up the bowling pin from the shelf. It dropped to the floor.

"Oh crap, the bandages."

It was less than a second between realisation and the feeling of teeth ripping against fabric, struggling and searching to find the end he had tucked within the folds. His head and hand contorting, twisting faster and faster. As the gauze fell, the sound rose.

Come on, come on!

The last few inches of gauze fell away. He started to claw at his right hand, pulling the bandages off in clumps. The gentle tapping increased, acting as a soundtrack to his panic.

Shit, shit, shit. It won't come off. Why won't it come off? Grab something, anything. Quick!

He reached out and grabbed the bowling pin with his free hand and wielded it like a baseball bat. As he turned, weapon in hand, his ears were met with silence.

Black smoke began to waft out of the viewing tube. At first it was just a wisp, stinging his eyes and causing him to blink.

No.

What the…?!

This isn't real.

The smoke shifted and changed, building up momentum as it lurched forward, now billowing from the tube. He hit at it with the bowling pin, but it danced around his attacks with a merriment and glee that only brought more fear. This was The Raven and his enjoyment sickened Jacob to his core. His mind raced, thinking about her.

Oh my God Alex, is this what you felt? I can't.

"Help me, someone, help me!"

The smoke began to take form. Jacob saw the darkest, densest black and what looked like fingers, reaching out, searching for him. He tried to bat them away but the tip of one brushed against his skin. Every nightmare, every wrong choice, every moment of pain he had ever experienced flooded into his mind.

Jacob froze. The screams were his own. Blood rushed through his ears overwhelming his senses. Smoke seemed to seep into his eyes, blocking out his peripheral vision. Spirals of smoke coiled together forming a misty arm stretching. The long fingers searching, hovering inches away, plunging forwards deep into his chest.

Stop! Get out. No. No. No. Shit. Get out.

The blackened nails dug deep into his flesh, clawing

through the fat and muscle and twisting through his bones. Cracks echoed in his ears and he inhaled sharply, compounding the pain. Jacob's muscles spasmed, trapping his hands into malformed claws. His skin went taut, pulling against itself, aching and ripping. His head lolled forwards, eyes rolling wildly. Glimpses of The Raven's arm protruding from his chest made him gag in repulsion. The acid rose into his throat, burning. The blackened nails cut like razor blades, edging slowly closer into the chambers of his heart.

The smoke danced, twisting into Jacob's arteries, flowing away in his blood. With his pulse rate fuelled by panic every pump of his heart forced The Raven's hold further, deeper into his organs. His back arched, forcing his head backwards and causing him to crack it hard against the wall. Intense pain rippled forwards, then stopped. The pain merged, pushing back against the source, blue flames danced within his vision. Crackles rang out so loud Jacob felt warm trickles of blood pool in his ears.

Just for a second, pure darkness and joy danced within him. His muscles twitched and tremored. He felt The Raven's rush at holding a life in his hands, feeling a pulse quicken, each beat bringing a new wave of excitement. Jacob's thoughts turned back to darkness, as the fingers took hold and the blackened nails plunged ever deeper into his heart. He saw her face and screamed the same anguishing cry he had heard leave his sister's lips six months before.

2

The man stared into the mirror whilst he waited for the laptop to load. His tired sunken eyes stared back at him.

"I'm getting too old," he said gruffly.

A coarse callused hand reached up and gripped the knot of his tie. Straightening it in the mirror, he smiled softly and stroked the arms of his suit to flatten out the wrinkles. The newspaper fell with a thud through the letterbox and he tripped over his own feet as he ran to pick it up anticipating what would be inside.

Unfolding the pages carefully and placing them on the kitchen table, he sneaked a look at the front page as he made breakfast. The headline grabbed his attention.

'The Raven strikes again'.

He felt a gleeful shiver course through his veins.

Beep!

Jumping at the noise he turned to the laptop and using one hand typed the password, as he placed the bread into the toaster with the other. He scrolled through the start menu, quietly berating himself for not putting the news icon on his desktop yet.

It loaded and he cautiously sat down, being careful not to crease his suit.

'Police believe The Raven has struck again as a 15 year old boy vanished last night from his room at the Elm Park children's home. The 15 year old, who cannot be named at present, was discovered missing in the early hours of the morning after one of the other residents raised the alarm. It is believed he was taken shortly after curfew. Police and social services are discussing the security measures in place and whether more can be done to protect these vulnerable children. The head care worker at the home refused to comment about the current security measures, however the police have confirmed they are currently investigating the boy's disappearance and haven't ruled out the possibility he has been claimed. Eyewitness reports state that the room appears to have been left largely untouched. There was a small hole in the window, but police are baffled about how a boy could have disappeared from the room without triggering the motion detectors in the corridors.

The term 'claimed' was coined by Veronica Pilton 5 years ago after a string of unusual disappearances. She used the description in one of her articles for the Daily News to describe the peculiar nature of the crimes. She said 'kidnapping makes it sound human and I believe from the witness statements I have received that whatever is taking these people is not human. It appears it is "laying claim" to them based on their past experiences.' The term has widely been used since whenever a new victim is taken.

Further information about the latest abduction will be listed as breaking news throughout the day.'

A sinister smile passed over his lips. He licked them gently, scrolled down to the end of the article and clicked on the email icon. The screen turned blue and an envelope appeared. Beep, beep, beep! The smell of burnt toast filled his nostrils and he jumped up to stop the alarm before it woke all his neighbours.

"Ha, I need to be more careful," he muttered, whilst laughing to himself.

Unflinching, his fingers reached into the toaster and fished the blackened lumps of toast free from their metal cage.

Sitting down at the kitchen table, he absently rubbed against the red blisters beginning to form. Skin popped and serum puddled on to the wood. Underneath raw flesh throbbed. His fingers pulled and picked at the loose skin, ripping it clear. His mind began to wander. He was intrigued to know what else they would release in the next few hours.

It will just be his name and maybe how he ended up there. I wonder if they will mention Alex. It'll be more worthy of the headlines when they realise they're related. I doubt they will have much more than. I was very careful.

3

Come on Jacob, wakey wakey. Open your eyes. OPEN YOUR EYES! Look at the world Jacob. Look at the exquisite desolation. The lights dance in the darkness Jacob. They dance for me. Open your eyes, watch the shadows. They're calling to you Jacob. Take a look.

He tried to fight it, but he couldn't. Tentatively he opened them and gasped.

I'm running! Why don't I feel like I'm running? What's happening to me? I can't stop. Why can't I stop?

Hush now Jacob. Faster. Faster. FASTER!

His legs pounded deeper into the ground, each stride reaching for a longer distance than the last.

Jacob tried to take control, he willed his legs to stop, but each time he tried they just got quicker. The world around him was beginning to distort. The street lights and shop signs blurred into a visual cacophony of light. Jacob searched for somewhere he recognised but everything was happening too fast.

Soon the lights began to fade, solid blocks of colour thinned into lonely streams. Then the street lights disappeared altogether. The concrete turned to gravel under his feet. He could hear them scrape on the loose ground then squelch as they slipped in piles of mud.

Not long now, you're nearly home.

He was laughing at him, dancing with merriment around his building fear. Obscurity closed in on the edges of his vision. His mind was hazy and his focus was fading. When he awoke he was engulfed in darkness.

Are my eyes closed? I don't think they're closed. Ow! Ah, geez that stings. Stupid! Don't put your finger in your eye. You've got enough problems without blinding yourself.

He blinked to take away the mild burning sensation. His hand stretched out again and brushed against the cold rock.

What the..?
Where am I?
What happened?
How did I get here?
No.
Think.
Get up.
Search.
There has to be a way out.

Pushing against the rocks, he stumbled to his feet. The ground felt sharp and cold against his skin. Uneven terrain threw him off balance. He collapsed back to the ground, misjudging his landing.

"Ah shit, that hurt."

The pain ripped through his left hand, fleeting but intense. He instinctively reached across, clasping his right hand shut before he even realised. Soft, sticky heat oozed from his skin, he felt it soak through the bandages.

The bandages!

Grimacing in pain, he unwound the last of the gauze from his right hand. The blood trickled down, hindering his efforts, making the gauze slippery and sticky all at once. He twisted the bandage one last time and freed his right hand from its sheath. With as much speed as he could muster Jacob wrapped his aching hand in the bandages. His nostrils flared against the smell of sweat and dirt, musky but pleasant. He felt the warm blood seep through as he twisted and wrapped them around his left wrist in a circle of 8, only stopping to pull the fabric tight.

He heard his whispers, "palm, wrist, palm, wrist, palm, wrist," Jacob laughed, more of a scoff, so much for his mantra of hope.

He leant down and rubbed his feet with his good hand. Loose particles of gravel fell away. Dirt stung like salt as it inched into the multitude of lacerations scattered along the soles of his feet. They throbbed and his mind flicked back to the memory of running bare foot through the streets so fast and out of control. His mind was spinning like the

11

feeling of a high speed rollercoaster looping the loop. His hand rubbed against his eyes, introducing dirt into the crevices. Wincing at the pain he suddenly heard The Raven's voice.

"You're mine now!"

Jacob felt the icy fingers slowly, steadily caress his neck. Circling, then plummeting down his spine. His shoulders lurched forwards causing his body to shudder. His Mum used to describe the feeling as if someone was walking on her grave. He tried to shake the sensation, but it lingered and danced like The Raven's shadowy smoke. He swung his neck round without warning desperate to catch a glimpse of his assailant. An icy finger jabbed at his ribs. He swung back, fists high, ready to fight.

"You'll have to be quicker than that Jacob," whispered The Raven.

4

His fingers searched for traces of fresh blood. The bandages had hardened becoming crisp to the touch. Jacob felt flakes of blood crumble through his fingertips. The smell of iron filled his nostrils and he tilted his head back to try and escape it.

What's that?

I can see light.

Is it dust? You see it on the ghost programmes, orbs of light, it's always dust. It's swirling, dancing in the darkness.

Where did it go?

He strained his eyes against the darkness, searching for another.

"There it is!"

It floated down and gently landed on his arm. Just for a second Jacob could see the tiniest crease on his top; he smiled, but then searing pain ate into his skin.

"Ah, it's burning. Water. I need water."

Panicking, Jacob leapt from the rocks and slid into one corner of the chamber, huddling as close as he could to the cold soothing gentle drip, cascading down the flint.

"Ah, no! Please, stop! No, please."

As the pain burrowed deeper through each layer of flesh, he drifted in and out of consciousness. The pain seared through his memories and teetered on an image of his Mum.

"Mu, Mum."

"Five more minutes and they'll be ready," she said.

"They smell yummy. I like chocolate."

"I know you like chocolate Jacob. You're my little chocolate monster. Come here mister. Let me get the chocolate out of your hair."

She ruffled his short brown hair with her soft fingers. He leant into her and breathed in the sweet scent of rose and vanilla mixed with the faint aroma of hot chocolate ponge. Her arms wrapped around his tiny frame. His head pressed against her chest. Her dark green fleece muffled the steady beat of her heart.

"Come on, it's time to get the cakes out."

His hand fitted snuggly in hers and they skipped through the living room giggling. When they reached the kitchen, she pulled the tray out amidst the onslaught of steam that raced out as she opened the oven door.

"Remember Jacob, it's hot, so you need to be patient. Don't touch the tray."

His wide eyes stared up at her smiling.

A gentle chirping of a phone could be heard through the wall.

"Wait here Jacob, I'll be right back."

Standing patiently, he breathed deeply. His shoulders sighed happily.

"One little bit will be okay. It must be colder by now."

His scrawny arm reached up to the counter with his neck and arm stretching. Tiny fingers searched for the fluffy warm sponge and the gooey chocolate. He couldn't wait to feel it dripping down his chin. His mouth began to drool.

"Chocolate, chocolate, chocolate. I'm the chocolate monster," he giggled.

His fingers found the sponge and plunged deep within, trying to scrap it free from the tin. Through his screams he heard her quickened footsteps echo on the wooden floor.

"Jack, I've got to go. NO. I've got to go now. Jacob's hurt."

Her arms scooped his up, lifting his squirming body close to hers. Water splashed rapidly on to his fingers. It felt like jumping into the swimming pool, the coldness took his breath away.

"It's okay. I'm sorry Jacob, I'm sorry. It's going to be okay, it's going to be okay."

She grabbed his jacket with her free hand and threw it into the back seat of the car. Fuzz the bear was swept on to the floor, rolling under the front seat. A metallic taste from the keys covered her tongue and she half spat, half dropped them into the bag hanging around her neck. Clicking Jacob into his car seat she checked the cling film wrapped around his wound. The skin was mottled red, wet and blistered.

"Why did I answer the phone? Look at my baby, so stupid, so stupid."

The drive to the hospital was fraught with worry. Every set of traffic lights made her lean every closer to the wheel, willing them to change. When she got there, the doctors were brilliant. They took control, sat her down and made her drink some sweet tea, while they bathed his hand and gave him medicine to ease the pain. Riley sighed and took her phone out from her pocket.

"Hi Michael, I'm really sorry. I know you're at your job interview but there's been an accident. Jacob's in the hospital. We were baking cakes for you and my phone rang. I told him not to touch the tray, but I guess the temptation of chocolate was too much for him. I raced him straight here and they have been great with him. They reckon he's going to have a scar though."

"Riley, calm down. He's going to be alright, accidents happen. I'm on my way now. I'll be about ten minutes. Give him a big hug from me. I love you both, see you soon. Oh by the way I got the job."

Riley ended the call and waited for Michael to arrive. When he got there, he scooped her up in his arms and hugged her unconditionally.

"It's not your fault. Don't blame yourself. So where's my boy."

Riley led him through the double doors to a row of cubicles. Michael rushed to Jacob's side. His lips gently brushed against his cheek and he smiled at his brave son. After a few minutes, they saw his wide eyes smiling up at them.

Oh my God, he's okay. Oh Jacob.

"I love you," they muttered with tears in their eyes.

Jacob reached across and hugged his Mum and Dad.

15

"Are the cakes ready now?" he asked.

She shook her head and laughed.

"You can have as much cake as you like when we get home, but I'm not going to be baking any for a while."

Michael's strong arms wrapped around her shoulders and he rested his head next to hers. Riley cradled Jacob in her arms and sat on the side of the bed, rocking him gently as he fell asleep.

Jacob wavered back into consciousness longing for her to hold him and rock him to sleep like she had done that night in the hospital. His eyes misted over and tears rolled softly down his face. As he looked closer more specks gently floated down. Each one momentarily lit up part of the room. He saw something etched into the stone but couldn't get near enough to see what it was. Haunting howls of laughter echoed around the chamber. Each one coinciding with one of Jacob's screams.

Jacob's flesh was burning.

5

His screams had dried up to a whimper, but the remnants of them still echoed deep within the caves. His body rocked slowly, back and forth. With his knees tucked up to his chin and his hands cradling his head, his mind jumped.

Think about them.

*

"Mum, she's beautiful. Can I call her Super Girl?"

"I don't think Super Girl is quite right Jacob. I was thinking Alex?"

"Alex, Alex. I like Alex. There's an Alex in my class at school, but he's a boy. Hi Alex, I'm your big brother. I'm going to look after you and let you play with my toys and watch TV with me and here, his name is Fuzz. He'll look after you because I've got to go now. Nanny is taking me to her house so Mummy can stay here with you."

**

The cold winter air, nipped at their faces. Moisture rose visible in the air with every breath.

"Ready, steady, jump."

Splash.

The water spurted up around their knees and trickled back down inside their wellington boots.

"Again, again," called Alex.

"This one looks bigger. Can we Mum, can we?" said Jacob, whilst pointing his finger wildly.

"Ready, steady, jump."

"Argh! You've soaked me. Just you wait, I'm going get you," Michael laughed as he chased them across the tarmac and on to the grass. His huge arms wrapped around Jacob whilst Riley grabbed Alex.

***

"Hahahahaha. Do the princess voice Mummy. The princess needs to come and save the day."

"Okay, Okay 'I'm here to rescue you dear knight from the evil dragon," she said in a high pitched squeak.

"Use my sword to cut me free," Jacob said in the deepest voice he could muster.

Alex giggled, bouncing gently on the bed. "More, more," she called.

****

"No. I want the toy this time. You got the last one. Mum, Mum, Alex took the toy and it's my turn to have it. I poured the breakfast, so I get the toy," he whined.

"You need to share the toys. Let her play with it for a bit. Oh man, the smoke alarm is going off again, ah, the toast," she called as she frantically waved a tea towel at the beeping box on the ceiling.

*****

The beeping got louder, twisting into screams and dragging him back to the realisation of where he was. His shoulders sunk and a gentle stream trickled past his nose.

I'm no good to anyone. I wasn't able to protect my Mum or Alex. No one will miss me. No one will remember me. I'll just be another forgotten face in the crowd. You win. I give up. Just kill me already. Come on. Just kill me.

6

Six months ago

Paintings and drawings scattered the walls. Football trophies sat along the windowsill, glimmering in the moonlight.

"Time for bed. Come on, before they lock the doors."

Alex scuttled across the floor of her room and clambered beneath the covers. Jacob reached across and carefully straightened the duvet, making sure the sides lined up exactly with the edges of the bed.

"Jacob. I'm scared. Can't I sleep in your room?"

"You know you can't Alex. Boys and girls aren't allowed to share rooms."

"We did at home."

"Yeah, but we aren't at home anymore are we. Come on, it'll be alright. Close your eyes and think of Mum. Fuzz is here to protect you."

Jacob lovingly placed Fuzz under the covers, gently lifting her arm and placing the tatty teddy into the nook of her elbow. He kissed her on the forehead and turned off the lights.

"Sleep tight, see you in the morning light."

Alex blinked against the darkness. She dreaded going to bed, her dreams would twist into nightmares and she would wake up screaming. She thought about calling out to him or making up some excuse so he would stay just a little bit longer, but she knew he had to go to his room and she had to stay in this one.

Jacob felt the soft fluff of the carpet under his toes as he walked the short distance to his room next door. The floorboard near the chest of drawers squeaked loudly as he stood on it absent-mindedly. The sound made him cringe. He reached out, grabbed the bandages and sat on the edge of his bed, twisting them carefully around one wrist then the next.

Flicking back the covers, he climbed into bed and closed his eyes. He let the waves of calm roll down his body and was just drifting off, when he heard it. At first he hadn't been sure what the sound was, it was shrill and piercing. He couldn't move, his muscles tightened and pinned him to the spot.

His rapid breathing matched his heart beat.

Just wait.

Listen.

Oh man, I can't hear anything.

Silence, shit.

Maybe I dreamt it. No, I couldn't have. Erm, what shall I do?

What shall I do?

The next sound he had heard was laughter. It cut deeper than the scream. He felt it tremor through his bones. The hairs on his arms stood and despite the warmth of the duvet, he instantly felt desperately cold.

Go. Get up. Something's wrong.

His feet treaded unsteadily towards the door. Shaking, he reached out for the metal door handle and pushed all his weight down on top of it, but it wouldn't budge.

Argh, they've locked them already. Why didn't I take the key yesterday when Matt put it down?

Because he would have got in trouble.

Yeah, but now someone else in in trouble and I'm locked in here. What if it's Alex? Erm, oh man, shit, wait, the hole in the wall.

He leant his body against the cool brickwork and placed his eye to the narrow gap, terrified of what he would find on the other side. His eye scanned around the room searching for her.

She was crouched cowering in the corner. Fuzz's eyes bulged from the pressure on his stuffing as she gripped him tightly across her chest. Her hand rested on the Nephrite jade necklace hanging around her neck. It had belonged to her Mum, Riley. Legend has it the spirit of each wearer is carried in the stone. It symbolised friendship, two lives interwoven for eternity.

Darkness surrounded her, billowing and engulfing.

Alex, Alex, do something. Grab something. Hide, run, do something!

Is that smoke?

No, there's no flames. There's no fire.

Little wisps of smoke danced, edging closer to her huddled body. It twisted and formed into a figure, jet black, stretching above her and towering seven foot high. He could smell dust, damp and sulphur.

No, not Alex. Come on Alex, move, move.

I can't watch this.

He tried desperately to close his eyes, but something inside willed him to keep them open. Large silent tears streamed down his face.

He called out to her, "Alex. Run! Run!"

She didn't move. Every muscle was frozen to the spot. He tried again, this time pleading with the creature.

"Take me. Take me and leave her."

The Raven stretched out his arm and plunged it through her chest. Her lips pursed into a scream. The same shrill piercing cry that had awoken him. The football trophies vibrated gently on the windowsill, reverberating from the noise. Beads of sweat rolled profusely down her forehead. Eyes wide. Her breathing was laboured. He could see the rapid rise and fall of her chest. Her limbs shook uncontrollably.

The long fingers clamped around her heart. The Raven's twisted joy danced within her bones. A subtle fleeting smile crossed her lips.

Why is she smiling? What it is doing to her?

"Leave her alone."

Jacob saw her trembling lips move, forming the same shapes he had seen them do for over 10 years. This time was different. No word was uttered, no sounds reached his ears. She was calling out his name. Tears mixed with sweat rolled silently down her face. He could swear she

21

caught his eye before she turned to smoke and disappeared.

7

Jacob lay on the floor staring into the darkness. His hand danced in the air above him. He used to be able to fixate on the motion but now all he could feel was the gently breeze his movements created.

Why can't I turn my brain off? I just want it to stop.

Ha, you're stuck here now. Never going to get out. Here forever, locked in the darkness. You should have jumped when you had the chance. The sparks from the tracks would have lit you alive as you died. The impact would have been much quicker than this. Bone shattering, sure. Your organs would have been torn to pieces, ripped to shreds as minute pieces of bones tore through. But no, you thought of everyone else.

Stop it! Stop it! Stop it! You know I couldn't do it. It wouldn't be fair. This is my curse. If I'd jumped, the driver, the passengers, the families wishing their loved one a safe trip from the platform edge, all their lives would have been changed. The curse would pass to them. They would sit and wonder. Ponder if there had been anything they could do. Replay the moment, over and over. I couldn't do it to someone else. I wouldn't wish this depression on anyone else. It's not fair. It's not right.

Ha, and all the scenarios are the same, right? Someone always finds the body in the end. Selfless to the last.

I'm not selfless. I'm terrified of dying. The inbuilt fear to survive at all costs runs through me. But if I die, when I die, I'm not afraid of death. I just hope the voice constantly in my ear dies with me.

The chamber was getting darker, his painful shadows brought around a darkness of their own.

He threw his head back and screamed, "What do you want from me?"

Sometimes he thought he heard whispers in the night time and laughter through the day, though he wasn't sure which was which any more.

"Jacob, I'm still here. I'm watching. I'm waiting. I did it with Alex too. She was strong but I broke her. Her little mind had seen so much grief. She called out for you Jacob, day after day reciting your name until her vocal chords rung dry in her throat. Even then she kept trying. Body broken, mind torn, but still clinging on to hope. Eventually the darkness and screaming echoes took their toll. Rocking back and forth just like you. Voices shrieking in her head. Torn and broken Jacob, torn and broken."

His fingers scratched into his skin, "Alex! Alex, I'm sorry!"

The repetitive pressure gave Jacob something else to focus on. His nerves fired off messages to his brain, but instead of adding to his pain, it soothed him. He felt the flakes build under his fingernails and the warm drips trickle down his arm.

He had started this process seven years ago when his Mum died. He hadn't even realised he was doing it until the police officer had grabbed his hands in desperation. Shock has many different outlets even for an eight year old. As Jacob had grown up he had found other ways to deal with the pain, pushing his body to the limits, swimming, running, lifting weights, building his muscles to control his mind.

In the distance a noise reverberated around the caverns. Jacob was only half listening, absorbed in his own thoughts until it echoed again. Someone was calling out to him in the distance.

It can't be, can it? This is just another one of The Raven's tricks. It's not real. She's dead. They're all dead.

There it was again, louder, clearer, as though his ears were now more attuned to the frequency.

"Jacob, help me!"

His pulse quickened and he tried desperately to control his breathing, panting, in and out, in and out.

It was her. It was Alex and she was alive.

He called out to her again, "Alex, I'm coming. Hold on."

He remembered back to when the burning lights fell. There was something on the rocks surrounding him. The words etched high above. Too high for him to read in the darkness, but maybe, just maybe he could reach them. His fingers searched to find any indents deep in the rock. The first was about a foot above his head. He pulled at the bandages, freeing his hand and stuffing them between the waistband of his trousers. He paused, pressing his fingers into the palm of his hand. The skin was tender to the touch and he hoped the red raw skin below had melded back together enough to take the strain.

Jacob didn't waste any time clambering up. The rocks jarred and sliced into his hands as his feet desperately tried to get a purchase against the wall. He managed to hoist himself up and jabbed his fingers into the second hole, almost losing his balance as the rock scrapped against his knuckles.

You can't do this. You're gonna fall. It's just a trick anyway. You won't find her.

Shut up!

He heard her voice calling out to him again, "Jacob!"

"I'm coming Alex. I'm coming."

Beads of moisture collected in the lines of his palms and he could feel his fingers slipping. He swung his arm up outstretched, using his adrenaline to push himself further. Toes scratching against the wall finding a place to rest, while his fingers searched for another hole in the rock. Slowly, Jacob managed to work his way up the precipice.

His fingers settled again, this time finding loose gravel and soft earthy ground. Jacob wedged his elbow into a crevice and pushed through the pain to hoist his body up on to the ledge. He used his hands carefully in the darkness to scope out which parts of the rock were safe.

He edged his fingers further from his body searching for the rocks ahead. They were sloping upwards but it was a steady incline and he knew he would be able to inch his way through. Pushing his back against the wall he kept

25

pressure against the rocks. He heard her again, she sounded so lost, so empty.

"It's okay Alex. I'm coming, hold on," he said, trying to reassure her, but he could hear the terror in her reply.

"Jacob, he's coming. Run!"

8

He ran towards Alex's screams with his arms stretched out in front of him, searching for safety through the darkness. Each scream seemed louder, more intense than the last. The Raven was with her, Jacob was sure of it.

Got to hurry up. I need to find her.

"Ow!"

Pain shot through his knuckles into his wrist. He stumbled to his knees, cradling his hand to his chest and muttering a barrage of swear words under his breath. Each word cleared his mind and somehow it helped with the pain.

I can't do this. I need to slow down. I'm no good to her dead.

He stumbled to his feet again and walked on blindly into the darkness. Each step was tentative, testing his footing before putting his full weight down. He waved his hands methodically in front of him like some weird slow motion Mexican wave, searching for low stalactites and cave walls standing in his way. The air stung against his knuckles. He pulled the bandages from his waistband and bound them around his right hand, just short of the blood throbbing tightness he was used to. It became harder to breathe, his nose was blocked, mucus mixed with tears and his eyes clouded over. His head fell into his hands and he wept whilst her cries echoed around him.

He felt his mind wandering again.

He saw the sprinkling of freckles encircled by her dusty brown hair. Riley's kind hazel eyes and the smell of her leather jacket. The sweet smell of roses against her skin. Just for a second he thought she was there with him again and everything was how it used to be. He felt her cuddling him and the lightest kiss upon his forehead as she tucked him in at night. The gentle tones of whispered lullabies singing in his ears. His breathing slowed and his mind began to focus again.

He called to Alex through the caves, "Think of Mum, remember Mum. She's always with you."

Forcing himself upright, he looked at the ground beneath him. Waves of black danced at his feet giving the illusion of being at sea. His eyes tried to find a point to focus on. Dizziness swept across his vision. Nausea surged and sank from the pit of his stomach. He reached out to steady himself on the rocks.

Once it had past, Jacob set off again. His left hand was splayed out in front of him and he felt the cold breeze as he waved it around. Alex's screams had settled to an intermittent whimper. Each step brought back a cascading flow of memories. He focused on the first night without his Mum.

*

In the hospital he had hugged Alex, rocking her gently as she lay on the chairs next to him. Her legs were pulled up tightly to her chest. Her face was red and blotchy from crying. With his free hand shaking slightly he wiped his own tears from his face before they gently dripped down on to hers. They both heard the doctor's voice but it was hazy and unfocused. Jacob tried to clear the fog, desperately starring at the doctor's lips hoping his brain would process some of the information. He felt numb. An unsettled calmness had fallen upon him. He heard one word, 'died'.

He'd known she was dead when he found the body. When he had shook his mother's shoulders desperately screaming her name, willing her to come back to them. When his tiny hands had pumped down rhythmically on her chest, replaying the first aid lessons he had had at school, but the odds had changed. He wasn't with his friends checking a dummy for life and knowing he wouldn't find any. It hadn't been a game that night.

Jacob's eyes, red and sore, fell away from the doctor's lips and down to his light blue trainers, though they weren't light blue anymore. Stained a dark crimson, his shirt was the same. He heard the word "changed" and flinched as clothes were hovered in front of his face. His hands settled on the folds of fabric. They were soft and warm. He pulled his eyes up from his shoes and saw a young nurse staring at him, her make up slightly smudged around her eyes.

He got changed, fidgeting as the ill-fitting clothes swamped his tiny frame. He waited for the nurse to finish helping Alex change and on her return he took her pale hand in his. They walked in silence down the corridor to a dimly lit room with two beds. Jacob had tucked his sister deep within the folds of the sheets, refusing any help from the nurse. He clambered into the bed next to hers and closed his eyes hoping he would wake to his Mum's voice.

He hadn't heard Alex get up, or felt her climb into the bed beside him, but suddenly she was there hugging him and rocking him like he had done earlier that night.

She pulled herself up to his ear and whispered sweetly, "It's okay Jacob, I'm here. Mummy will always love us."

He lifted the sheets high above his head and rolled over to face her. His left hand found her right and he held it tightly. Their fingers merging together, pressing into the mattress. They cuddled each other, whilst Alex rested her head into his chest and they both wept softly.

Jacob's mind came back to the present with a jolt. The ground fell away. He scrambled to regain control. Hands scraped against the gravel, loose rocks fell into the caverns below and his legs dangled into the darkness. Pulse racing, chest pounding. Beads of sweat formed on his palms and he fought to find something to hold on to. His fingers scrabbling, twisting to take hold.

"No!"

His voice caught as he plummeted down through the darkness. Arms and legs flailed outwards. Panic rose in his throat, gulping, he tried desperately to keep the vomit down. His body thudded against the rocks, twisting his falling carcass ninety degrees. His chest heaved against the pain. Muscle contracted from his toes to his hip as grit dug and grated against his flesh. Edging his body along the ground, he feared debris would still tumble down on top of him.

After a few metres he heard a whisper in the darkness, "Stop."

What was that? There's someone here. Oh, please be Alex, please. Did I hit my head on the way down? I can't hear anything.

"Stop."

It wasn't Alex. He strained to hear the voice. It was older and much closer.

"Stop! You'll do more damage. I'm coming!"

Jacob looked pointlessly into the darkness, staring, hoping to see a flicker of light or shadow. There was nothing, just the emptiness and a murmur of calm.

The rocks are falling. Someone's coming.

Breathe.

Turn over.

You need to be ready to fight them off.

Forcing himself on to his back, he propped himself up against the cold weathered rocks. He held his fists up to his face, guarding himself from attack. Adrenaline pumped through his blood. His breath whistled in his ears as he panted, inhaling sharply and holding it, searching through the echoes.

This might be The Raven. Be ready.

The sound of the rocks ricocheting, a scrambling from above and the gentle tread of feet on gravel was getting closer. He felt the air around him move. A light breeze indicated someone was nearby. The hairs on his arms stood to attention. He waved his fists wildly into the darkness hoping they would find their target. Suddenly his eyes were flooded with light. He winced in pain and clamped them closed. Through the red glow of his eyelids, he saw a shadow of an arm move across his face.

This is it. I'm going to die. I'm going to feel its long

black fingernail draw across my neck. Its laughter is going to ring in my ears for eternity. Brace yourself.

Why hasn't anything happened? One, two, three, four, five. Nothing. What's going on?

Shit! Something just touched me. I felt it stroke my face. Wait, what's that smell? It smells like perfume, faint perfume and something earthy. Wow dirt, lots of dirt.

Afraid but curious, he peered through a crack in his eye lids. The figure was blurry.

"Stay still. This is going to hurt."

Before Jacob had the chance to answer, the figure poured water onto his leg. It stung like acid.

"Stop! Aw man, please stop."

Opening his mouth to scream, he gagged as a cloth was hastily shoved inside, muffling his cries. He fought against it, desperately trying to use his tongue to push it free. The taste was vile, a mixture of dirt and blood. His eyes focused and he stopped.

Her long auburn hair fell across her face and she brushed it away with a flick of her wrist. Her glasses were scratched and chipped but he could see her green eyes smiling at him from beneath the damaged glass. He noticed the scars on her arms, they were long and varied, travelling up from her wrist to her shoulder. Some were thick white and others had almost faded back into her natural skin tone. She caught him looking and pulled her arm away. Shuffling backwards, she tried her best to hide herself from view.

"I gorr. I gorre," he tried to say apologetically, but his garbled response made her retreat into the shadows even more. He pulled the cloth from his mouth and tried again.

"I'm sorry, sorry, I didn't mean, erm, I didn't mean to stare, it's just, er, you're, you're real."

The sound of his voice caused her to recoil into the wall.

He's staring. He's a real person. A real person is here and they're staring.

His heartbeat pounded in his ears and his pulse

quickened. A smile formed on his lips. He hid it with his hand and tilted his head upwards slowly.

Chin, lips, nose, eyes. Don't stare. Don't stare. Oh shit, you've spooked her.

Her face was lit by the glow of flames dancing around her fingertips.

Is she magic? Maybe, she's The Raven in disguise. Maybe he's possessed her. This is all part of his game. No, wait a minute.

The metal of the lighter glinted from the flame.

Finally she uttered, "I'm Wisp," it was barely auditable and Jacob had to strain again to hear.

"Erm, Jacob, I'm Jacob," he muttered.

The words sounded strange, he blinked so hard, his eyes hurt. For the first time in days he wasn't alone.

I wonder if she heard Alex too? Was she going to help?

His mind cleared as Wisp smiled, a gentle but damaged smile.

Is this one of The Raven's tricks. He's not real, is he? Can I trust him?

She looks 16 at the most, but the layers of dirt, wow I think she has been here a while. Do I ask her? Will she think I'm being rude. I don't want to upset her.

Ask her. You need to know.

"How long you been 'ere?" he asked, still hoping his feeling was wrong.

"Erm, I've lost count. I used to know, but my watch stopped about three months ago. I've only got this lighter because, well, er…"

She glanced down at her arms and Jacob followed her gaze. He saw the burns now, they were scattered up along the outside of her arm, trapped within circles of freckles.

"Did you have it with you when you were taken?" Jacob asked.

Please say yes.

"No, The Raven, he, it, enjoys, when… so, erm, it provides them so I can..."

Her voice faded down to an inaudible squeak. Jacob

32

filled in the blanks. She saw the repulsion on his face, it was only a glimmer, but it was too late.

He thinks I'm crazy. He doesn't understand. Why did I even bother?

The light vanished and he could hear the sound of feet on gravel as she rose and began to clamber up the rocks.

Jacob called after her, "I'm sorry, please, please don't go," the desperation made his voice quiver.

The noise stopped and he was met with silence.

Wisp worked her way up the rocks. When she reached the top she hoisted herself up on to a ledge and waited. Keeping her breathing shallow, she listened for Jacob to move below.

What do I do? I haven't seen a person in ages and now I'm seriously considering walking away.

She bit down hard on her lip, the pain gave her focus.

I have to go back for him.

Flicking the flint on the lighter, she found a foothold and began to carefully edge her way back down the rocks.

Jacob sat helplessly in the cavern panicking.

How are you gonna get to Alex now? You're alone again, back in the darkness and Alex is who knows where.

Can you even walk?

So stupid. You had a friend and you let her walk away.

Why did you even open your mouth? Stupid, stupid, stupid!

It was a few minutes before he heard the gentle padding of feet on gravel edging closer. He felt the panic begin to subside as the flicker of light danced within his eyes.

9

They sat there staring at each other. Neither knew what to say. Jacob felt the words build and disperse on his lips without making a sound.

Talk to her. You've got to say something. Geez, it's been ages since anyone spoke. Come on, think of something.

"Er, erm Wisp? Is that a nickname?"

"Yeah," she said without looking up, "My name's Willow."

Willow? Willow? Oh Willow Matthews. I've seen the news reports. She looks like her Mum. She's been here ages. It was last year.

"Willow. So why are you called Wisp? By the way I'm 15. What about you?"

Her eyes rose to meet with his.

"16. My family called me Wisp because I was so quiet. I spoke in whispers. The girl's voice I heard, was she calling to you?"

"You heard it too," he said excitedly, "She's my sister. She was claimed six months ago. I... I thought she was dead."

"Don't take this the wrong way but if she's been here that long, she might be wishing she was dead. What's her name?"

"What do you mean? She's called Alex, she's only 11."

"This place messes with your head and after a while you're not sure what's real anymore."

They both fell silent. Wisp looked at his leg and saw the red raised skin speckled with dark black flecks of gravel. It looked like the biker's road rash she had seen on YouTube. She inched towards him and set about bathing it again. He flinched as water rolled across his skin. Every hair tingled as it ebbed through the gullies of flesh. The lighter threw up shadows across the cave. He could just about make out tiny specks of black, washing down towards his calf.

Reaching for his hand, she undid the bandages and lightly stroked the angry skin below. The water began to sooth the pain and the tingling sensation began to fade. She soaked his bandages washing out the crisp, dry blood and causing the cavern to have the faint smell of iron. She flicked the blade of her knife out of its metal casing. Jacob didn't ask, but he knew it was another 'gift' from The Raven. Bandages ripped against the sharpened metal and she tore some fabric free. After wrapping them around his leg she carefully placed the small pieces she had cut away around his hand.

"How do you feel? Can you stand?"

Wisp held out her hand and Jacob stumbled slowly and awkwardly to his feet. His leg ached but he was able to put weight on it.

"Yeah, I'm alright. I can walk just about."

He stumbled a few steps to prove it.

Wisp held the lighter inches from his face and Jacob could feel the warmth on his skin. It reminded him of long bus journeys to school on hot summer days, when the sun would be magnified through the glass and cause his skin to begin to glow a dark shade of red. He didn't mind the heat; it gave him a chance to look at her. He saw her doing the same.

His unkempt brown hair was sticking up around his ears and his brown eyes darted away from hers. Beneath the dust, dirt and blood, she could see his tanned complexion. Her eyes gazed down to his torn black Papa Roach t-shirt. The skin underneath was red and blemished. He was wearing pyjama bottoms which hung loosely around his navel. The outline of his abs were visible below his t-shirt and she could see his hip bones protruding slightly. His feet were scarred with crisscrossing lines of red. Flaps of skin hung loosely across his soles and tiny speckles of gravel were engraved in the flesh.

"So, how long ya been here?" she said while still looking at his feet.

"A few days, maybe a week," he replied.

What does she think of me? I've been here a week at most and I'm cut and broken. She's been here over a year and she's holding herself together. I must look so helpless.

She reached out and brushed her hand down his shoulder.

"It gets easier. After a while you'll just start to forget."

Forget, what does she mean forget? I'm getting out of here before I forget anything. Find Alex, get her out of here. That's it, no time to forget.

"Do you know where Alex is?

"Not exactly, but, we might find her eventually. I've been here, well, a while and I still get lost. You're the first person I've met. I think that's why he lets me roam; he knows I won't find my way out."

She hung her head and a single tear rolled from her eye. Jacob leant across and took her hands. Callouses were scattered across her fingertips, feeling rough to the touch. The palms of her hands were scratched and scarred. He gave them a gentle squeeze. Lifting her head, she looked at him and smiled that same sad smile.

"We're gonna find her and then we're gonna get out. You can see your brothers again."

"Wait, how do you know I have brothers? I've never told you that. You're The Raven aren't you? Come to trick me again."

She raised her fists high, swung her arm in a perfect arc and felt the bones in his cheek crack against her knuckles, before he even managed to utter a word.

Jacob raised his arms, cowering to cover his face.

"No, no, I'm not, I promise I'm not. I saw them on TV. I promise."

"TV? What do you mean TV?"

She edged away from him, pressing her sleek frame into the rocks.

"Erm, when you were claimed, they, erm, your family, they, er, went on TV. They thought you might have run away, but, but then the police linked your disappearance to

The Raven."

"They thought I ran away?"

"Yeah, I think they hoped you had because the reality of you being somewhere like this was too much to bear."

"I miss them. Sometimes I think I hear them. Mum calling me for dinner. Dad moaning about the TV. Corey shouting and laughing about something his friends have done at school and Liam in the garden kicking his blasted football against my bedroom wall for the umpteen time."

Her voice went quiet, her nose felt stuffy and she blinked repeatedly trying to clear the tears from her eyes.

Jacob pulled himself up and stumbled to his feet. He cautiously walked three steps towards her. The muscles in his arm went tense, shaking slightly. He reached out and tentatively settled his arm around her shoulders. They rose, the muscles in her back tighten but she didn't pull away. As he hugged her a deep sigh left her lips and her shoulders fell. Her hands reached up encompassing his muscular frame. Resting her head in his chest, she softly wept. The gentle beats of his heart reminded her she wasn't alone.

10

Wisp held the lighter high above her head. The flickering flames illuminated the shaft directly above them. Shadows swayed against the rock face.

"Time to climb," she said, whilst tilting her head back and pointing her eyes to the ceiling.

Clasping her hands together she took his weight and boosted him up. His fingers fumbled for a hand hold and loose rocks crumbled down like hail stones.

"Hey, watch it. Hurry up, you're heavy."

Jacob winced and took hold of the rocks again, pulling himself up slowly until he was four or five metres above her. Gravel dug under his nails, scratching and scraping his skin.

Jeez this is tough, almost there, just the last few feet.

Wisp worked her way up the rocks and met him at the top of the shaft.

"What took you so long?" he laughed.

"Just giving you a chance to catch your breath."

Her thumb struck against the flint of the lighter. It took a few tries before the flames sparked into life. Jacob could see the shadows dance around her face, the gentle smile upon her lips and the kindness in her eyes. She reached out her hand and he took it. Her fingers gently caressed his palm. Her knuckles were rough. Dry dirt from the creases of her palms mixed with his sweat. He felt the grainy texture staining his fingertips. He thought about pulling his hand away to shift the dirt from his fingers, but decided to leave it in situ, unsure if his actions would upset her.

Wisp took the lead and led Jacob through the twisting caverns by the gentle glow of the lighter. Ducking and swerving around hanging stalactites.

How does she know all the rocks? I'd be lost already. It's a labyrinth. My feet are killing me. I need to stop.

No, you can't stop until you find Alex.

"How many more of us are there?"

Wisp didn't answer. Jacob tried again.

"Er, have you heard Alex calling out before?"

Wisp paused then squeezed his hand and whispered, "Yeah, a few times. She was erm, she was crying, calling your name," her voiced quivered as she spoke.

The flame blew wildly to the left and Jacob felt Wisp tremble. He followed her movements as she crouched down low, adjusting her shoulders to fit amongst the jagged rocks.

Click.

Her thumb slid down from the lighter and the flames softly dispersed into the darkness. Jacob could hear her shallow breaths and felt the heat of each one on the side of his cheek.

"Stay down! Don't react," she whispered.

His hands shook uncontrollably, feeling his heart pounding in his chest, beads of sweat began to form on his forehead. Panting, bile rose in his throat. The rocks felt like they were moving underfoot. Shuffling, he tried to regain his balance.

It's The Raven. What do I do? Shit, I can hear him. He's singing.

"I'm coming, I'm coming, I'll find you. I'm coming, I'm coming, there's no place to go."

The calmness in his voice and the eerie tone made Jacob's hair stand on end, it was all accentuated by The Raven's laughter, cackling through the caverns, travelling on the wind. Jacob's hand gripped Wisp's so tightly, he imagined his own knuckles now a deathly shade of white. He could feel the uncontrolled tremor emanating from their palms and travelling the length of their bodies.

"Wisp, where can we hide?" Jacob whispered, trying to control the shakiness in his voice.

"It's too late, just think of your family and hope it'll be enough," she replied terrified.

Think of Mum. Think of Alex.

The smell of rotten egg perforated the air around him. Shaking, his hand pulled at his t-shirt, lifting it over his mouth and nose. He caught hints of his deodorant, masked beneath the aroma of dirt. As the stench clawed its way through the cotton, he exhaled sharply and vowed to only breathe through his mouth. The pungent odour overpowered his senses, jarring in the back of his throat. He wanted to cough and tried to stifle it. His shoulders started to shake. He felt it rising in his throat and clenched his jaw shut. It scratched; clawing its way up until a loud splutter left his lips. Hastily, he used his hand as a muffler and noticed a cold chill accumulate in the air around him.

Thick black smoke danced around their still bodies. Each wisp sung as it warped over them.

"I'm here, I'm here and I've found you. I'm here, I'm here and there's no place to go," the voice echoed with a delightful glee and a malevolent undertone.

Jacob could feel the curls of smoke converge over his body. Heat rose in his lungs, burning. The air felt dry to his lips. He tried to lick them and felt them crack under his tongue. Iron rose to meet his taste buds. A weight pressed on to his chest, forcing him down into the dirt.

No, come on, fight it. FIGHT IT. Breathe.

Smoke coiled amongst his bandages, bleeding into his wounds. It felt like hundreds of needles plunging into his skin. With every muscle tense, he felt them shake in anger. The darkness was taking hold.

The Raven's joy lingered and twisted around Jacob's body. Creeping through his bones and edging its way up his spine. He clamped his free hand over his eyes and tried desperately to focus on his Mum and Alex.

Dark thoughts crawled through his optic nerve. He saw blood dripping down their bodies, falling and covering the dead. The smell overpowered his senses. The screams all at once, were deafening, hurting his ears. His breath quickened, feeling panic rapidly inching its way down his body. He couldn't keep up. Everything was spinning, faster and faster until his eyes were coated with black.

Help me.

Got. To. Keep. Calm. Got. To. Take. Control. Think.

Of. Mum. Breathe. Think of Mum and breathe.

Jacob imagined his Mum there beside him. Wisp's hand turned into hers and he regressed to his happy eight year old self.

*

"Mum where are we going?"

"We need to help your sister. She's too little to use the swings on her own."

They giggled and laughed as they took it in turns to see who could push her the highest. After a while Jacob's arms were getting tired.

"Mum, can we get an ice cream? Please! Please Mum."

The coins clinked gently as his Mum put her hand into her pocket. She pulled a few coins free and placed them into his palm. Together they walked to the ice cream van until the distant sound of music buzzed from Riley's pocket. She fumbled in search of the phone.

"Here, you go ahead. I'll be right behind you."

The kids ran on in front. "I'm gonna get a 99," called Jacob.

"Well, I'm getting rainbow sprinkles on mine," said Alex.

"Jack!"

Jacob had turned around thinking she was calling him back to her, but she was deep in conversation.

He saw smoke twisting from the corners of his vision, catching him off guard. The memory continued to play. The chirpy music from the ice cream van vanished, hidden behind the shrill piercing scream that haunted his nightmares. He saw a hand gesturing to Alex and leading her away. His light blue trainers slipped on the wet grass. He started to fall, unable to put his hands out in time. His chin hit the ground and he cried out, whilst desperately trying to keep his eyes on Alex. Crawling to his feet he tentatively started to run, but his feet betrayed him every time and he fell. Over and over. Run, chin, ground, run,

41

chin, ground. All too soon, it was too late and she was gone.

Riley, grabbed him by his shoulders, shaking him. Spit flying from her mouth as she shouted. Her nails dug into his thin t-shirt marking the skin below. He stammered and stuttered trying to get his words out. Trying to explain it wasn't his fault.

"I'm sor, sorr, sorry. I tr, trie, tried to find her."

His Mum continued to scream, to shake. Her eyes bulging in their sockets, red and blood shot. Lips downturned.

Tears poured down his face, his own eyes red and puffy. With his bottom lip quivering, he started to stare past his mother's enraged face and into the tree line, searching for a glimpse of his sister.

The wet dirt made his cheek cold and clammy. It was enough to pull him away and suddenly his mind fought against the memory.

This wasn't what happened. We ate the ice creams then we mucked about rolling down the hill. Alex was sick on me and I had to get the bus home covered in regurgitated sprinkles. This wasn't what happened!

Jacob felt The Raven's hold waver just for a second. He reached out for the lighter and clicked his thumb down against the flint. The flame danced above his fingertips.

Wisp's words replayed in his mind, "Stay down, don't react."

He turned his face and was horrified to see the terror in her eyes, but all the time she was still, her body unmoving and her breathing as shallow as it had been before.

I can't stay down. I need to do something. I need to fight.

Jacob forced himself over on to his back and held the lighter with his arm outstretched above him. The air turned blue and ripples of flame dispersed like lightning bolts inches away from his hand. Gritting his teeth, he managed to cope with the pain as the flames licked at his skin. An insane cry echoed through the caves and the thick black smoke dispersed.

Jacob covered his mouth and began to cough, hacking and spluttering against the burning air. It felt like his lungs were dissolving inside of him. He dropped the lighter and fumbled around in the dirt trying to find it. His hand recoiled through instinct as his skin brushed against the hot metal. The sensation in his lungs was getting worse and he reached over to Wisp, desperately trying to clutch the water from her belt.

He felt the warmth of a hand in the nook of his back and heard a whisper from behind him.

"Get up. Now!"

Wisp's fingernails dug into his arm and dragged him across the stony ground. His long fingers just had time to clasp the lighter tightly before she pulled him up and away from the gas.

"You shouldn't have done that," she growled, as Jacob coughed and spluttered from the remanence of the sulphur.

"He was inside my head, he played with my memories."

Jacob's face was red and his fists were clenched. His shoulders arched forwards as he inhaled and shot back in a fit of coughing.

Wisp didn't say anything else and stood glaring at him. He could feel the anger in her stare and wondered whether he had done the right thing.

After a while, he heard her mumble, "it'll pass".

"It felt so real and now every time I try to remember it, The Raven's alternative plays like a filter over the top. I can see both versions, but the real memory is fading and The Raven's is building in clarity."

Wisp was in front of him inches from his face.

"Stop!"

He looked up at her, his eyes wide and searching.

"It's what he does. If you try to regain the memory, you'll lose it forever. Just let it settle."

"Has it done this to you?" Jacob asked in a whimper.

Soft tears rolled down her face as she stumbled over

her words.

"Yeah, I, I can't picture them now without, without seeing the blood pouring down their scarred and twisted faces. He plucks out their eyes with his long blackened fingernails. I close my eyes and, and, and hear their screams. Their voices, they, they call my name and I can't. They're so little and I, I… "

Tears streamed down her face as she relived the fear and the terror all over again.

11

"I heard him. He's here. He's coming for me. I knew he would. I knew he wouldn't leave me. See Fuzz I told you, I told you he would come."

The tatty pink teddy bounced around on her knees. She couldn't see him, but felt the bobbled fur, matted and joined, slide under her fingertips. The stitching on his left leg was frayed. Stuffing poked through and Alex prodded it gently back into place. She lifted Fuzz to her nose and gave him a hongi. Holding him there, she breathed deeply. Dust and damp masked the smell she was searching for. She pushed harder and breathed deeper until her lungs couldn't hold any more air.

"Nope, where are you?"

Turning Fuzz round she tried again. Pushing harder, breathing deeper and there it was, the faintest smell, rose and vanilla.

"Hi Mum, I knew you were there. I told you I would find you. Jacob is coming to find me too and then we can all be together again."

Alex lifted the bear and tucked him inside her shirt.

"I'll leave your head out so you can breathe Fuzz, okay?"

His fur rubbed softly against her skin and she tilted her head slightly to kiss him. Her fingers rested on the Jade necklace around her neck. She felt the cool stone glide against her fingertips and smiled.

"So Mum, where are we going to go when I get out of here? Can we go to the funfair? I like the funfair. I like candyfloss and bumper cars. I want to leave here now Mum, it's dark and it smells. The Raven feeds me and stuff, but it's not like your cooking Mum. It doesn't taste very nice and I don't like it. I don't like him, he's mean to me and he took me from Jacob. What do you think Mum, do you think he's mean?

I cry all the time, but I know I've got Fuzz with me and

45

you're here now Mum. I can't be sad when you're here. They told me you were dead Mum, but I knew they were lying. I told Jacob they were lying. He just hugged me. I like it when he hugs me. The Raven tells me you are dead too. He shows me horrible pictures and I don't like them. He shows me, you and Jacob bleeding and stuff. It makes me cry. Those pictures are in my head Mum, every time I close my eyes. I want to go home now. I just want to go home."

Alex tucked Fuzz further into the folds of her shirt and pulled a tatty piece of cloth up to her shoulders. Her legs lay on the cold bare ground causing her to shiver. Pulling the cloth tightly around her chest she squirmed trying to get comfortable. Her eyes closed. Blood thick and oozing, pouring from Jacob's face flashed like a neon sign in her mind. The muscles in her face, tight and grimacing tried to force the image away.

"No, I don't like it. I don't like it Fuzz. I need to keep my eyes open. I need to stay awake. I don't like it when I sleep. Must stay awake. Must stay awake. Must stay awak…"

Her body was exhausted, every muscle ached. With her stomach churning and her eyes burning, she began to twitch and shake. Minutes later, a shrill, high pitched scream echoed through the caverns and Alex pulled Fuzz closer to her chest.

She whispered, "I'm sorry Fuzz, did I wake you? You sleep now. Jacob will be here soon, won't he Mum?"

12

A rusted clasp. Curled and yellowed pages crisp to the touch. Worn leather adorning the cover along with the clawed hand framed with metal. It had been six months since he had last opened the latch. It squeaked slightly as he pulled back the clasp. The pages rose as the pressure was released. A sweet musty smell of paper and ink filled the air. He breathed deeply, savouring it. Blotting paper lay on top of the ink well. He slid it to the left and picked up the fountain pen. Flicking the lever on the side of the pen, he placed it in the ink and snapped it closed. The blotting paper soaked up specks of black, growing and merging. Gently he pulled the old stained fabric bookmark, lifting the pages with it. Fluttering on the breeze, his hand smoothed them down and held them in place. He picked up the pen and started to write.

Long pen stokes recorded his latest claim. Name, age and date, nothing more. He flicked back through the pages, each one headed with a name. Some with one date others with two.

"She was weak. She didn't last long, but oh what a meal. Hmmm, he was stronger; it took longer to break him. I remember the taste. The bitter tang, popped and sizzled on my tongue. The aftertaste like burnt cherries and the sweet crackle as it seeped into my bones. Oh so good. Not long now and I will feed again, soon one of them will be ready for a full meal. The new one is going to be trouble though. I need to break his spirit, but now he knows his sister is alive, he's not going to stop until he finds her.

Huh, maybe he needs to find her then."

He stood up from his desk and smoothed down the creases in his suit. Tugging at the sleeves to help the shoulders fall into place. The pages of the journal fell closed and he clicked the clasp shut. His hand rested on top of the metal fingers. Dusty brown leather began to unravel from the cover, twisting up and around. Looping around his arm it settled on his flesh, moulding and shaping within his pores. Bones cracked and separated as the metal frame lifted and fused into skin. His hand pulled away as the book was fully consumed by his body.

"Right, time to get to work."

He left the house, locked the door behind him and set off down the road.

Let's see what they are up to. I think it's time to pay Alex a visit.

Feet pounded into the pavement and a voice whispered in his head, *"please stop, please let me go."*

You know I can't do that. We need each other. You would have been caught a long time ago, if I wasn't calling the shots. Maybe it's time you paid Alex a visit. I think that might just push her over the edge, don't you.

The shop lights began to blur, each stride faster than the last.

It's almost time for her surprise. I wonder if she'll recognise you. How long has it been?

Seven years.

13

"Listen, can you hear that? It's coming from down there," Wisp said whilst pointing past a large pile of rocks.

"It's faint, but I can hear it. It sounds like someone's crying. What do we do? Shall we go to them? It might be Alex."

"We can look if you want but don't get your hopes up."

They walked on, calculating each step and taking care to make as little noise as possible. The caverns twisted sharply to the right sloping down. Jacob took the lead, steadying himself as he slid.

"Be careful," he called out to Wisp, "It's steep."

Wisp followed taking care to keep her arms and legs away from the jagged rocks.

"It looks like there's been a cave in."

He tilted his head scanning for loose rocks.

"I think we'll be safe enough, it looks secure for now."

Wisp followed his gaze and stretched her arm out above her. Brushing her fingertips against the rocks to test the structure.

"I think you're right. Let's not stay here too long though, just in case."

The only option was to crawl through an opening to the left. Jacob held the flame up and peered inside.

"I think we can fit. It doesn't look too narrow. You wait here and I'll try to get through."

He pulled his arms across his chest. His shoulder wedged into his neck. His cheeks compressed inwards, forcing his face to gurn. Twisting and shuffling he tried to keep his momentum going as he pulled his body the last few feet. He hung out of the hole, whilst his hands felt around in the darkness.

"Is there anything there?"

"I can't feel any ground. I'll push myself a little further but if there's nothing there, I'm just going to fall."

"Be careful."

Jacob placed his hands flat against the tunnel wall and pushed. His torso wiggled free. Hanging there for a moment, he tightened the muscles in his legs to try and maintain his balance. His fingers brushed past something. It felt soft but greasy. The oil coated his fingertips. He reached out, stretching further and found a thick soft mass, smooth and overgrown. Sliding his fingers down, his nails caught against it. Oil coated his palm as he ran his fingers down searching for its origin.

Skin slapped against skin. The impact sent pain in both directions, echoing towards his fingertips and elbow. A hand gripped, pulling.

Jacob fell head first towards the ground, screaming, "Get off me. Get off me."

He wrapped his arms around his head, tucking his body up, desperately trying to change his trajectory.

"Jacob!" screamed Wisp from inside the tunnel.

"There's someone here."

The first blow crashed into his ribs. Kicks littered his chest. He drew his knees up. His hands clawed wildly searching in the darkness.

"Stop, please stop," called Jacob.

One final blow landed sharply on Jacob's chin. His head jarred backwards, smashing into the rocks. A scream bounced across the walls. Everything faded and Jacob was left with white noise ringing in his ears.

He awoke to talking. A firm husky voice and the subtle tones like a whispering meadow. Opening his eyes he struggled to focus. When they finally settled, he stared straight ahead.

He looks a mess.

A man sat in front of him with his back against the rocks. His hand pressed against his head. Blood trickled between his fingers and soaked his dark brown hair, tracing the outline of his beard. His wide frame made Wisp look miniscule in comparison. Wisp's voice seemed distant.

"I'm sorry about your ear. You were hurting him. I had

to make you stop."

"It's okay, I've had worse," Todd said nodding his head towards Jacob, "It looks like he might be waking up."

Wisp bent down and lightly stroked Jacob's face. He felt the warmth of her hand against his shoulder gently nudging him upwards until he was leaning against the rocks. The world was spinning and it reminded him of looking through a kaleidoscope.

"Ow, my ribs."

Wisp looked at Jacob and sighed, "You've got to stop getting hurt."

Jacob winced and smiled slightly, "Yeah, I'll get right on to that," he muttered, "So who's this then?"

"Sorry about before mate, I'm Todd, but in future if you don't want a kick in, don't grab me."

"Yeah, I'll try to remember that," grimaced Jacob.

"So, what's your deal?" asked Todd.

"I'm Jacob. Ow. I'm trying to find my sister. We heard someone crying, so we, we thought it might be her," he said between breaths.

"Oh, I didn't think anyone else was here. There goes my rep. I've been here almost nine months now and sometimes I…"

"It's okay you don't need to explain yourself. You've gotta do what you can to survive. I get it. I cried when I first got here. I'm sure I would still be crying if I hadn't found Wisp. She's… well, I wouldn't be here without her," Jacob averted his gaze as he spoke.

He caught a glimpse of Wisp in his peripheral vision, shying away from his comments.

"Erm, yeah, anyway, so where were you before here?" Wisp interrupted before Jacob could say anything else.

"I was nowhere really. I lived on the streets. I used to go the shelter at St Paul's. Mostly, I didn't get in but sometimes I was lucky," Todd said embarrassed.

"That's where The Raven claimed you, wasn't it? I remember hearing about it on the news," Jacob said before he had given the words a second thought.

51

"Hmmm, I made the news. I wonder how long they looked for me. Bet it wasn't as long as that girl Willow. Her family were constantly on the news and in the papers. I saw the posters everywhere. I sometimes think I'm better off here. No one cared for me before. At least The Raven feeds me."

"So, hi. I'm that girl Willow," she muttered.

"But, you said your name was Wisp," he replied defensively.

"Wisp's my nickname."

"I'm sorry, I didn't mean to offend. It's just, it seemed like they really loved you. I always wondered why you got claimed. I mean, a loving family, friends who cared about you, good grades. Why would The Raven want you?"

Wisp tutted, "What, only people like you have problems? People like me should just be happy. We've not allowed to let things get on top of us. What have we got to worry about? Everything's great in my life, right? You don't get it. It doesn't matter where you come from. I didn't choose to feel this way. I didn't choose for The Raven to claim me and take me away from my family, but here I am, stuck, just like you," there was venom in her voice.

Todd looked at her apologetically, "I didn't mean that. I just, you know. I'm sorry."

Jacob looked on, wondering if he could say anything to defuse the situation. Instead he tucked his chin into his chest and stared motionless at the dirt under his thumbs. The rattles of the cave echoed through the silence. Wisp sat twirling her auburn hair around her fingers whilst Todd rubbed at the dry blood staining his cheek. Jacob sighed.

Well, that went well. I got a kick in and Wisp ripped him a new one and now we are just sitting here. I've got to say something. Look at the size of him and Wisp brought him down with words. I'm guessing he's not used to people. He seems to put his foot in his mouth more than I do and that's saying something.

So Todd, how old are you?" Jacob mumbled.

The sound of a voice made Todd jump slightly.

"17."

"I'm 15, Wisp's 16. I'm sorry but I need to get out of here. I need to keep looking for my sister."

"Older or younger?" asked Todd.

"She's only 11," answered Jacob.

"Oh man, I'm sorry."

"I just need to find her," Jacob's voice broke slightly.

He felt Wisp's hand slide into his and squeeze. The warmth of her hand made him hope again. Turning to her, he smiled and leaned in close to her ear.

"Thank you," he whispered.

"We'll find her, but we need to go now, she's waiting for you," she said.

As they started to work their way back through the hole, Wisp turned back to Todd. "Are you coming?"

14

Water dripped down the walls, dribbling to the floor and formed a small puddle. Fuzz lay nearby soaking it in like a sponge, the white fur around his ears slowly turning a murky brown. Light streamed into the cavern, filling every crevice. Alex sat huddled in the corner with her arms shielding her eyes, vigorously rocking. Aching muscles in her shoulders and hips willed her to stop. She pushed through the pain, using her thighs to prolong the movement. A voice called out her name over and over.

Grimacing, she pressed her head down harder into her arms. The voice tried again, this time more controlled, quieter, as though it was trying to wake her from a bad dream.

She continued to rock, eyes shut, faster and faster.

Soft, hot breaths landed on the nape of her neck.

She shivered; her hairs were standing on end and her stomach heavy. Slowly, she raised her head, whilst her fingers dug into her arms, pressing so closely across her body. Opening her eyes, large bright spots blotted her vision.

It took ages for the spots to begin to fade. As they did Alex caught glimpses of a figure. Square shoulders, outlining his tall thin frame. His dark grey suit hung in perfect alignment. Deep wrinkles scattered his brow and his tired sunken eyes stared straight ahead, unfocused. Calluses accentuated his knuckles. A troubled sigh left his lips.

"Uncle Jack, you can't be here. I'm dreaming this, aren't I? You're not real. You can't be real."

"I'm sorry Alex."

"What for?"

"For what I did and what he's going to make me do."

"I don't understand, what do you mean?"

Jack's lips moved but the words belonged to someone else.

"Too late, time's up. I think we need to show her, don't you Jack?"

"Uncle Jack, Uncle Jack, it's not really you. I know it's not you. It's The Raven. It must be The Raven. Stay away from me. Stay away," she cried out panicking.

The long sleeves of the grey suit began to tinge a darkened shade of orange, glowing and flickering in the light. Flakes of suit fell away, turning to ash as Jack grew, now towering high above her. His sunken eyes still stared straight ahead. The grey suit burnt away, morphing into flowing black robes, dancing in the amber glow. Alex stared transfixed.

"Leave him alone, please leave him alone."

Cracks and pops filled the air as his bones broke and stretched. Jack didn't react but Alex pressed her hands over her ears, trying to block out the noise. Her fingertips pushed hard into her skull. She could feel the blood pushing back against them and hear every gasp and gulp. The callouses on his knuckles tore open stretching along his fingers, forming long scars reaching from wrist to fingertip.

Alex's feet scrabbled on the floor, kicking up clouds of dust as she pushed herself into the furthest corner on the cave. The Raven's towering figure slowly edged towards her.

"Don't try to hide from me Alex. There's nowhere to go. I've got something to show you. I think you are old enough to know the truth."

"I don't want to see anything you want to show me. I just want to go home."

"You don't have a home Alex, remember. You used to have one, but then it all got ripped away. Do you remember Alex?"

Alex stared straight ahead, putting all of her efforts into blocking out The Raven's words.

I know what happened. I don't need to listen to him. He's just trying to get into my head.

But what if he does know something?

He doesn't. It's just another way to try and get to me.

He might though. I've always wondered.

He doesn't. Stop it. Stop thinking about it.

"What's wrong Alex? Are you wondering what it might be? Here, let me show you."

Before she could pull away, taut bony fingers reached down and grabbed her shoulder. Jagged nails pierced through her flesh leaving deep indents. Her body convulsed sending her skull careering backward. The shadowy figure towered above her blocking out the rock face behind. Her teeth clamped together, the muscles in her neck stiffened. Hot prickles cascaded over her eyes. She tried to blink.

I can't move.

Try again.

It's not working.

"Don't worry Alex, that feeling? It's just me, I've taken control. Can you feel your muscles tighten, twitching deep within? Don't fight it. Let it settle. It'll help you focus. Look up and take it all in."

The cave began to dim and white lights shone on the rocks. Shifting and changing, the lights shaped into familiar faces. Alex felt her stomach churn and her spine tingle as the scene played out above her.

*

Jacob's hair lurched wildly to the left, standing on end. He ruffled his fingers through it and stood in front of the mirror teasing it backwards and forwards, trying to regain control of the dark brown mass. Alex pulled at his trouser leg.

"What ya doing? Hurry up. Mum said I have to brush my teeth."

I was so young, look at me. I remember this. I don't want to see what happens next.

Alex reached out for the toothbrush and giggled as Jacob brushed her hand away. "Hey."

"Haha, too slow."

The scene suddenly changed. Alex tried to pull away but her muscles betrayed her.

It's our living room. I can still hear me and Jacob upstairs.

"I said no! You can't come over tonight, the kids are about to go to bed and I just want an early night. Just give me some space. I'll phone you in a few days. No, Michael, I said no."

Riley slammed the phone down on to the stand and slumped into the comforting folds of her favourite green chair. Her fingers circled her temples then slid down to rub her eyes.

"I know he means well, but after the week I've had I just want some peace. I better check on the kids."

She rushed up the stairs, taking two at a time.

Alex could hear the conversation from upstairs but the scene stayed in the empty living room.

Why am I being shown an empty room? Mum stayed upstairs with us because I wanted another story. There's nothing there. What's the point?

Alex tried to focus on the snippets of conversation she could hear from the bedroom. As her ears honed into the voices, her eyes lost focus.

Click.

Light shone on the far wall.

What was that?

Oh wait I remember, the lights downstairs were on a timer. Mum said they would make people think we were at home.

Alex continued to stare, taking it in.

There's Fuzz, I can see his nose sticking out from under the chair and that's Jacob's favourite shirt. My school uniform is crumpled up in the corner. Mum must have been getting ready to do the ironing.

What was that?

I'm sure I just saw something move. There it is again. It's a shadow. Someone else was here.

She looked closer, watching every movement. The figure paused for a moment in front of the lamp. Square shoulders, tall and thin.

Uncle Jack?

She heard herself calling from upstairs, "Mummy, I can't find Fuzz. I can't go to bed without Fuzz."

"Okay, I think I saw him downstairs. You snuggle up and I'll go down and grab him for you."

Alex remembered the warm, gentle kiss as her Mum pulled up the covers and shuffled them softly around her ears so only her nose and eyes were visible.

She heard the floorboards creaking under foot. The shadow moved, darting to the left.

He's gone into the kitchen. Oh, please no, I don't want to see what happens next. Please stop. Please.

Riley reached the bottom step and leapt playfully into the living room.

"Now Fuzz, where did I see you? Ah, there you are."

She bent down, reaching under the red plastic chair.

"Gotcha! Right you, I've got a tired little girl who can't go to sleep without you, so up you go."

Her Mum's frame was silhouetted on the wall as she reached the foot of the stairs. Alex saw a shadowy arm reaching out and missing by inches. Riley bounded up them two at a time unaware.

"Here you go, he was hiding under your chair. Sleep tight, don't let the bed bugs bite."

There was the gentle padding of footsteps and a simple sigh as she reached the bottom step.

"Wine, I think, then some TV before bed."

Alex saw her Mum's shadow heading towards the kitchen.

Don't go in there Mum. He's waiting. Just run, run away.

Alex's muscles strained. Tension built in the corners of her eyes as she fought to close them.

"Seen enough? But we haven't even got to the good part," heckled The Raven.

Two shadows reappeared from the kitchen. Arms outstretched, one blocking, the other trying to take hold. Alex heard a thud then her Mum staggered into view. The man's hand was clamped across her mouth. Teeth chomped against his palm.

Bite him Mum or scream, please do something.

Her arms waved wildly trying to loosen his grip. Riley's body tumbled to the ground. The weight of it smashed through the red chair.

Get up Mum! Push him off.

The man was on top of her, pinning her to the ground. Her nails dug into his flesh. Dragging down, clawing at his face. Blood pooled in her nail beds and smeared over his cheek. He pulled away and scowled.

"Don't fight me. Do you really want your kids to see this? Lie still, no one needs to get hurt."

Alex felt the tears streaming down her face.

We were upstairs. Why didn't we hear anything? Why didn't we wake up? We could have helped her. We could have saved her.

His fingertips pushed and pulled against Riley's cheek, silencing her muffled cries. His free hand fumbled in his pocket then re-emerged, holding the silver duct tape.

"Maybe once I'm done, he'll stop asking questions that don't concern him."

Alex couldn't see her Mum's face; her eyes were drawn to the duct tape. She watched as his fingers pulled at the end and ripped a long strip free from the roll. He moved his hand from her mouth and slammed the tape down across her lips.

Shifting his weight, he sat down hard on her stomach. Riley squirmed. Reaching for her arms, he pinned them down at the wrist and unwound the tape, binding it in circular motions. She fought against him, twisting her body to the left and forcing her shoulder blades into the carpet trying to break free. He laughed. Leaning forward he placed his lips close to her ear and whispered.

"Don't bother struggling. That's just in case you try

anything stupid."

He pulled at Riley's trousers, shuffling them down below her knees and ran his fingers along the top of her knickers. Riley's head butted against the floor. She tried to use the momentum to get free. He slammed his palm hard against her face and laughed again as it ricocheted off the floor.

"Nice try Riley, but come on did you really think it would be that easy. Always remember I'm better than you. I'm stronger than you. I'm in control."

He ran his hand gently down the side of her face. Riley pulled away. Alex watched as he lifted himself from Riley's stomach and his fingers pulled at the zip of his jeans.

No! Stop!

Riley felt the change in pressure and raised her knee hard into his groin. He bent double, rolling backwards towards the fireplace.

Yes! Mum, come on, fight back.

Riley rolled over on to her stomach and pushed herself onto her knees. Her fingers fumbled out in front of her reaching for a piece of broken plastic. Managing to grab it she jabbed it into the tape. Small perforations grew into gaping holes as she pulled her wrists in opposite directions. She rushed to pull up her trousers. Then her hands pushed down on to the ground and she tried to steady herself as she rose to her feet. She felt the bobbles of the carpet underfoot. The room swung wildly to the right. She gripped the cupboard tightly, waiting for the nausea to pass. Riley managed to regain her balance and grabbed a photo frame of Michael and the kids. Swinging wildly, it collided with her assailant's shoulder. Glass shattered down his arm and crunched into the carpet. Yellow teeth growled and the veins popped from his neck. His hand was on her head, fingernails digging into her scalp, twisting strands of light brown hair around his palm. Tugging sharply, she fell backwards.

Alex heard footsteps from upstairs. The distinct click of

the bathroom light. A door closing and the gentle splashes of wee hitting against the sides of the pan.

Jacob's up. Please come and save her Jacob, please.

He can't. You know that. She dies.

Elbows and knees hit against the floor, against each other, rebounding off walls and flesh. Riley's hands clawed at his clothes. They settled at the base of his back. The coldness of the steel chilled against her skin.

What did she find? Oh, he was in the kitchen. I recognise the handle. Mum!

Wrapping her fist around the handle she yanked it free from the waistband of his jeans. The glint of the blade caught on the lamp's light. He jerked backwards and to the right, anticipating her movements. The blade caught on his forearm, tearing down against the flesh. Blood bubbled up from the wound. His knee landed with a thud on her shoulder. Riley winced, dropping the knife. He snatched at it, his little finger a little too close to the blade.

No, please don't. Just drop it and leave. Please. I don't want to see this. Stop, I'll do anything, please. Stop!

Alex's eyes stayed transfixed on the knife but her ears heard the sounds from upstairs. Jacob's feet could be heard shuffling again. The door to his bedroom creaked as he pushed it open and an awkward groaning emanated from his bed springs.

Why didn't you come downstairs Jacob? You could have stopped it. We would have all been happy if you had just come downstairs earlier.

"Don't make me do this Riley. I only came here for one thing. Just let me finish what I started. You know, all I ever wanted to do was help, but you kept pushing me away. Funny how things have a way of falling into place isn't it?"

Riley's head shook. Her eyes were red and puffy.

"Okay, if that's how you want it. This is your fault."

He held the knife, his fingers twitched slightly, throwing dancing shadows on to the far wall.

Alex desperately wanted to close her eyes.

"You can't stop now. We're almost at the best bit, just a few more seconds. Personally, I love watching as the blood sprays," echoed The Raven.

The metal glinted again as it plummeted. She threw her head to the right avoiding the blade. Pushing her shoulders back into the carpet her body bucked against him, throwing him off balance. He lunged forwards. His left hand thumped into her shoulder. Her chin fell open and a muffled scream made the tape vibrate. Shuffling on to her chest he redistributed his body weight. His hands froze inches from her throat. He held it steady. The tip of the blade indented her skin. Her eyes pleaded with him and her legs kicked wildly into the ground.

He turned away and Alex finally saw his face. Uncle Jack. His eyes seemed vacant. The knife twisted downwards and dug into flesh. He dragged it across her neck and heard the muffled gargles of blood build in her throat. It sprayed like a sprinkler in summertime. Her legs writhed against the floor until the last drops of blood drained from her throat. The soft fabric of the green chair was now a mottled shade of brown.

"Shall we zoom in a bit Alex? Watch the last bit of colour drain from her face? Hear her final rasping breath? goaded The Raven.

The image changed. Riley lay motionless. A bloody footprint was embedded on the cream carpet just to the side of her head. Matted brown hair entwined with the crimson red. The house shook as the door slammed. Alex heard footsteps again, this time more rushed, worried and searching. A voice called out.

"Mum? Mum? Are you here Mum?"

Jacob's skinny legs cast shadows on the wall, stretching taller. Alex heard his breath catch in his throat. The mumbled cry, confused. Sticky red blood causing his feet to slide on the carpet, then his knees giving way inches from her body. His hand reached for his favourite shirt and Alex's school uniform pressing them down against her throat. His free hand tore at the tape across her lips. He

62

kept calling her name, even as his small hands pummelled against her chest. His mouth softly pressed against her lips, willing her to life with each breath.

More footsteps, this time softer followed by a desperate scream. Fuzz clenched within her fist.

"Call 999 Alex!"

She saw herself fumbling for the phone. Looking at the numbers, trying to remember which was which. She placed her finger over the number one and counted. Her finger hovered above the number 9 and pressed it three times in quick succession. Alex heard her own voice, so tiny and afraid.

"I need an ambulance. My Mummy's been hurt. Please come quickly. There's lots of blood."

The lights on the rocks faded and Alex could hear nothing but The Raven's voice.

"I think that's all. Don't you Alex? I don't think you really need to see what happens next. I'm sure you remember it or have you tried to block it out. Let me give you a quick recap. The police came. The ambulance came. They couldn't do anything. You and Jacob got taken to the hospital. From there you both ended up in a temporary foster home for the night because they couldn't contact your Dad. He seemed to have vanished. Strange, isn't it? Just when you needed him the most he wasn't there. The next day you both got interviewed. Neither of you could tell the police much about what happened. After all when your Mum needed you the most, you were both upstairs asleep. Neither of you woke when she fell to the ground or fought for her life. It took her killer to wake you and well as they say the rest is history.

Jack is there anything you would like to add?"

Alex finally felt her muscles loosen. She screwed her eyes up, blinking repeatedly trying to erase everything she had just seen.

His voice was wavering, laced with regret, "Alex, I'm sorry."

"That's enough for now, don't you think? I mean all

that information in a matter of a few minutes and to find out that dear old Uncle Jack wasn't who he seemed. Let's give the girl a second to process it all.

Right time's up. Now to really get this party started."

15

Gravel, scrap, step. Gravel, scrap, step. Gravel, scrap, step.

Jacob sighed and rolled his eyes.

He's doing my head in. Just lift up your feet. It's really not that hard. I just want to make the noise stop.

Gravel, scrap, step, gravel...

Jacob winced, "Todd, you alright back there? It's just, er, you sound a bit tired."

"Yeah, I'm fine. My ankle's throbbing a bit, not sure what I've done to be honest. I'm sure it'll ease off in a while."

You kicked me very hard, repeatedly, so I sure hope it eases off for you. We wouldn't want it to linger around for a while like a bruised rib or anything.

Jacob kept looking straight ahead. Wisp turned, lighter in hand and caught his eye. She glared.

Shit, Jacob, please don't say anything. We all know why his foot is hurting; it's the bloody elephant in the room. Let's all just ignore it and hope it goes away. Come on Jacob. We are all in this together. He's just as broken as the rest of us. He just hasn't been around people for a while.

"Let's stop for a bit. I need to get my bearings again anyway. It's been a while since I've been this far out," Wisp called from a few paces ahead.

Jacob's shoulders sagged and he kicked the gravel against the rocks.

"Any chance you could give it a rest mate. That noise is doing my head in," said Todd.

Teeth grinding and eyes closed, Jacob stretched out his fingers, determined to not let them bunch into fists. Slumping to the floor, he perched on top of some jagged rocks as far away from Todd as he could manage. One rock stabbed deep between his shoulder blades.

Shit that hurts, but it's worth it, just not having to listen to him for a while.

Space. I would give anything for some space.

"Why have you squashed yourself over there Jacs? There's more space over here," chirped Todd.

"I'm fine here and it's Jacob not Jacs," replied Jacob sharply.

"Okay then. So Wisp, how long have we been walking do you reckon?" mumbled Todd, "It must be a good few miles by now. Either that or you've just been leading us round in circles."

He bumped his shoulder playfully into Wisp's with a wink and a nod.

Wisp's eyes glared and her lip snarled, but she remained silent. Todd pulled at his collar and shuffled his fingers around the rim, whilst mindlessly scratching at the red blotchy skin below. Twisting towards Jacob, she held out the water bottle. Nodding, he accepted the silent gesture and began to swig a few mouthfuls before passing the bottle back. After sipping at the cool water, she placed it carefully in the space between the elongated belt loop and her trousers, pulled the leather tight and slid the metal clasp into place.

"Do you reckon we'll find her soon?" Jacob whispered.

"I think we're getting closer. I just haven't been down these tunnels as much, so it's taking me longer to find my way around. Plus we haven't got much lighter fluid left. If we don't find her soon we'll be searching in the dark again."

Jacob closed his eyes and rubbed his temples.

"I've got to find her Wisp, whatever it takes. She's been here too long already."

"I know. We'll find her in the dark, bleeding and broken if we have to," Wisp replied.

"You've already got those last two mate, so we're half way there," muttered Todd.

Jacob's stare bore into the ground. He examined every inch of the fine dust beneath his feet. Grunting to himself, he exhaled a painful sigh.

Two thirds you moron and most of my broken bones are down to you.

16

Tossing and turning, his sheets twisted around his legs and droplets of sweat clung to the short hairs on the back of his neck. He wiped away the salty water and sat bolt upright. His fingers pulled at the sheets, before he swung his legs clear and carefully placed the soles of his feet into the spongy carpet.

"Alright Crimp, I'm coming. I can't sleep anyway. What's the matter, hey?"

The cat purred at the sound of his voice then turned to the window and continued to hiss. He followed her gaze and tugged the curtains open to show her there was nothing there. Next door's blossom tree tapped against the glass, gently creating the rhythm of the wind. The midnight sky reflected his tired face back at him through the window pane. His short brown hair clung to his head, dripping wet, whilst his beard had begun to look overgrown and off centre. An old white scar sat under his right eye and down along his cheek. He ran his hand through his hair, yanking at the greys and grimacing as he pulled it away, wet.

"Eurgh! I need a shower," he exclaimed to the empty room.

Crimp followed him as he plodded down the corridor, pushed the door and grabbed hold of the pull cord. He yanked down hard and winced against the imposing LEDs bouncing light in all directions. Rubbing his eyes, he let his vision settle before gripping the sodden edges of his clothes and pulling them free from his body.

The shower head lay trailing in the bath so he bent down, scooped it up and hooked it back into the highest setting.

"I need to fix that," he said as he twisted the dial and shuddered whilst the water warmed up to an acceptable temperature.

Water jetted out steadily, washing away the hot sticky

moisture clinging to his skin. He sighed and momentarily let his worries follow the water down the drain. His hands pressed against the cold ceramic tiles and his head slumped forwards, resting gently on to the wall.

"I should have been there. I should have done something to protect them. Why did I let fear take me away from my kids? I could have stopped this from happening."

Tears mixed with water, washing them away like lost memories. He patted the wall trying to find the dial again. Gurgles rumbled through the pipes. Stepping backwards towards the taps, he fumbled for the towel. He rubbed the tears away as he sunk his face into the warm fluffy folds and pushed the towel back through his hair. Turning to the mirror, he wiped away the steam that blotted his vision. A black misted veil coated the polished glass as he attempted to wipe it clean. Their faces were embedded in the surface, their eyes unblinking, staring and pleading for his help.

Michael's jaw went slack, his eyes stared straight ahead, welling up with tears. The towel dropped with a quiet thud onto the tiled floor. His breath caught in his throat and he had to will himself to breathe again. Stumbling backwards, he flung the door open, leaving soggy footprints in the cream carpet leading to his room. Crimp scuttled through his legs and raced back to safety. The heavy wood slammed behind him as he entered, causing the dresser to shake, a photo to tumble and glass to shatter on to the floor. Crimp leapt from the window ledge and hissed loudly.

"Bollocks," he muttered as wet flesh met jagged glass.

He collided with the corner of the bed as he hopped backwards. The mattress groaned and he scrambled back to a sitting position. Leaning down, he yanked the shards of glass free. His fingertips recoiled at the sharp edges, losing their grip and dropping the clear blood stained pieces back onto the floor. Blood dripped through his fingers, whilst smoke poured down from the ceiling. Crimp screeched and hissed, scratching against the base of the bed.

"What's wrong Crimp?" he asked without turning round.

Her eyes were fixed on the ceiling. He turned slowly, his fingers twitched with anticipation. A cold shiver trickled down his spine. He fought to control his breathing as his lungs pressed hard against his ribs with every breath. Catching sight of two yellowing eyes peering from the smoke, he froze.

A fist formed. Long black nails gently stroked the white edge of his scar and followed the line down to just below his chin. They dug down into his flesh as the smoke clawed towards his lips, prying them open and dragging the darkness to the back of his throat. Air slipped past, flowing into a single scream. Crimp matched the tone and screeched. Her eyes never leaving her master, whilst his eyes stayed fixed on the photo of Alex, Jacob and Riley as it lay smashed and broken on the floor. The edges of his vision faded as his feet motored into a sprint. The door to his flat rested ajar and Crimp cried out into the crisp night air.

17

"Just listen to my voice as it echoes in your mind. Take your time and listen now for it's all you're going to find. Just listen to my voice as it twists within your head and very soon you'll be wishing you were dead."

The Raven's words played over and over like an irritating song she wished she'd never heard. The only pauses were filled with Uncle Jack's last words to her. She exhaled sharply, her eyelids burnt against her tears.

Make it stop. Please, just make it stop.

Uncle Jack said he was sorry but he didn't look sorry. He didn't look anything. His eyes had just stared straight ahead. It was as though he didn't see me at all. Maybe it wasn't him. Maybe it wasn't real. It could all just be another trick. It needs to stop. I need to make it stop.

The palm of her hand slammed into her right temple sending shooting pain to the back of her skull. Each blow was like the waves of a tide, building up and washing away the words. Every time the pain retracted the words reappeared embedded in the synapses. Her fingers drew towards her palms. Tightened muscles held them in place as her hand repeatedly crashed into her head. A fog sat above her temples falling down across her eyes.

"Keep trying. Hit yourself harder, see if it works.

No.

Okay.

Then just listen to my voice and let me take control. I'm hungry Alex, so hungry. Let me eat your soul."

The song danced within the forming mist. Playing over and over until she couldn't take it anymore.

The muscles around her mouth pulled taut. She felt her skin quiver as the noise expelled from her lips and burnt the back of her throat. Her right wrist rose and wedged itself between her teeth, dampening the sound. 18 tiny red marks blemished with hints of blue began to form, denting the skin where her teeth took hold. Fingers twisted against the locks of her hair. Her left hand pulled down sharply, gripping tighter and tighter until clumps fell loosely on to the rocks.

"Come on Alex, the face of the man who killed your mother is still here staring at you. I can feel his disappointment in you Alex. You're beloved Uncle Jack. He's still in here you know. Every now and then he tries to fight back, but it never works. I'm too strong.

Every time you scream. Every time you hurt yourself. Every time you think of her. I get stronger Alex and if you stop, well, I get stronger then too. Your despair fuels me. I can feel it bubble inside like candy rocks within my bones. You remember candy rocks, don't you Alex, Jacob used to buy them for you and you'd giggle as they danced on your tongue. Where's Jacob now? Oh yeah, he left you just like everyone else. Everyone leaves you and why wouldn't they? Your Dad. Your Mum. Uncle Jack. Jacob. All of them, gone.

Just let me in and I can silence all your pain. I can make it stop. That's what you long for, for the pain to stop. It's what everyone longs for. I've been inside so many heads. Planting my seeds and watching them grow. That's how I know. I've enjoyed watching you grow, seeing the darkness take hold like a firethorn and now you are nearly ready, so close."

Alex's hands fell by her sides. Her mouth closed and her eyes stared vacantly straight ahead.

He's wrong about Jacob. Jacob is coming. I know he is. I've heard him calling. He'll be here soon and then we'll fight back. I'll fight back.

Come on Alex, don't you think I'm in here too. I can hear your thoughts. I know you think he's coming but I can assure you he's not. He's too busy with his new friends. He doesn't have time for you. They're trying to leave and they're not bothering to look for you. Why would he want his whiny little sister cramping his style?

Lost and broken, that's all you are. Lost and broken, that's all you'll ever be. I'm all you have left Alex, so embrace it. That feeling you're been trying to hide. No matter how much you hope, it's hopeless in the end. Everything is hopeless Alex. Once you accept that, it'll all become easier for you.

Her mind fell silent for a second. A single tear rolled down her cheek. Her eyes burnt. Her breathing was unnervingly steady and controlled. Anxiety bubbled quietly inside like a million pin pricks all at once. Her fingers and toes twitched, dancing to a tune no one could hear. Then it started again.

"Just listen to my voice as it echoes in your mind. Take your time and listen now for it's all you're going to find. Just listen to my voice as it twists within your head and very soon you'll be wishing you were dead. Then just listen to my voice and let me take control. I'm hungry Alex, so hungry. Let me eat your soul."

18

The group tentatively removed their hands from their ears.

"What was that? It didn't sound human," said Todd.

"I'm not sure. I've never heard a sound like that before," Wisp added.

"I've heard it before," Jacob said sadly, "Once, the night Alex was taken. It was her. The Raven must be with her again. God knows what he's doing to her."

Wisp's hand softly brushed against his shoulder.

"Are you sure?"

"Yeah."

As he finished talking, Jacob's chin fell against his chest. He pulled his t-shirt up to cover his nose and rubbed the seams under his eyes. After jerking the black fabric down again he could feel wet cloth against his skin. His fingers interlocked and twisted back and forth, rubbing across his palm in a circular motion. Wisp's hand ran down his shoulder and rested on top of his knuckles. He lifted his chin slightly, though his eyes were still downcast. Her other hand caressed his cheek and gently raised his chin so his eyes were now level with hers.

"Look at me. It'll be okay. We're so close to finding her. It won't be long and then you can hug her again. You'll have your sister back soon. Trust me. I'll get you there."

She's lying Jacob. She works for me. They all do. They're not leading you to your sister. They're just keeping you busy while I get to play. There's a special present on its way. I hope you like it. I made it myself.

Jacob pulled away. Running his fingers through his hair he turned towards the wall and let his shoulders sag.

"You keep saying that, but we're not any closer, are we? Maybe he sent you to find me, just to keep me busy or to keep me away from her."

"You know that's not true. Why would you even say that?" Wisp paused, "He's in your head isn't he? What did

74

he say? I hear him sometimes in my head, but you have to fight against it. Everything he says is a lie. You can't believe him. Jacob, please."

"He's in my head, but it doesn't mean he's lying though. Maybe it's all just part of his game. I don't know any more Wisp, I just don't know. He said he's sent me a present."

"I don't like the sound of that," muttered Todd from a few steps behind.

"Me neither. Presents from The Raven are rarely good and even when you think they are there's always a sting in the tail. Please trust me Jacob. I want out of here as much as you do."

"Maybe you're right. It's just he changes things, makes you see them his way. It's like all those little details get twisted slightly until you think night is day and day is night. I don't know, I guess, let's just keep going."

Hmmm, you've decided to trust them. Good luck. Your present is waiting. Just a few more metres and turn left. You'll find it.

"He said the present is waiting up there. What do ya reckon?" asked Jacob.

"It's a trap. We need to go the other way," Todd said with certainty.

"But what if it's not? Or if the trap is him telling us to go left, so we go right and whatever is waiting for us is there?" Wisp said tripping over her own words.

"Okay, after three say left or right, majority wins. Agreed?" The others nodded, "one, two, three."

They all spoke at once and avoided each other's eyes as they muttered their choices.

"Okay left it is. Two votes to one," said Wisp as she took the lead, "I've got the light, so I guess I'll lead the way. Let's go."

She walked ahead before either of the boys could disagree. They fell in line and followed her footsteps down the tunnel; watching the light and shadow dance on the rocks. Wisp stopped just short of the crossroads.

"Ready?" she asked.

"Ready," they both replied, their tone giving away their uncertainty.

Wisp took a final deep breath and held it as she turned the corner, expecting the worst. She blinked, holding her eyes closed for a few seconds longer. Drawing out the mystery or the pain; she wasn't sure which it was going to be. Jacob's voice made her open them faster than she was planning to.

"He lied. There's nothing here. Nothing at all," the disappointment mixed with fear was clear as his voice broke.

"Maybe he wanted us to go right after all," added Todd.

They stood like three points on a triangle, staring at each other, unsure of what to do next.

"I guess we keep going. Let's go back to the crossroads and decide which tunnel to try," Wisp said.

Just as they turned, dust danced on the wind. The flame on the lighter flickered and faded. The tunnels filled with growls and panting. Jacob turned slowly. Darkness engulfed him. His hand shot out behind searching for Wisp's.

"Wisp, Wisp are you there?"

His hand settled against something warm, "Wisp?"

He pulled his hand away at the sound of gnashing teeth. Sharp claws rested on his thigh, dragging down slowly, inching deeper into his skin. Jacob squealed, spinning sharply with his hands flailing. His right found nothing but air, but his left thumped hard against wet fur. He saw the eyes of the creature; the dark yellow glare pulsing from the beast. It shot up again with its claws poised. Jacob wasn't quick enough. His shoulders smashed against the rocks. Clouds of dust caught him off guard. Exhaling in a series of coughs, Jacob closed his eyes, his lungs on fire.

Snarling teeth hovered over Jacob's neck. Beads of sweat collided with hot breath as he forced his elbow under its jaw. Lifting his right forearm up across his face, he used his left arm and both his feet to push against the beast. Wet fur clung to his toes and its racing heart pounded against them. He pulled his knees back into his chest and steadied himself with his shoulders, pressing them into the dirt. His muscles twitched like pistons waiting to fire. Feeling the full weight of the beast bearing down on top of him he drove his feet in hard against the fur. It flew across the tunnel. A single yelp left its lips, followed by an almighty thud that echoed around the cave as it hit against the rocks.

Jacob ran his fingers down his arms and across his chest checking for damage. His lungs burnt against his breath and his chest ached. Rolling on to his knees, he dug them into the dirt and exhaled exuberantly. His short lived relief was suspended by the gentle cry of Wisp from further back.

He clambered to his feet and ran blindly in the direction of her cries, sensing her movement, but unable to make out exactly where she was in front of him. Dots of red, like distant cars on a motorway, swooped ever closer. Jacob felt specks of gravel digging into his palms as he dropped to his knees.

"Wisp? Wisp?" he said quietly under his breath.

"Jacob? Help me!"

"Where are you?"

"I can't be too far away. Stretch out your arms and I'll do the same."

Fingers searched through gravel and dust until they met. Jacob pulled himself towards her, wrapping his arms around her shoulders. Her warm breath crawled over his skin. He felt her muscles twitch and shiver as he pulled her closer.

"I've got you. It's gonna be okay."

"I don't think we can get out of this. They're everywhere."

Leathery wings swooped towards them. Jacob ducked into the dirt, his free hand shielded Wisp's face as the bat like creature sunk its fangs into his forearm. He winced and pulled his arm away as blood trickled from the wound.

Its huge eyes filled its head. Jacob stared at it transfixed, until his mind refocused on to the pulsing pain, as black poison was being pumped from its fangs. Shaking his arm wildly, Jacob tried to knock it off. Its wings flapped as Jacob tried to grab hold. He managed to grip the tip and swung his arm back hard into the rocks. Black venom dripped from his wounds as he pushed the folds of skin together like a massive zit.

Wisp pulled the water bottle free from her belt and swotted at the bats. Jacob screamed whilst his fingers searched for the lighter. Settling on the cold metal he flicked the lid and felt the notches on the wheel dig into his skin. The flame jumped into life.

"Wisp, where's the rest of the lighter fluid? Quick, I need it."

She fumbled in her pockets and produced a small rectangular bottle.

"Here."

"Thanks."

He battled to lift the nozzle from the plastic encasing it. Wisp saw the problem and grabbed at it.

"Like this."

She flicked her fingers up in unison and the nozzle came loose.

Shrill squeaks and long wings bombarded them. One flew straight at Jacob. His heart pounded against his ribs. His arms flinched. Instinctively his fingers outstretched, dropping the lighter. The bat swerved to the right as Jacob ducked down further into the dirt. He scrambled to find the lighter amongst the dust. Grabbing it, he flicked down on the flint.

"Right, let's hope this works. Get behind me. On the count of three I'm going to light it up."

Wisp gripped Jacob's arm tightly.

"One, two, three."

His hand clamped down around the bottle, forcing the liquid to jet out in a steady stream. Deep orange flames leapt into the air. The squeaks morphed into shrieks. Jacob squashed his shoulders up over his ears, feeling the blood pumping through his temples.

It's so hot. Ah shit, it stings. I feel like I'm on fire. Maybe this wasn't the best idea.

Steady heat built in the air, forcing Jacob to take shallow breaths. Each one felt like swallowing hot chili peppers. He turned his head away, gulping down a few quick breaths before repositioning the stream. Bodies thudded into the rocks one after the other. One swooped down from the ceiling passing straight through the flames. Its leathery wings caught alight. They were still beating wildly as it coursed sharply to the left. Singed hairs glowed orange, burning down to the flesh. Jacob let go of the lighter and snatched at his shirt, pulling it up over his nose and mouth. His eyes opened wide and his forehead grimaced, before he grabbed Wisp's arm and dived to the floor as it plunged towards them. The flaming body smashed into the gravel, sending up a small plume of dust and smoke. The red glow of its eyes danced within the flames until the leathery wings turned to charcoal. The final shrieks faded away, sending small echoes rippling through the tunnels. Jacob and Wisp turned to each other.

"Is it over?" Wisp whispered.

"I don't know. I hope so," replied Jacob.

Wisp's hand slid into Jacob's and she squeezed it tightly as she leant in to kiss him. Spotting yellow eyes watching them from inches behind Jacob's head, Wisp pulled away sharply, clambering to her feet and stumbled backwards towards the rocks.

"What's the matter? What did I do?"

Jacob's question was answered with a heavy growl. His stomach flipped and his arms tremored. Slowly he turned his head. In his peripheral vision he caught sight of a yellow glare. Tucking his arms around his face, he tumbled towards Wisp's new position, pulled himself to his knees and stumbled to his feet. Wisp squirmed, her clammy t-shirt pressing against the cool rocks.

The eyes continued to stare.

Their chests rose and fell, panting in the darkness. Pin pricks of pain stung their eyes and caused their noses to twitch.

Seriously, enough already. Come on, make your move. Why isn't it attacking?

Wisp's nails dug into his waist and pinched the pale skin beneath. The gentle scrap of feet against gravel echoed through the tunnel. She inched her way backwards. Jacob stayed with her, his eyes never leaving the beast.

A burning pressure built across Jacob's eyeballs. Using two fingers he pulled at his eyelids forcing them to stay open.

I've got to blink. I can't last much longer, but if I take my eyes off it, what'll it do?

His eyes screwed up, it felt like his whole face was blinking. Every muscle tightened and retracted in unison.

Wisp screamed.

Jacob's eyes sprung open, expecting to see the beast hurtling towards him. Or to hear its teeth ripping into Wisp, but the yellow glow remained at a distance.

"What is it?" he whispered.

"Something just grabbed my leg."

Jacob didn't stop to think. He lifted his leg and stamped down hard behind where Wisp was standing. A creature screamed. Jacob lifted his foot again and slammed it down even harder.

Shit! I wish I was wearing shoes.

"Stop! Stop! It's me," Todd whimpered from below them.

Jacob paused. His eyes searched the darkness, resting on two small glints of white barely visible amongst the dust. He bent down reaching out for Todd's arm.

"Here, can you stand?" he said whilst tugging at Todd's elbow, pulling him to his feet.

"Yeah, I'm okay. Sorry, I didn't mean to scare ya. Jeez, you're actually quite strong. That really hurt."

"Sorry."

Jacob inhaled sharply and spun his head round.

"Oh shit! Wisp it's gone. Did you see where it went?"

"No, I was too busy thinking I was about to have my tendons ripped out. Seriously, why did you grab me?"

"I didn't think. I'm sorry," muttered Todd.

"You should be sorry. We're stuck down here in the dark with creatures attacking us and you think it's the right moment to grab me. Don't you ever think before you act? So friking stupid and now we don't know where the beast has gone or when it's going to be back. Just think first Todd. Think."

"I'm sorry alright. I just… I, oh, whatever."

"Whatever! That's all you've got to say. Whatever? Really?!"

"Let's argue later. We need to get out of here. Silly question, but do you know anywhere that's safe?" Jacob said hoping to defuse the situation.

"Nowhere is safe, but I can get us out of here. Will that do?"

"Yep, that'll do."

19

"This is ridiculous. How are we going to find our way in the dark? I just keep walking into things. There's got to be another way," said Jacob.

"I'm sorry, but I'm not the one who used all the lighter fluid," retorted Wisp.

"I did it to save both of us from those things."

"I know. Sorry. It was a good idea. It's just, it's gonna make finding Alex so much harder. I might have hid a can of lighter fluid in the tunnels, but I don't know where I am to be able to find it."

"Erm, I could help," whispered Todd, "I have a lighter, it doesn't have much lighter fluid left but it might be enough to find your way. Here, if you want to try."

Wisp fumbled around, trying to find Todd's hand. Taking the lighter, she struck down on the flint. Nothing happened. She tried again, still nothing.

"This thing's useless. It won't light," she said as she thrust it back in Todd's direction.

"It's temperamental, that's all. It's had a rough life. You just need to know how to handle it. Here."

His thumb rested on the metal frame and he shook the lighter up and down three times before quickly striking the flint. A tiny flame emerged, barely enough to light the air around it. Todd moved his thumb down slightly and carefully turned the wheel to adjust the flame. As it grew, the cave slowly became illuminated again. He leant across Jacob to pass the lighter back to Wisp.

"Thanks. This will help."

"Yeah, thanks Todd. I'm sorry for before," Jacob added.

"It's okay, I get it. It's hard being here. We haven't been around people in a while so it's gonna take time. Really, it's okay. I guess we're even now, hey?" said Todd as he nudged Jacob's arm.

"Yeah, let's call it quits," Jacob said smiling.

"Well, this is great. I'm glad we're all friends again, but can we get a move on. I don't think this lighter is gonna last much longer and I need to find my bearings," said Wisp.

The group walked on with Wisp in the lead. She built up her pace as the boys shuffled behind trying to keep up. They walked down endless tunnels, twisting and turning, left then right, over and over. Jacob sighed.

I don't think she knows where we're going. It was a shot in the dark I guess. We're never going to find Alex? We're all gonna die down here, just wandering until we drop.

"Hey, stop here a minute," Wisp said.

"Why?"

"This looks familiar. We might be back on track."

"How can you tell? It all looks the same, rocks and dirt. Rocks and dirt, that's all there seems to be," muttered Todd.

"And darkness, don't forget darkness," Jacob added.

"Have you two finished? You're right, it looks the same if you don't know what you're looking for, but luckily for you I do," she said smiling, "I marked the rocks to help me find my way around. See?"

Wisp held the lighter up to the rocks. The boys strained their eyes trying to see anything that looked different. It took them a few moments to spot the W etched into the stone.

"Smart. It looks just like part of the rock."

"Yep, barely noticeable unless you know what you're looking for. I wasn't sure who or what else might find them and try to track them so I tried to be cautious," Wisp smiled, "It means we aren't too far away from where I hid the lighter fluid. It should be down this tunnel and to the right."

Wisp ran her fingers along the rocks, feeling each bump and notch.

I hope I'm right.

The right wall fell away revealing a small opening.

Wisp peered round the edge of the rocks examining the tunnel. Turning back to speak to the boys, she froze. Her jaw went slack and her eyes fixed on a point behind them.

Jacob read the terror on her face.

"What's wrong?"

Her arm rose pointing, her mouth dry and her lips unable to move. Jacob turned slowly. He instantly knew why she was so afraid. He gulped against the panic rising in his throat. Todd was a beat behind. He let out a gasp as he spun to see what they were staring at. The yellow glare shone out of the darkness, fixed on the three of them like the sights of a gun.

Todd stepped out in front, shielding the others. He took a deep breath, closed his eyes and started walking. The beast didn't move. Todd felt his pulse quicken. The adrenaline coursed through his veins and his muscles tightened.

I've got to do this. I'm the one who let it get away. Now, I need to be the one to stop it. Eight more steps and I'll be in touching distance. Seven- It's eyes are burrowing into my head. Six- This is going to hurt. Why am I doing this? Five- is it too late to turn around? Four- Open your eyes. What am I even going to do when I get there? Three- it's still staring at me. Why hasn't it moved? Two- Clench your fists, get ready to fight. One- I'm ready. I can do this. Zero - wait where did it go?

An ear splitting scream filled the air. The gravel ground into dust as Todd spun round. His eyes focused on the yellow glare reflected in the metal of the lighter. Their mouths were stretched, white teeth showing. His feet slipped as he tried to run back to them.

Where are you going? This is their fight, not yours. You're already mine. Why are you trying to help them? You're never leaving this place. You know that. I'm all you have Todd. I'm your family now. Let my beast, do its job. It's not going to kill them, just destroy their hope.

The slow ebb, eating away. It's much more fun, don't you agree? Forever in the distance stalking. Always watching, waiting for that moment. You know what it's like. You've felt it before. They've got too hopeful. They need to be reminded just where they are. What they are and who they belong to.

"No. I don't belong to you. They don't either. Stay away from them," screamed Todd.

Todd ran at the beast, fists clenched. Jacob and Wisp's faces were still. Their eyes transfixed. Todd willed them to move.

His nails dug into his palms and he screamed out, "Blink Jacob! Don't look Wisp."

The words sounded muffled to Jacob and it took his brain a few seconds to process the cry. He blinked, the heavy cloud resting across his eyes started to fade. He rubbed at them, watching the white pixels turn to black. His hands fell and rested in front of his face, ready to fight. Wisp did the same.

Its dark matted fur glistened. Long, sharp white teeth protruded from its drooling mouth. Flecks of white bubbled and smoked where the spit hit the dirt. Its tail raised high above its body. Muscular legs toned and visible from beneath its skin tracked down to sharp claws, which settled on the rocks. It stood waiting.

They encircled it and watched.

Jacob was the first to move, lunging forwards. Todd followed then Wisp. Arms flailed. Jacob hit wildly at the air. Pausing, he stepped back and took a deep breath. His left hand jabbed into the beast's neck. Wet fur caught on his dry skin. The beast veered to Jacob's right. Todd grabbed at its tail, pulling back sharply as he took hold. It spun towards him, claws outstretched. Letting go in panic, he stumbled. His foot ricocheted off the floor and collided with the beast's snarling jaws. Wisp swung out her arms swiping at its paws. She felt the wet fur rub against her skin. The thud as flesh met bone, echoed around the cave walls. Jacob landed another blow, this time hitting its back legs. Todd kicked at its face. Spittle landed on his skin, burning small round splashes into his leg, but he kept kicking, wincing through the pain. Its yellow eyes remained focused on Jacob as each blow pummelled its fur. He averted his gaze. Bones popped and cracked against the backdrop of grunts and thuds.

As it lay bleeding, the three of them looked up nodding to each other in unison. They each took a step back. Drawing in breath, they sighed and slumped to the floor in exhaustion.

"Did we do it?" asked Todd.

"I think so. I'm not sure," Wisp replied.

A gentle clicking filled the air, slowly at first, building up in pace and volume. The noise erupted as the limbs of the beast reformed. Its bones rubbed over each other, cracking and popping back into place. Muscles shifted, pulling the skin taut as they realigned.

"Shit! We can't fight this. We need to run. Now!" shouted Wisp.

She clambered to her feet and started putting some distance between herself and the beast.

"I'll try to get the lighter fluid on my way past."

Jacob and Todd ran through the tunnels after her, following the sound of her voice in the darkness.

"Yes, I got it," she called out to them.

She's amazing. How on earth did she manage to grab the bottle, when we had a 6ft beast chomping at our heels?

Jacob managed another 400 metres before he gave in to temptation, turning his head slightly, searching the darkness for the tiniest glint of yellow.

"I think it's gone again for now," he muttered as he slowed down to a gentle jog.

He wasn't completely sure the others were still close by. The echoes of the caves distorted his senses. He strained to hear anything to pinpoint their location. A gentle drip turned into a steady gush. Jacob ran his fingers along the sides of the wall, searching for rainwater. The gushing stopped. He sighed, closing his eyes in the darkness.

Yellow lights streamed across the black. Jacob opened

his eyes, watching the flame grow. His breath quickened as he watched the yellow flames dancing in Wisp's eyes.

"No!" he screamed.

Taking his head in his hands, he fell to the floor and rocked. His fingers rested around his ear lobes, whilst his palms pressed into the holes. He watched as the yellow flames subsided.

"What's the matter with you?" she asked as she moved the lighter away from her face.

Jacob looked up confused and muttered, "Huh, your eyes were yellow. I thought he'd got to you. It was just the flame reflecting, I get that now, but for an instant I honestly thought I was going to have to fight you too."

She heard the waver in his voice and reached out.

"Not a chance," she replied.

"No more fighting please, I'm getting too old for this," said Todd from a few metres behind.

His cheeks glowed a scarlet red and his hands were pressed firmly on his knees. His shoulders rose and fell in pace with his breathing.

"Everyone alright? I thought we were goners back there," said Jacob.

"Yeah, but you should know he was in my head. He said it's always going to be there waiting, watching, ready to pounce. It wasn't going to kill you through, just ebb away at you like a dripping tap. I don't think we have seen the last of it. Sorry."

"Todd, it's okay. It's not your fault. It's what he does," said Jacob, "Let's just find my sister so we can get out of here. Alex! Please answer me. Alex!"

They all stood like statues, afraid the scuff of a shoe or the intake of breath would cover the sound of her reply. Jacob counted in his head, each second making him panic more.

Ten - Nothing. She's got to be here. I know she's here. Fourteen - Come on Alex, just answer me, please. Fifteen – maybe we've ran too far away from her when we tried to get away from the creature. Maybe that was The Raven's plan all along. Keep us distracted. Keep us away from finding her. Twenty...

The faintest cry echoed off the cave walls. Jacob strained to hear, concentrating on the silence.

"Jacob, I don't want..." Alex's voice broke and wavered as she spoke.

"It's her! It's her! Wisp did you hear her too?"

"Yeah, I heard her, but, but Jacob, she doesn't sound good. I think you need to be prepared, erm, she might of changed. This place does different things to different people and we, well, we don't know what The Raven's shown her or told her. She might not be the same Alex you remember."

"I'll get her back if you can get me to her. I'm not going to lose her Wisp. I can't. Please!"

"I'll get you there. This way! Quick."

20

"Michael. Wake up. I hope you like your new clothes. I couldn't bear staring at you any longer. Now come on. It's time for a family reunion. How long has it been since you saw them?"

Michael rubbed at his face and slowly opened his eyes. His hand reached out and took hold of the table next to him. When he pushed against it, the muscles in his legs wobbled and he tumbled back on to the hard wooden floor. His head rolled backwards and his eyes followed, searching the room for the voice. They settled on a dark figure perched on a worktop in the corner of the kitchen. Tapping fingers, drummed on to the marble. Michael rubbed his eyes again, running his hand over his face and back down over his hair.

Where am I? What did he say? Family reunion? My kids?

"What do you want?"

The figure landed on to the wooden floor, with an almost inaudible tap. Michael felt the sweat gather in between his fingers. His palms slid off the floor as he fought to get traction. His feet pressed hard against the wood. Fabric and sweat dug between his toes. Rubber squeaked, leaving black marks on the wooden panels as he propelled himself into the corner of the room.

"I want you to answer me!"

The Raven's hand descended and rested on to Michael's shoulder.

"One way or another."

Michael felt a clamping pressure build in his neck. His vision blurred with spots of red. He tried to shake off the feeling, but his head jerked sharply to the left, ricocheting off the corner of the table. A warm trickle of blood ran across his forehead. The muscles in his hand begun to spasm. His fingers went tight and jerked sharply. Pain shot through his shoulder, fizzling to his fingertips.

"I'll ask you again. How long has it been since you saw them?"

"Sev... seven years," he mumbled through the pain.

"Thank you. Next time, answer me the first time I ask. Okay?"

The Raven's arm lifted from Michael's shoulder and the pain instantly ceased, leaving behind a knot. Reaching across his body, Michael kneaded his muscles trying to release the building tension.

"So, seven years? I think that's long enough, don't you?"

"What do you want? Are you the person that took them? Where are my kids? There's a reason I haven't seen them. It doesn't mean I don't love them but... I'm no good for them. They're better off without me."

"From my point of view, yeah, they are, but then I have a soft spot for dark brooding despair. They were four and eight when you vanished from their lives. I don't know for sure, but I would guess if they had a choice between you and foster care, they would have chosen you every time. I wonder if they still will."

"Why am I here?"

"I just want to reunite a family but I think you might need some internal encouragement though, someone to guild you through this turbulent time. Someone to help you reconnect with them."

"Stay away from me and leave my kids alone."

"Where would the fun be in that? I think it would be much more exciting if I just helped you along a bit. Let's give it a try, see if you're a perfect fit. I think you will be."

Smoke bellowed from the intimidating frame now towering about Michael. It engulfed his skin, twisting and wrapping around his limbs. Black dust danced around his face. Rolls of fat protruded through the gaps as the smoky hand crawled up and rested between nose and chin. Forcing his head back, the smoke formed into fingers, prying at his jaws. He struggled as it crawled over his tongue. A bitter char coated his taste buds. Five sharp crescents dug into his scalp as the other arm made from a plume of malformed broken smoke reached down past his teeth.

Michael swallowed, his saliva tasted like old pub ashtrays and he could see curls of black smoke as he exhaled. The ripples burnt with every breath. Pressure built under his skin, pushing and pulling like someone trying to force themselves into an ill-fitting jumper. Tremors started at his fingertips, raising and quaking through his bones.

What's happening? Get out of me. Shit! No! Stop please. Stop.

Is this what they felt? They must have been so alone.

A single tear managed to free itself and trickle down following the gulley of his scar before everything went black.

I'm in your head now Michael and do you know what? I think I like it here. I might even use it as my new home for a while. I'm sure Jack won't mind. After all you are practically family.

"You don't mind, do you Jack?"

Everything's surreal. I can feel my head turning. I can still see everything, but nothing is working. I'm trying to talk and nothing is coming out. Wait? What? Jack?

Michael watched his own hand rest on the cold metal door handle, the sensations of touch were there but it felt like the circuit was broken somewhere in between his hand and brain. The snaps and cracks of bone played in his ears, but he felt no pain. He imagined his eyes widening as his finger morphed taking on the shape of a two tooth key. It fitted snuggly into the lock. The hinges creaked slightly as his other hand applied pressure, pushing the handle down sharply and tugging.

Hunched in the corner, tucked behind a broken shelf and some old plastic bags was a man. His clothes hung in creases around his frame, resembling discarded washing. His head was down and he looked frail and weak. Michael noticed the scars and calluses glimpsing from under the cuffs of his shirt and across his knuckles. The man looked up. His tie hung loosely around his neck. Deep wrinkles scattered his brow and his tired sunken eyes stared straight ahead.

"It's been a long time Michael," Jack whispered after clearing his throat.

"Jack, no time for a catch up. We are about to have a family reunion, but don't worry, I'll be back for you soon," Michael could hear his voice, but they weren't his words.

Let me speak to him. He's the scumbag that kept me away from Riley. He stopped me from seeing my kids grow up. He tried to turn their mother against me. I deserve the chance to talk to him. I deserve the chance to rip his head off.

But that would spoil all my fun. I'll tell you what, you play nice and stop trying to fight me and maybe just maybe, I'll let you get a few kicks in before I change outfits again. Right, I think it's time for the reunion.

"Bye Jack," the voice called as the door slammed and the key turned in the lock.

21

"Hey, I think we're getting closer. Her voice is louder, I'm sure of it," Jacob said happily.

"Yeah, I reckon we can't be too far away now. Call out to her again?" Wisp replied.

"Alex. Alex!"

"Jacob, where are you? I'm so tired," her voice was louder but more distant.

Wisp caught a glimpse of Jacob as his hand rubbed across his face wearily. His finger and thumb pinched the bridge of his nose then fanned out across his brow, before finally settling in his short brown hair. Her hand reached out for him but he turned and pulled away.

"I know you're worried. I am too but you're gonna see her again any second now."

"Yeah, I, just… she's always been the strong one and now she just sounds so alone. I don't know how I'm meant to protect her. Wisp, I think he's already won. She's not my Alex anymore. I'm terrified I'm going to get her back, only to find I've already lost her."

His nose tingled and a gentle thud settled over his left temple. Todd took over the lead whilst Wisp's arm settled across Jacob's back and she pulled him closer. His head rested on her shoulder, shaking slightly from the trembling waves of tears pouring down his face.

"Alex. I'm Jacob's friend. Answer me if you can hear us. We're coming to get you. Don't worry," Todd called out over and over, barely leaving any time to hear her replies.

"Todd, you've got to stop and give her time to speak. We won't hear a thing over the boom of your voice," said Wisp.

"Sorry."

Todd tried again, this time leaving a break in between his calls. He held the lighter out in front and stepped further down the tunnel.

A tiny voice answered "Are you really?"

"Yes, we're coming. Hold on."

Todd swayed the lighter back and forth, up and down, searching for the smallest crevice, anything to indicate she was nearby. His eyes caught the edge of a rock glinting in the dusty light. Bending down he ran his hand along its edge feeling the smooth contours beneath his fingertips. He followed them round, watching as the rocks arched and twisted until his hand fell away into the darkness.

Shit, that was close.

"Guys, I think I've found something. The tunnel drops away here. It might lead us to a cavern. Whatcha reckon?"

Jacob broke away from Wisp's gentle comfort and rubbed his shirt around his eyes, letting the fabric soak away his pain. After pulling his shirt back down, he paced over to Todd and bent down to join him on the edge. He ran his fingers along the rocks, following the same line as Todd had done. Lying down on the stone, he dangled his arm into the abyss and searched for the sides.

"Alex," he called into the darkness.

"Jacob"

"She's down there. Her voice is much louder. It's possible; it might lead to a cavern. Hand me the lighter, then grab my legs. I want to see how deep it is."

Todd's hands settled on the ripped remains of Jacob's pyjama bottoms.

"They aren't gonna hold," announced Todd.

Jacob squirmed slightly as Todd pulled at the fabric, shuffling it up over his knees. The warmth of Todd's palms rested on his calves and he felt the slightly sweaty grip force them into the dirt. Wisp's hands joined Todd's in holding him steady. Jacob grasped the lighter and clicked for a flame. It grew out of the metal and he swung his torso back into the hole, arms outstretched, with the lighter gripped tightly in his hand.

Where are the sides? I can't feel them. There has to be sides if we are going to get down. Maybe if I push a bit further. Please, come on. I've got a feeling about this.

94

She's down here somewhere.

"Anything?" asked Todd.

"Nothing yet. I'm trying to find the sides."

"How deep is it?"

"I'm not sure. I can't see the bottom, but it might only be a few feet away or it could be a massive drop. I don't think we can chance it. Anyone got anything we can drop and listen out for?"

"Erm, yeah, hang on. Todd have you got him?"

"Yeah."

Wisp rose to her feet and scurried back down the tunnel. She returned a few moments later carrying a few tiny pebbles and one larger rock.

"Okay, move over a bit. I don't want these to hit you as I let them go."

Jacob pressed his stomach in against the edge of the hole. The coldness of the rocks made his muscles tighten. Once he was in position Wisp let go of the first pebble.

"I didn't hear anything but it was tiny. It probably broke up as it hit the rocks. We need something bigger," said Todd.

"Okay, I'll try this one. Let me put the others down. I might need to position it better."

Jacob's voice echoed as he spoke, "Okay, hurry up though. This is starting to hurt."

Wisp shuffled into position and counted to three, then dropped the rock and held her breath.

Please let this work. One, two, three, four...Was that a thud? I think it was a thud.

"Did anyone else hear a thud?"

"I think so," replied Todd.

"Yeah it was. Can you pull me up please?"

Todd and Wisp each grabbed a leg. Their faces reddened as they strained against Jacob's weight. He wiggled his hips into the dirt, trying to give himself some traction. It took a minute or so to hoist him completely free of the hole. Jacob rubbed absently at his stomach as the others fired off questions.

"So did you find the sides?"

"How deep do you reckon?"

"Can we make it down without hurting ourselves?"

"Do you think she's really down there somewhere?"

"Okay, hold on a minute. Yeah, I found the sides. I don't think it is break your neck deep, but possibly break your leg deep. I think she must be down there. Her voice was so much louder when she called to us. So now we need to work out how we are going to get down there safely," replied Jacob.

"Have we got anything we could set alight? Maybe we could drop it down there and get a better look at it," suggested Todd.

"Your pyjama bottoms have seen better days. We could cut some of the fabric free, pour some of the lighter fluid on it, set it alight and drop it in," said Wisp.

"Good idea, as long as we only use some of the fabric. I'm not walking around in my pants."

"I don't know, that could work too," Wisp smiled and giggled.

She unclipped the knife from her belt and flicked the blade free with her finger. The metal slid across the fabric and she worked it through the strands until she held a piece of cloth in her hands. Next, she wedged her fingers under the nozzle of the lighter fluid and prized it free. Tipping the bottle upright, she squeezed and watched as little droplets of liquid squirted out from within. Hovering over the void she held the soaked rags at a distance and tentatively waved the lighter underneath, then dropped the rags into the darkness, watching as particles of dust caught fire as they fell.

The three of them dropped to their knees and hung their heads over the void examining the structure as the flames danced to the rocks below.

"I was right. We can make that jump if we're careful. Look, there's definitely an opening off to the side. It kinda looks like the one we had to crawl down when we found Todd. I'll go first," Jacob said excitedly.

"Hang on a minute, it's still a steep drop. How can you be sure we won't get hurt?" asked Todd.

"I can't be 100% sure but if we dangle from the edge by our arms, it won't make the drop so bad. It's like they tell you to do if you're upstairs in a house fire. I'll show you what I mean and if I don't make it then you don't have to follow. How about that?"

Jacob dangled his legs into the hole and placed his hands into the surrounding dirt. It coated his palms like chalk.

I hope this gives me extra grip and doesn't just turn to sticky wet mud.

His shoulders rose and fell slowly as he tried to calm his nerves.

His nail beds turned a mixture of dark red and shocking white. Tremors rippled down his muscles causing his arms to shake as they took the strain. He hung suspended for a moment before his grip loosened and begun to slip. He felt the sweat forming on his fingertips. It glided over the smooth edge of the rocks. Wisp reached out and clasped her delicate fingers around his wrist. Todd fumbled slightly then managed to do the same.

"Thanks. I could feel myself slipping."

"Well, now we've got you we might as well try to lower you down a few more inches," said Todd.

They lay on their stomachs and winced as the dead weight of his body forced their shoulders down awkwardly into the rocks.

"Okay, we'll let you go on three. Ready?" said Wisp.

Jacob grunted back a yes and tried to mentally focus on how he wanted to land.

"One, two, three," they said in unison.

As their grips loosened Jacob plummeted towards the rocks. He managed to use his knees to absorb some of the impact and rolled slightly to the left to counteract the loss of balance.

"Jacob?" called Todd.

"Jacob? Answer him!" shouted Wisp.

"I'm okay. It hurts less than I thought it would," he said whilst rubbing his elbow and knee in quick succession.

"Jacob? Jacob. I'm down here," called a voice in the distance.

"Alex!"

Jacob hurried to his feet and rushed over to the opening. His heart was pounding with anticipation.

"Oh, please let it be real," he whispered.

As he reached the tunnel, his face fell and his hands locked behind his head. He rocked back and forth, drawing his elbows in against the sides of his head.

"What's wrong?" Wisp called from above.

"It's blocked. There are loads of rocks piled up. It's going to take ages for me to clear it," he replied.

"Jacob, where are you?" Alex called from somewhere behind the rocks.

"I'm coming Alex. Can you see a tunnel? I think I'm on the other side, but there are rocks in the way."

"I can't see anything. It's pitch black in here," she replied whilst crying.

"Use your hands. Can you feel around? See if you can find any loose rocks or an opening. Any luck?"

Her voice broke and her breathing was uneven as she replied, "I'm scared Jacob. Every time I move something bad happens. Mum told me to stay still. I don't want Jack to come back again."

Why is she talking about Mum and Jack? What's The Raven shown her? What do I say? She sounds so lost and confused.

"Erm, it's okay Alex. I'll start digging."

Jacob crouched on his knees, balancing the lighter on the ground he began to claw at the rocks. The sharp edges dug into his fingers. Dirt built up under his fingernails and he could feel the sides slicing into his fingertips. Slowly pebbles crumbled away from the wall. Jacob prised his fingers into the gaps searching for some purchase over the rubble.

Wisp called down to him, "I'm coming down to help.

Watch out!

Todd can you hold my arms, like we did for Jacob?"

Wisp slid into the void legs first. Her fingertips clung to the edges of the hole as Todd shuffled his body into position. He wrapped his fingers around her wrists.

"You okay? I just felt your joints pop," Todd asked.

"Yeah, I can just feel it pulling. It's not pleasant but it's not for much longer. Let me go on three. Ready?"

She dangled further into the cavern.

"Yep, one, two, three."

Momentarily Wisp felt the air pressing against her body. She pulled her arms up to cover her face, clamping her palms firmly to the back of her head. Drawing her knees up to her chest she landed, rolling wildly across the cavern floor.

"Ouch! Shit! You said it didn't hurt much. Ow!"

"You must have landed funny. Bones all still intact?" Jacob asked while still scrabbling at the rocks.

"Yeah, I think so. Gonna have some bruises though. Move over and let me see."

Wisp grabbed the lighter from the floor and waved it close to the rocks.

"This has been sealed on purpose. There's too much filler in between the rocks for it to be a coincidence. Jacob, your fingers."

"I know, but I can't stop. They're numb now. I hardly feel the pain."

"Stop!"

She grabbed his hands and held the lighter as close as Jacob could bear to examine them.

He snatched them away again, "I don't have time."

"You do because I'm here now. Let me take over just for a bit. Here, use the water to clear some of the blood and dirt off."

She held the water bottle out in front of him. Jacob took it and placed it on the rocks.

"No! I've got to do this. Either help me or go away. Alex doesn't have time for us to argue."

Wisp sighed, "Okay, you win."

She leaned closer and began to scratch and pull at the rocks. After a few minutes, she stopped and leaned back on her knees.

"This isn't working. We need something to chip away at the dirt. If we can loosen the filler, we can loosen the rocks."

"The knife?" Jacob asked while still digging.

"We can try," replied Wisp.

She reached to her belt and felt the cold metal casing rub against her palm. After wiggling the casing free, she flicked the blade out and dug the sharpened edge into the muddy filler. Dirt fell away as she slid the blade through the cervices. Using her fingers she grabbed at the debris and began to yank handfuls of rocks away.

"Yes, it's working. You're amazing," Jacob said gleefully.

"Teamwork," she replied, "It's really deep. There must be at least four or five layers of rock."

"He really doesn't want us to find her," whispered Jacob.

"Or for her to leave," added Wisp.

The two of them continued to dig. Wisp chipped away at the dirt, whilst Jacob heaved away chunks of debris.

Above, Todd was building up the courage to drop through the hole into the cavern below. His shoes slid on patches of mud. He skirted around the edge, trying to find the best angle.

"Hmmm, I could try here."

Bending down he examined the space with his hands.

"It feels rough. Maybe this angle is better. Hmm, maybe, I don't know. I think maybe I should try another place."

Todd circled the hole over and over, coming up with a different reason to stay each time. He ran his fingers along the bumps and recesses. He leant down to try and grip the edge. His foot slipped, shooting into the void. Desperately, he clambered for something to grab, anything to hold on to. His body weight carried him through the hole, one leg in front the other flailing behind. He screamed as he plummeted, catching his hand on the jagged rocks as he fell. Wisp and Jacob twisted their heads round, feeling the strain in their necks.

"Shit!" they said in unison.

Todd thumped into the ground sending up a plume of dust into the air. Wisp jumped to her feet and leapt five steps in one bound. Kneeling at his side, she placed her hands on his shoulders and shook him gently. Jacob was a few seconds behind.

"Todd? Todd? Todd!"

He grumbled and moaned incoherently. Wisp tried again.

She grabbed his shoulders, shaking him more vigorously, "Come on Todd, wake up!"

"Wha…what happened?"

"You fell. How do you feel?"

"My head's spinning. I feel sick. I think I'm going to throw up."

Yellow bile with darkened chunks of brown splashed on to the rocks inches from Wisp's feet. She stumbled backwards whilst he coughed a few times to try and clear the taste from his mouth.

"Every time I move I get sharp stabbing pains in my left arm and the world seems to be moving."

"I think you might have concussion, possibly a broken arm. I'll come round and take a look. Stay still while I get the lighter."

Jacob grabbed the lighter and passed it to Wisp.

"I'm glad you're okay, but I need to keep digging. Wisp will fix you up. Don't worry."

He went back to the opening and continued to prise rocks free from the wall.

"It's okay. I get it. So what's the damage?" Todd asked wearily.

He struggled to stay still as Wisp gently examined his body with the lighter. She ran her fingers up his left arm, pressing gently and watching his face for any changes. As she reached just below his shoulder he began to wince. The closer she got the harder he bit down on his lip, trying desperately not to scream out. A lump protruded through his skin. It looked red and angry with a white shine where the bone was pressing hard against the skin.

"The good news is you've only managed to cut your arm and I think your shoulder might be dislocated not broken. Everything else seems to be intact," Wisp replied.

"And the bad news?" Todd asked after vomiting again.

"We need to pop it back into place."

And I've only every seen it done on telly.

"Oh great!" mumbled Todd.

Jacob stood up and walked over to where Todd was lying.

"Do you need any help?"

"I'm going to try and pop it back in. I might need your help if I can't manage it."

"Okay, are you sure you want to try alone first?"

"Yeah, I think both of us doing it might cause more damage."

"That alright with you mate? If Wisp doesn't need my help can I borrow one of your shoes? I'm almost through."

Todd grunted and Jacob took it as a yes. He bent down and tried to undo the laces, but his fingers kept slipping from the thread. Wisp saw him struggling and went over to help. Jacob sighed and pushed himself back against the wall to give her more space. The laces were covered in a combination of sticky blood and soaked mud making them wet and slimy. Wisp grabbed at the plastic end and yanked it free. The laces unravelled. Undoing the last loops she wriggled the shoe free from Todd's foot.

"Thanks."

Jacob slipped his own foot inside and tied the laces, pulling tightly to ensure the shoe was secure. He went back to the opening, sat down and positioned his leg in line with the main body of rocks. His foot pounded into the rocks over and over while Wisp took hold of Todd's arm and tried to remember what she was meant to do.

Todd and Jacob's screams synchronised, each one louder than the last. Jacob was getting more frantic with every kick. Wisp was on her third attempt, she was hoping to hear the satisfying pop as Todd's shoulder clicked back into place.

"One more try," she said as she raised his arm slightly.

Wisp pulled sharply. Todd and Jacob let out an anguishing cry. The final rocks crumbled away. Wisp didn't hear the pop as his shoulder went back in; she was too distracted by the face appearing in the opening. It was dirty and wet. Brown hair matted together in long strands framing the thin face. A black ribbon glinted slightly in the light. Wisp followed it with her gaze trying to find where the ribbon ended and the hair began. Hazel eyes stared wildly at the lighter, transfixed by the flame. Her fingers stroked absently at the green marbled necklace which hung loosely around her neck. Pink fur hung from her elbow.

Jacob reached out to her but she just sat staring at his arm. He shuffled closer and she recoiled slightly still within view.

"Alex," Jacob said softly, "It's me. It's okay. I'm here."

Alex's hand crept out from the opening, though the rest of her body stayed hidden in the darkness. Jacob mirrored her movements. His fingers brushed against her arm and she screamed as bloody streaks of red smeared across her pale skin. Alex scurried further into the tunnel clutching her elbows. She pawed at the blood, scratching it from her skin.

"I'm sorry, I've just cut myself. That's all. Look."

Jacob grabbed the water and poured it over his fingertips, washing away the blood soaked mud.

"See. It's me Alex. I'm real."

Alex stopped. She watched the lumps of mud float and dance in the water. Her eyes rose slowly from the floor and stared at Jacob. Her head tilted to the side and Jacob could just make out her tongue sitting behind her teeth.

She gently patted Fuzz with her free hand and stroked the necklace one last time.

"Jacob?" she asked hopefully.

22

Wisp tugged at the belt, unwinding it from around her body. She picked up the knife and lighter bottle lying on the ground and shoved them into her pockets. Leaning over Todd she refastened the belt buckle and gently placed it around his neck. He winced slightly as it brushed against his shoulder.

"Sorry. Try it now. I've made it tighter so it'll fit better."

Todd thanked her and slid his hand inside carefully lowering his forearm against the belt and allowing it to take the weight from his shoulder.

"That's alright," she replied, "How does it feel?"

"It feels better than it did. It only hurts when I breathe, move or laugh so as long as I don't do any of those I'm fine," he said with a half-smile half grimace on his face.

Wisp's lips fell into a sad smile and her eyes were downcast.

"Should I go over?" she whispered.

"Maybe in a bit. Has she moved yet or stopped staring?" Todd asked quietly.

"No, she's still just inside the opening. She won't let Jacob in but won't come out either. She keeps muttering about their Mum and someone called Jack."

"Isn't their Mum dead?"

Wisp sighed, "Yeah but I think The Raven's got inside her head."

"He's good at finding your trigger and manipulating it. He did it to me."

"I'm sorry, I haven't even asked. How did you end up here?"

"Erm, well, I was a good kid then I got bullied at school and used drugs as a way out of it, which got me kicked out of my flat and I ended up on the streets. I kept my head down and tried to make the best of it, but it's hard. I never knew where my next meal was coming from or if I was going to wake to find my kit bag stolen. Once, I was sleeping in an underpass near Southbank. I'd just managed to drift off when a couple of guys were on their way home. They decided me being there offended them so they came and woke me up with a boot in my chest. I don't remember much from that night, but you can still feel the dip in my skull if you put your hand here. Someone else must have spotted me because I got rushed into hospital. After they fixed me up they arranged for me to go to St Paul's Shelter for the homeless. That's where The Raven found me. I've never felt worthy of anything so it didn't take much for him to get into my head and well here we are."

Wisp felt a cold shiver run down her spine. Her eyes felt hot and the base of her nose began to tingle. She reached for his good arm and stroked it gently, squeezing his hand.

"Thanks. I think you should check on Alex. I'm alright."

Wisp bit her bottom lip unsure on whether to leave.

"Are you sure?"

"Yeah, go."

"Okay, I'm going to try and talk to her. Shout if you need anything."

"Cheers."

Wisp rose to her feet and walked the few steps to where Jacob was sitting. His arm was outstretched and Alex's dainty hand lay within his palm.

"Hi Alex, I'm Wisp. I'm Jacob's friend. Do you want some water?"

She held the bottle out in front of her and Alex's gaze shifted slightly. The ripples glimmered in the light of the flame. Alex watched intently and mirrored the movements with her fingers, before cautiously reaching for the bottle. As she did so Fuzz came loose from his makeshift pouch and tumbled towards the muddy puddle. Wisp realised and caught him in mid-air. Alex looked at her perplexed, dropped the bottle and screamed.

"Here, here, take him," Wisp said trying to comfort her, "He was going to fall in the puddle. I didn't want him to get wet."

She waved the teddy close to Alex's face as though she was a toddler. Alex snatched at it and drew it in close to her nose. Her body shuffled back into the darkness. She sighed and breathed in deeply over and over, moving the teddy as she did so. Jacob watched, his mouth hanging open slightly and his eyes aghast.

What's wrong with her? What's she doing? She's just muttering about Mum and Jack. She won't come near me. What do I do? How can I show her it's safe?

He thought about what his Mum would have done. Closing his eyes, he started talking.

"Once upon a time there was a brave Princess called Alex. One night long ago, she was taken by an evil sorcerer and locked away in the darkness. She was very sad and lonely but she had her trusty companion Fuzz with her to keep her company. He protected her from danger and looked after her until her brother Prince Jacob and his band of loyal friends Whispering Wisp and Tireless Todd came to look for her. They followed the sound of her voice for days and fought off monsters before finding her trapped behind an enchanted wall. Whispering Wisp had the magnificent idea to use a magic knife to chip away at the wall and remove the evil sorcerer's magic. Prince Jacob struck the final blow and the wall came crumbling down. Inside Princess Alex was alone and lost. The evil sorcerer had been unkind to her and shown her some horrible things. She didn't know if she could trust the Prince or his friends. When Fuzz was almost injured in a nasty fall, Princess Alex worried Whispering Wisp was going to try and take him away but then she realised the fair maiden with her auburn locks was actually saving Fuzz from crashing into the most dangerous river she had ever seen. Almost at once Princess Alex knew it really was her brother Prince Jacob and..."

Jacob stumbled over his words. He didn't know how to

107

finish the story. He desperately wanted to say how she fell into his arms, cuddled him and they were suddenly transported back to a happier place and time but he couldn't.

I don't know what's going to happen next. I can't tell her it's all going to be okay, because it might not be. We might have found each other but we're still stuck down here and I don't know how we're going to get out, especially with Todd's arm out of action.

"and she crawled out of the tunnel and gave him the longest hongi in the world." Alex said as she crawled out into the light and sat down in front of her brother.

One hand cradled Fuzz whilst the other stroked Jacob's hair in the same way his mother used to. Alex leant in closer and sniffed, breathing in his scent. Her face softened and she gently rubbed her nose on his. A smile blossomed on her lips and she wrapped her arms around him, pulling him into her embrace. He grabbed her and squeezed so tightly. Wisp turned to look at Todd and smiled. She cheered silently, waving her hands in small circular motions. He tried to do the same then stopped abruptly as the pain kicked in again.

Alex whispered in Jacob's ear, "I missed you but I knew you would come."

Her shoulders jerked slightly and her eyes became puffy and red. Jacob felt her tears soak into the black cotton of his t-shirt. His head rested on hers and his arms wrapped around her, pulling her in closer.

He rocked her slowly back and forth, then placed his lips to her ear and whispered "It's okay Alex, I'm here. I'm not going anyway without you. I love you."

23

Alex lay on Jacob's chest and Wisp rested her head on his shoulder. Todd was pacing the width of the cavern searching the walls with the lighter in his good arm.

"Alex, before, erm, you were muttering something about Mum and Uncle Jack. I didn't understand what you meant. What were you saying?" Jacob said quietly.

Alex sat bolt upright. Her shoulders arced up forcing her chest into her chin. Every muscle tensed and froze. Her eyes danced wildly, dashing from left to right. Jacob could see her chest rising and falling faster and her face drained to a ghostly white.

"He was here. He showed me Mum. I, I had to, he made me..."

"Who was here? The Raven? What did he show you? What did he make you do? Alex, please talk to me. He showed me stuff too, but it wasn't real."

"But this was real Jacob."

"Please Alex tell me."

Alex started to cry again.

"It was The Raven and Uncle Jack, they were both here. He showed me Mum the night she died. He made me watch."

"Oh Alex," he said hugging her, "but what does that have to do with Uncle Jack?"

"Uncle Jack killed her Jacob. I saw him. His eyes were empty, but it was him. He tried to get her to do something. Then when she fought back and grabbed the knife, there was a struggle. He got the knife from her and dug it into her neck and twisted it. The blood poured out and sprayed everywhere. Her eyes were searching. They were looking for us to save her but we didn't. We were upstairs asleep and Mum was downstairs fighting for her life. You got up to pee but you went back to bed. If only you had come downstairs. Maybe he would have stopped if one of us had got up to look for her. We could have saved her Jacob. It was our fault. I should have made her stay upstairs with me. I should have made her read me another story or lie with us until we both fell asleep. He would have gone away then and she would still be alive. But I didn't, you didn't and she's dead. We killed her. Uncle Jack had the knife, but we let her die Jacob. We let her die."

Alex's sobs were loud and uncontrollable. Her tiny body heaved and trembled. Her lungs burnt, longing for more oxygen with each sharp intake of breath. Jacob stared blankly. The colour drained from his face and his fingers pinched and scratched the skin around his wrist.

Wisp didn't know what to do. She noticed Jacob anxiously scratching at his skin and could see Alex's obvious despair. She reached for Jacob's arm and placed her hand on top of his fingers. Forcing his hand away from his wrist, she slid her fingers in between his. He tried to scratch at her skin but she wedged her fingers higher, trapping each fingertip between her knuckles. She was reaching out for Alex too, but Todd got there first. He stumbled as he tried to sit down and landed ungracefully behind her. Scooping her up with his good arm, he pulled her close to his body and rocked her gently, placating her with gentle whispers. She crumbled into his chest and wept.

Jacob struggled trying to wrench his fingers free. His eyes were stained red, bloodshot and bleary. Wisp let him have his wish and unlocked her fingers from his. Instead, her hands rested gently on each side of his face and she shifted her weight, straddling him with her legs.

Bending forwards, she whispered, "You didn't kill her. It's not your fault. Look at me. It's not your fault."

Jacob blinked. Salty tears rolled down his cheeks and she caught them with the side of her hand, brushing them away. Her eyes stayed focused on his momentarily then flickered down to his lips. Moving her head closer, she kissed him softly where the tears had been then gently placed her lips on his. A warm feeling bubbled inside, nervous energy fired off sparks and his stomach churned.

110

The feelings clashed then settled. Sadness tinged with joy, fear blurred by hope. He felt his lips soften, moving silently matching her movements. Her eyes were stinging and red. She blinked to clear the building water away and their tears mixed like streams flowing into a river.

Alex broke the silence, "Jacob, I want her back. She talked to me while I was alone and I want her back."

He broke away from Wisp, caressing her face with his hand as he clambered to his feet. Pressing his forearm into his eyes, he wiped away the residual tears, breathed heavily and moved to where Todd was sitting. Alex smudged her face against Todd's chest, hugged him and shuffled over to Jacob.

Her brother held her in his arms and said, "I want her back too. I know we aren't going to make new memories with her, but we still have so many great times to look back on. She's with us Alex. She's in us. She's the reason we both had hope we would find each other again. She made us strong. We have to be strong now. We need to find a way out of here and show The Raven, Uncle Jack and whatever else they throw at us, we can and we will win."

A few minutes passed before Alex and Jacob rose to their feet. She led him down into the opening where she had been kept captive. He looked around using the flame to examine the walls. Leaning down, she picked up the tatty piece of cloth she had used as her blanket and folded it over her arm.

"You might be able to find a way out. It was so dark in here I couldn't find anything, but you might have more luck. Have a look, I'm going to crawl back out and give this to Wisp maybe she can make a proper sling for Todd with it."

Jacob felt around the walls searching for any hand holds they could use to climb up with. The rough edges of the rocks jabbed and poked into his skin. He closed the lid on the lighter and stood in the darkness. His senses searched. His eyebrow rose as he listened to a gentle

111

cascade of water.

Jacob slid the metal lighter in between the elastic of his pyjama bottoms. Closing his eyes, he focused on his breath, in and out, calm and slow. Splaying his fingers out in front of him, he started to walk, listening for the slow dribble and splash to become more defined. His fingers crunched into the wall and he shook his hand to shake off the pain. On the last shake, his little finger brushed against the wall. Cool droplets settled on his nail. His hand held there for a moment, angling upwards so gravity would force the soothing drips to trickle down towards his wrist.

If I can find where the water is coming from, maybe I can find a way out.

Jacob retrieved the lighter, flicked open the lid and snapped his thumb against the wheel. A flame shot free and swayed with his breath. One hand traced the water upwards the other followed with the lighter. Soft wet dirt dug beneath his nails and he forced his fingers into the tiny faucet and pulled down sharply.

"Yuck, it's so slimy but it's not budging. There has to be another way in but I can't see the ceiling. It's just darkness. Maybe we could scale the walls, but I don't know how high we would even have to go. This is hopeless. I better go and tell them the bad news," he mumbled.

Jacob crawled back through the opening. The flame illuminated his face.

"Any luck?" Todd asked without looking up.

"What's wrong?" said Wisp. Her eyes settled on his shrugging shoulders and the worry lines wrinkling his brow.

"There's water dripping through the wall and there has to be oxygen getting in from somewhere, but the walls are sheer and there's no way we would be able to climb up, plus I can't tell how far up we would even have to go," Jacob sighed, "It looks like we're gonna have to hoist each other up and go out the way we came in."

"How the hell am I gonna do that?" said Todd, cradling

his left arm in its new sling.

"I don't know. Maybe we could lift you up somehow. Wisp any ideas?"

"Erm, let me think about it for a minute or two. We'll find a way. Don't worry."

Alex scurried around them collecting the rocks they had dislodged from the opening. Piling them up under the hole and racing off to get more.

"What are you doing?" asked Todd

"If we pile these all up, it might give us some extra height. We could use the water from the walls and the dust and dirt on the floors to make mud like the puddle over there. If we use enough mud we could make it like cement, join the rocks together. Maybe use the lighter to dry it out. I don't know if it'll work but it's better than just sitting here."

"How did you think of that?" Jacob asked impressed.

"We learnt about mud houses at school," Alex replied, whilst twisting strands of hair around her finger.

"It's worth a try," said Wisp.

The three of them scuttled about collecting the rocks. Todd moved closer to the discarded rock pile and rolled rocks along the ground using his good hand. He tried to turn his face away from the others to hide his disappointment.

I'm not going to get back up there. I can't use my arm and they won't be able to lift me. I'm too heavy. I reckon this is it. I'm just gonna be trapped down here forever.

Unless... The Raven, he might takes pity on me.

Ha! I doubt it. He feeds off despair. Being trapped down here; I'll end up being his next meal.

"You okay Todd?" asked Alex.

Todd blinked and shook his head as though he was waking from a dream. His right hand rubbed his temple and slid a little too easily through his greasy hair.

"Erm, yeah, sorry. I was just thinking if this doesn't work you guys need to leave me behind. I mean, I'm not light and you aren't going to be able to lift me up. I can't climb out on my own, so yeah, I was thinking you should leave me down here and then when you get out you can send help back to find me."

Alex bounded over to him, swooped down and kissed his forehead.

"We aren't going to leave you behind," she said with certainty.

"I think we're nearly done then all we have to do is dry it out. Anyone got any suggestions of the best way of doing it?" Wisp asked trying to move the conversation on.

"The lighter fluid might work, but I reckon there will be a lot of smoke. We could try to sleep here tonight and see how dry it is in the morning. Maybe we might have thought of some other ideas by then. Failing that, another day or two down here would give Todd's arm a chance to settle. I know it won't fix it, but it might be less painful for when we have to lift him up. Whatcha reckon?" replied Jacob.

The others nodded.

"Do you think one of us needs to stay awake in case The Raven pays us a visit?" Todd asked.

"It's not a bad idea. Maybe we can take it in shifts," replied Wisp.

Todd nodded, "I'll go first. You all try and get comfortable and get some rest."

"Thanks," they said in unison.

Wisp lay with her head resting on Jacob's chest. Alex lay down next to him with her arms wrapped tightly around his stomach. Jacob lay awake watching the darkness. His eyelids felt heavy and his breathing shallowed. All his muscles began to relax and his head bobbed towards his chin before jolting upright again. Each time his eyes shot open, only to close again moments later. Eventually he succumbed; a tiny smile emerged on his lips as he dreamt about his Mum.

24

"I reckon it's hard enough. I told you it only needed another day," Alex said while standing on tiptoes on top of the rock pile.

"So, let's go through the plan again.

I'm going to stand on the rocks with Alex on my shoulders. She is going to reach up and climb out of the hole. Then I'll do the same for Wisp. I'll give Todd a leg up and he'll use his right arm to lever himself out of the hole. You two can pull from up there and I'll try to support his feet from down here, then Wisp will lower her belt down. I'll jump up and grab the end. You'll both help me up until I can reach the sides of the wall. Then I'll drag myself up and out. What could possibly go wrong?"

"Don't say that," Wisp said whilst playfully hitting him on the shoulder.

"So, everyone ready. Alex you're first."

Alex went around the circle and hugged them all. Her brother knelt down near the mound. Jacob rotated his shoulder slightly as Alex climbed on, whilst Wisp's hands braced around Alex's legs. Shakily Jacob stood up wincing from the stabbing pain emanating from his ribs. Wisp noticed him squinting and tucking his elbow in against his ribs to try and give some support.

Alex wobbled unsteadily, curling her toes to try and keep her balance.

"Okay, I'm going to stretch up now and grab hold. Try not to move."

Her fingers searched for the rock's edge. Fumbling, her knuckles grazed against it and her fingers took hold. She waited until she was sure her grip would hold, tightening her muscles, she felt the weight of her own body dragging her back down towards the others below.

Come on, you can do this. It's just like climbing out of a swimming pool, just without the water and a massive drop instead.

The dirt scratched her skin, filling the crevices on her elbow. A dust cloud swirled as she exhaled. Pressing her hands into the dirt, her arms trembled taking the full weight of her body.

"I've made it up. Wisp you're next."

"Nah, I think we need to change the plan. Jacob you're going next. I'll give Todd a leg up and you can help Alex pull him through up there."

Jacob began to protest. Wisp nudged him gently in the ribs. A flash of white shot in front of his eyes and he bent over clutching his side with his arm. His eyes glared then softened.

"You won't be able to lift him alone. Up there you'll have Alex and the counter balance of the floor to help you. Trust me, it's the better option," Wisp said.

She knelt down and clasped her hands together. Jacob placed his foot inside.

"Just like old times," he muttered before he transferred his weight.

She jerked her arms upwards, thrusting him into the air.

Alex lay on the ground. She pressed her shoulder into the floor and dangled one arm through the hole, whilst the other gripped tightly to the side. Jacob's right hand snatched at her, holding tightly. Her muscles trembled and she fought against them to stay in control. Jacob's left hand searched for purchase on the rim of the hole. A sharp intake of breath and an almighty push forced him upwards. Alex rolled backwards, her momentum pulling him up and over the edge. His hands scrambled momentarily until he managed to regain his balance and work his way out.

Wisp removed her belt.

"Here," she said, "you better take this up otherwise I'll be stuck down here."

Todd looped the belt over his neck and rested it under his sling.

"Are you sure about this? I'm not exactly light," he asked.

"Yeah I'm sure, so let's get on with it before I change

my mind."

Wisp knelt down again, using her toes to steady herself. Breathing deeply and calmly, she cracked her knuckles before locking her fingers together ready to take his weight.

"Everyone ready up there?" she called.

"Yeah."

Todd's foot pressed down hard into her hands. The imprint of his trainer etched into her palm. He could feel her shaking, slowly at first, then building into a full tremor. His right hand waved aimlessly above him until it collided with something warm and squishy.

"I'm hoping that's one of you," he called as he gripped it tightly.

Another arm lunged out of the darkness. He felt the air swoosh as it passed by, before the hot sticky limb clamped around his wrist and heaved. Every tendon wrenched. His entire body weight hung on one arm. Todd flapped his left arm back and forth until it was clear of the sling. Reaching up, he managed to grab hold of the edge and push. Sharp bursts of red and white popped and fizzled in front of his eyes. He screwed them shut and bit down hard on his lip, tasting the warm metallic blood oozing through every bite. His head lolled to the side and everything went black. Jacob and Alex saw his eyes roll back and lurched forwards, grabbing hold of his trousers. They levered the rest of his body free from the hole and shuffled him towards the cave wall.

Wisp called out to Jacob, "Everything okay?"

Jacob panted and leant over the hole, "Yeah, we got him up. He tried to use his left arm and passed out from the pain. Give us a minute to catch our breath and we'll get you up too."

Jacob and Alex lay staring at the stalactites hanging above them. The steady rise and fall of their chests unsettled the dirt. As the pace slowed they looked across to each other and nodded. Clambering to their feet, Alex went to check on Todd again and freed the belt from his neck, before taking up her position around the hole with her brother.

"Okay, we've lowered the belt down. You might want to use the lighter to check where it is before you reach for it."

Wisp placed her hand within her bra and it rested on the metal casing. A few seconds later she sparked up a flame, held the lighter above her to work out where the belt was and repositioned the lighter back within her bra, feeling the hot metal against her skin. She stood on the rock pile, bent down into a squatting position and pushed her feet into the dried mud, spring boarding herself up into the darkness. Leather slapped against her skin and she tried to take hold. She felt the air rushing against her legs and the impact of rock against bone spiralling through her shins.

"Hold on. I'm going to try again."

This time she repositioned her arm before starting her leap. Her fingers found the leather. Her weight caused the belt to jerk down sharply. After lifting Todd, Alex and Jacob had learnt to turn their shoulders into the dirt to get more traction. They both twisted into position and tugged over and over, until they could hear nails scratching against rocks, huffs and puffs mixed with grunts, then a thud.

"Made it," said Wisp.

She tumbled a few feet away from them both. Jacob crawled over to her carefully, making sure to avoid the hole. His hands felt about tracing the outline of her body before settling on her long auburn hair. He followed the locks with his fingers and rested his hands on her face. Using his thumbs he searched for her lips, tilted his head and leant in. Her hands rose from the dusty ground, smearing cold wet mud over his cheeks. Wisp turned and settled her lips on his, kissing him softly. Jacob's lips mimicked her movements, mirroring each one. As Wisp pulled away, Jacob's lips followed, trying to prolong the moment. Her hand rested in the nook of his neck and gently caressed his hair.

"Did I pass out?" mumbled Todd from somewhere behind them.

Jacob broke away and replied, "Yeah, we managed to pull you up though. How does the arm feel?"

"Which one? Doesn't matter really, they both hurt like hell. Where's the lighter? I don't want to move against until I know where that poxy hole is."

Wisp slid her hand down from Jacob's cheek and rummaged in her bra.

"What's the matter?" asked Jacob.

"It's not here!" Wisp replied anxiously.

"Where is it then?" said Todd

"I don't bloody know. It was in here before I got out of the hole. Then I pulled myself out and rolled over here. Can you feel it near you?"

Jacob's hand scoured the ground, moving backwards and forward, left and right.

"It's not here."

"So we're out of the hole but we're back to searching in the dark. Just when you think your luck's about to change," Todd sighed, "Could it have fallen out on the way up?"

"No, it was in my bra, I would have felt it slip out, or hit my legs or something and I definitely would have heard it hit against the rocks. It's got to be here."

Jacob called out to Alex, "Do you know where it is? Alex? Alex! Where are you?"

The hairs on his arms stood to attention. He could feel the air temperature dropping with every breath. A tingling sensation rippled over his lips. He rubbed his fingers together and curled his toes trying to bury them into the dirt. Pounding beats filled his ears, the noise increasing rapidly. His eyes scanned the darkness for any sense of movement. Wisp's hand found his and they shuffled backwards huddling up against the side of the tunnel. Cold rocks dug sharply in between his shoulder blades.

Todd called out, "Alex! Jacob! Wisp! Is anyone still there?"

"Stay still," answered Jacob.

Jacob screwed his eyes up, rubbing his fingers across his forehead. Butterflies churned in his stomach and his heart jumped in his chest.

"Lost something?"

A sharp intake of breath held in his lungs. His eyes rolled to the ceiling, trying to recall the owner of the voice.

Dad? It can't be Dad though. No one knows where he is.

Silence.

Jacob clamped his lips and teeth together afraid to utter the words. His free hand rose to shield his mouth. He desperately wanted to close his eyes or scream out Alex's name. His head pitched back and forth gently colliding with the rocks. His ears concentrated for the slightest sound. It didn't take long to hear it, the click of a lighter and a single flame hovering in the darkness.

Jacob could make out the stocky outline of a man. Closing his eyes he searched through his memories to the last time he had seen his Dad.

He picked us up from school one night and took us all out for ice cream. Alex sat up on his shoulders and he had to duck as he walked through the door. Once we ordered, I asked him about the scar on his face, he told me he got into a fight when he was younger. I had chocolate ice cream with sprinkles, though most of it ended up on my chin and Dad used his sleeve to wipe it off. Alex still had ice cream on her hands when we left. She wiped it all over his brown hair and along the neck of his football shirt. I hugged him so tightly when he dropped us off. The smell of sawdust clung to his clothes, mixing with his aftershave.

The man lifted the lighter up to his face and snapped it shut. Jacob glimpsed a white jagged line running along his right cheek.

A bolt of dazzling blue like lightening crackled from the ceiling. The tunnel was awash with colour. Jacob, Wisp and Todd sheltered their eyes. As the light settled, Jacob let the tiniest crack appear from under his eyelid.

Thousands of black and white pixels danced into view. He opened his eyes further, straining and blinking repeatedly against the glare.

The outline of the man became more visible with every blink, his shape had a vague familiarity about it. Jacob's eyes rested on the figure standing behind him. Wisps of black smoke coiled around her tiny frame like a boa constrictor catching its prey. Small dimples appeared on her skin as veins of smoke twisted off in every direction. Her head hung awkwardly, tongue drooling and eyes closed.

"What have you done to her?" Jacob shouted.

"Wait! No hello? No hug? Just straight to the point," The Raven replied.

"Let her go."

"Why would I do that? She's my daughter. I'm just getting to know her again."

"She's not your daughter. You're not our Dad!"

"Tut tut tut."

Jacob rose to his feet, fists clenched. Wisp stood behind him with her hand clutching the knife's metal casing. They started to walk towards Alex, making sure to avoid the gaping hole in the ground. Todd was propped against a rock cradling his arm and looking on with uncertainty.

"Oh, am I going to get my hug after all?" The Raven goaded.

"Hug this!" screamed Jacob as he ran towards him with his fist raised.

The black smoke uncoiled from Alex, dropping her to the floor with a thud. Then it built and twisted, joining together like a swarm of vicious bees. Sharp points protruded from the surface piercing Jacob's hand as he swung. His arm locked like a statue, black lines of smoke travelled through his veins, pumping through his body with every beat of his heart. Jacob yelled.

The walls shook.

Todd cried out in pain, desperately trying to block both ears with one arm. The plumes edged towards him, dancing and twisting in the blue light. Crawling into his mouth and pulling at his cheeks from within. His jaw dropped open, clicking from side to side as the smoke surged inside. It built in his throat forcing hard against his Adam's apple making it enlarged and malformed. Silent coughs made him convulse. His skin twitched like mice under a carpet.

Wisp slid her hand around her head, trying to cover both ears. Her left hand rested against the knife and manipulated the blade into position. She tried to scramble to her feet, but the noise and dust had created a haze like a sand storm, making it impossible to stand. She crawled with stealth and precision, using her knees and elbow to propel herself along the ground. When she was inches away she lay down waiting for her chance. Screwing her eyes up tightly, she felt the air grate against her cheeks. Pushing through the pain she leapt from the spot and ran full pelt towards the man. His hand moved, gesturing for her to go away. The air whipped around her sending her hurtling towards the rocks. Puffs of dust rose as her body made contact with the ground.

"Silly, silly girl. I live in every shadow including the corners of your mind. I know what you are thinking before you even form the thought," the voice boomed but Michael's lips stayed firmly closed.

The four of them were immobilised. Jacob and Todd were frozen in black smoke, whilst Wisp and Alex lay motionless on the floor.

Michael's head shook violently. A thick black liquid spewed from his mouth, dripping down his chin and splashing on to the ground below. He coughed repeatedly, each time expelling more of the liquid from his lungs. His chest crackled as he tried to find his breath. Eventually he spoke.

"Don't do this. Let them go. They haven't done anything. Kids, I'm sorry for leaving you. I stayed away because I thought it would keep you safe. I love you, you've got to know that. Please let them go, take me, I'm begging you."

"Blah, blah, blah. Why do you always beg? Enough."

Alex's eyes fluttered open. Her little finger drew lines in the dirt before reaching up towards Fuzz and her necklace. The figure towered in front of her blocking part of her view. Her eyes scanned around the tunnel searching for the others. Jacob's skin crawled with lumps of black. His arm was pinned upwards and his face was still stretched into a scream. Todd's hand was clamped across his head covering his ears and Wisp's face was out of view but she could see her legs moving, pulling upwards into the foetal position.

What do I do? Wisp doesn't look like she's under his control, but the others aren't going to be able to help.

"It's family movie time. Jacob you better get comfortable," said The Raven.

Jacob's legs crumpled beneath him and he fell backwards onto his bottom. The black cloud fogging his mind began to fade and he felt the muscles in his neck loosen. He rotated his shoulders to the crunch of bones shifting. His eyes bulged wildly, darting from left to right. Smoky fingers pried through his synapses. Grabbing at his lips he felt them moving but there was no sound.

"Your inane chatter is superfluous to requirements. All you need to do is watch," said The Raven.

Blue lights shimmered from the stalactites. The walls twitched and shook flickering from black to white. Jacob felt the nervous energy in the air. His hairs stood on end, pins and needles climbed upon his nerves giving the sensation of ants crawling over his skin. Jacob's mind lapsed into the darkness.

I felt the darkness. I saw the faces of all the people he claimed. Their last breaths, their depression and despair. It felt like the coldest snow nipping at every muscle, but there was joy too, uncontrollable, exhilarating joy.

Stop it. Stop thinking like that.

He's still in here. I can feel his fingers prying, searching through my memories.

You're right and I'm not letting go, so enjoy the ride.

The walls were pure white while the rest of the tunnel was submerged in darkness. The dust swirled and rose around them. Jacob could feel the air build, brushing past his skin like sandpaper, as it settled pictures materialised on all the walls, the dust acting as tiny pixels.

They watched as a woman lay in a hospital bed. A young boy came running in and was lifted up onto the bed. Wisp and Alex stared transfixed, riveted by the image. An older woman entered the room. She was carrying a large hessian bag, filled to the brim with clothes and toys.

"Hi Love, how you feeling?"

"I'm alright Mum, just tired, 26 hours and counting."

"Mummy, Mummy look what I got."

"Oh you brought Fuzz," Riley said as she tickled him and ruffled her fingers through his hair.

"It's for the baby," he said holding it up in the air.

"She'll love it, if she ever comes out," laughed Riley, "Ow!"

"More contractions Love?"

"Yeah, the nurses say it shouldn't be long now. In fact this one is..." Riley screamed and gripped the bed sheet, "Get Michael," she said through gritted teeth.

Riley's Mum stroked her hair and kissed her on the cheek.

"Okay Love. Come on Jacob, we need to find your Dad. It's nearly time to meet your sister."

"Bye Mum," Jacob said jumping down from the bed.

"See you soon," Riley called after him.

Jacob ran into the hallway and towards the nurses' station. His Nan trotted behind trying to keep up.

"Hold on Jacob. I'm not as young as I used to be."

"Sorry," Jacob said as he took her hand.

They walked down past the nurses' station and out into the adjoining corridor. Michael was sitting on a bench, holding his head in his hands.

"What's wrong Daddy? Mummy is asking for you," Jacob said whilst climbing up on to the bench.

"Nothing Jacob, nothing at all. I better go and see your Mum."

Michael rose to his feet. Riley's Mum tutted and rolled her eyes as he walked past.

"Not now Debbie," he replied angrily.

I don't remember that. Why was Nan being so rude to Dad?

The scene jumped back into the hospital room. Riley was panting on the bed. She screamed just as the door swung open and Michael walked into the room.

"Where have you been?"

"I needed time to think. I'm in trouble and I don't want you to get involved. I think it would be better if we lived apart for a bit."

"Seriously? How much trouble are you in? This is not the best time for this conversation. I'm about to give birth to your daughter."

"No, now's not the best time, but I don't want to put you all in danger. I'm sorry. I've got to go. I promise, I'll stay in touch and help you out with money and stuff."

"Money! You think I'm thinking about money. You complete bastard."

"Okay, fine, whatever. Look, I'll be in touch, once you've calmed down a bit. I'm sorry. This is for the best. I know it might not seem like it but I'm trying to keep us all safe."

"Calmed down, seriously I'll give you calmed down if you keep talking like this. You can't just leave me. Whatever it is we can work it out together."

"I'm sorry Riley. They're after me. I'm just trying to keep my family safe. I'm sorry."

He leant towards her forehead but her arm swung up wildly batting him away.

"Who's after you, that lousy lot from the pub? Please don't do this Michael. What do I tell Jacob?"

"You are better off not knowing. Just stay at your Mum's for a while. Please. I'll sort it all out. It's just a misunderstanding, but I've got to go, just until it all settles down."

He stepped back towards the door.

If you walk out now don't bother getting back in touch. You won't see Jacob or this baby ever again."

Michael's shoulders fell and his head drooped. His feet shuffled along the tiles and he ran his fingers through his hair. Riley's face turned a cherry red. Her features were unrecognisable as she clamped her jaws together. She heard footsteps then a swoosh of the door rocking back on its hinges. The hum of the air conditioner filled the silence. Hot tears trickled down her cheek. A deafening scream left her lips and a nurse rushed into the room, shocked and perturbed.

"No need for all that noise. Here have some gas and air," suggested the nurse.

The scene jumped again.

Michael was standing at the traffic lights frantically pushing the button. He started to pace along the kerb.

"Come on! Come on! This is taking too long.

The green man flashed and beeped on the crossing. A low buzzing met with distant ringing. Michael shoved his hand into his inside pocket and pulled his mobile free of a clump of papers. Some caught on the breeze and he chased after them angrily, whilst an impatient driver accompanied his dance with tooting horns. One fluttered down and rested onto a leaf floating in a puddle. He muttered and swore under his breath as he retrieved it. His index finger thwacked against the screen and swiped to the right.

"What do you want?

No! I don't know what you're talking about.

That's ridiculous. Why would I steal from you?

Maybe you need to talk to him then."

A woman grabbed her kid and covered his ears blocking out the profanities leaving Michael's lips. He slammed his finger on the end call button and shoved the phone back into his pocket.

The dust vibrated off the walls and fell back in a haze on to the cave floor.

"Michael, I think you have some explaining to do," said The Raven.

"Jacob, Alex, I'm sorry. I was in trouble, some blokes thought I had stolen stuff from them and I had to get away. I thought I was keeping you safe. I changed my name and moved into a tiny bedsit in Fulham. Your Mum didn't even know what was going on. I was trying to protect you all. Now stop it. Please stop it."

"That's not everything though, is it Michael? If you won't tell them, I will."

The black droplets quivered and levitated off of the cold floor. Jacob watched in disbelief as the droplets landed on Michael's face, seeping in between his eyes and crawling up his nose. Michael tried to cough but his mouth slammed shut, absorbing each shudder. Jacob dropped to the floor and Todd screamed. Black liquid oozed from their skin and formed into tiny spheres. Each one rose and floated towards Michael.

Alex and Wisp glanced at each other. A single nod from Wisp signalled her intentions. She reached for the knife sitting near her left hand. Alex hastily nodded back before swiping her leg into the back of Michael's knees. Jacob realised what was happening just in time to roll out of the way. Michael crumpled like a game of Jenga, landing first on to his knees before slamming his face into the ground. Wisp raced to join Alex. They each grabbed a foot and pushed. Todd clambered to his feet and joined them, narrowly missing the hand swinging for his ankles. Jacob rolled in beside Wisp. His hands gripped tightly and heaved.

"Wait, what are we doing? He's our Dad," said Jacob.

"It's not your Dad anymore. It's The Raven," said Wisp.

Michael's arm with blackened veins clawed at the dirt. His eyes glowed yellow and his teeth gnashed against the air. He pushed himself on to his side and wriggled free from their grip. His body twisted, crawling towards the group. Todd kicked out uncontrollably, his foot slammed into Michael's face. The impact forced him backwards making his legs disappear into the abyss. The yellow glow faded and Michael's brown eyes pleaded with them. Alex and Jacob reached out to grab his arms as he fell into the hole.

"Pull me up. Please, I don't want to die."

They looked at each other, their eyes pleading to find another way. Rocks and pebbles sounded like raindrops as they fell through and collided with the ground below. Alex pulled back sharply as a crack appeared in the rocks under her elbow. She heard the rocks rub together before they crumbled away. Instinctively they let go and scrambled backwards, turning away to shield their eyes. A goading smile formed on Michael's lips as his body slipped into the abyss and plummeted down into the darkness.

Thump.

Alex screamed out, the moment the thud hit her ears. The others glanced at each other unsure of what reaction they were supposed to have. Todd broke the confusion.

"RUN."

Shaking heads. Pounding feet. A single cry of relief as Wisp saw a glint of blue reflecting awkwardly from under a rock. Bending down her hands brushed against metal. She scooped up the lighter without breaking her stride.

"Got it," she said hurriedly as they dashed down the tunnel back into the darkness.

25

Glass bottles smashed on to the floor sending shards of debris into the corners of the room. Stray biscuits crumbled as they struck his arms. Bags of flour plummeted from the shelves and exploded on impact causing plumes of white to litter the air. Jack coughed, covering his mouth with the crease of his elbow. He noticed his tie was covered in white specks. Once the air cleared, he brushed himself down as best he could. The pins and needles had swarmed together turning his lower extremities numb a few hours ago. Despite his best efforts there was not enough room to stand or stretch out.

Beneath him, the wooden floorboards began to creak, low and steady. Tucking his head in his hands he braced for impact. Splinters of wood randomly pinged from the floor piercing his trousers and poking into his legs. Burning pain flickered where the points touched his skin. He winced. Black smoke curled through the gaps like tentacles lapping at his flesh. He lay still as they slithered up his legs, across his chest and over his arms. They came to rest just below his chin. The smoke shimmered as clouds of flour were sent back into the air, before settling like a light blanket of snow. Jack opened his mouth in readiness. The smoke began to climb again, slipping over his tongue and sliding down his throat into his lungs. It hijacked his blood cells, hitching a lift throughout his body. His heart mottled as the blood pumped, darkness clinging to every cell. The synapses of his brain fired little flurries of black smoke until its shade resembled tarmac.

Jack squirmed into a squatting position in front of the door. His hand reached up for the handle as the familiar cracks of bone rang in his ears. His finger turned in the lock and the door opened with a creak. He stood and leant against the door frame waiting for his bones to click back into place. As his hips realigned he stepped over the threshold and into the kitchen. His shoes clacked against the wooden floor as he walked over to the worktop and grabbed the kettle. Carrying it to the tap he turned it on and watched as a torrent of cold water poured inside. Placing the kettle down back on its base, he hit the switch and listened to the liquid bubble and pop as it boiled. Reaching for the upturned cup on the draining board, his hand knocked against a glass. He grabbed it and rewashed it before drying it with a tea towel. He placed it back into the cupboard and straightened it up before examining the box of teabags, selecting one he waited for the kettle to boil before hanging the teabag over the side of the cup. Water splashed up the sides as he poured. His shoes clacked again as he walked over to the fridge for the milk. He poured it in and carefully took a saucer from the cupboard. Resting the saucer on the table he took his first sip. It sent a wave of warmth rolling down his body.

"Ah, that's much better," he said to the empty room, "Well that was unfortunate, but killing their own Dad is definitely going to eat away at them. Collateral damage. I can feel their panic. It's bubbling up inside. With a few choice words, I'm sure I can tap into it. Then maybe I will finally be able to eat."

He looked down at the creased suit and the speckled tie.

"Hmmm, this won't do."

He savoured the final sip of tea before twisting his legs free from the table and standing up. After washing up the cup and saucer he dried them and placed them back within the cupboard. The three steps to the door were accentuated by the gentle rhythmical tapping of his shoes. He turned into the hallway and climbed the stairs. On the landing he removed his shoes then pushed the white wooden door with his right hand. The door to his bedroom opened flawlessly and he stepped inside. Unlatching the wardrobe he peered inside. Every suit was the same identical shade of grey. Sharp crisp lines made them hang as if someone was already wearing them. His hand rested on one, then slid across to the next. He stepped back and undressed, making sure to put each item of clothing into the wash basket. Taking the new suit from the hanger, he dressed slowly and methodically. He flicked up his collar then wrapped the tie around his neck. His fingers were well rehearsed in tying a Winsor knot and did so with precision. Staring into the mirror, he adjusted the knot two millimetres to the right.

His feet slipped into matching grey slippers and he proceeded to go back downstairs into the living room. Sitting on the edge of the settee, he adjusted the pillow behind him before leaning back and placing his feet up on the footrest. He picked up the remote and tapped the standby button. The television burst into life.

"Oh good, just in time for the news."

26

"Do you think he's dead?" asked Alex.

"I don't know. He might have survived," said Todd.

Jacob took over.

"Alex, yeah he's dead. I'm sorry. It wasn't really Dad though, not anymore. The Raven had taken over. We tried Alex. It's not your fault."

"It is my fault. I kicked him. I pushed him. Maybe we didn't have to push him. We could have just ran. It might have been enough."

"It wouldn't have been. He was attacking us. As it is we just delayed him. The Raven probably survived. I don't know about your Dad but he was probably dead as soon as The Raven possessed him. The Raven was never going to let him go back to his normal life. He would have just ended up down here like one of us," Wisp said.

"If that's true, we did him a favour," added Todd.

"Not helping," said Jacob.

Alex cried uncontrollably. Jacob tried to hug her but she pushed him away.

"Do you know what your Dad was talking about?" Todd asked quietly.

"No, Mum never said much about it. She had some complications when Alex was born so I was at Nan's for a week or so. When we did go home I remember some blokes coming round and kicking down the door. They shouted a lot and we ended up staying at Nan's for a bit longer. Mum told me they were friends of Dad's. She phoned him to say they were looking for him. A few more days passed and then Mum said it was alright for us to go home again. We only saw him a few times a year after that. He was always really cagey if I brought it up, so I just stopped asking," Jacob replied.

"The Raven obviously wanted you to know something. Why would he go to all that trouble otherwise?"

"Maybe because he's sick and enjoys revelling in our

pain."

"Yeah, but he had a reason. Whatever he knows he thinks it'll break you. He must do."

"I don't really care. That's the past and right now all I want to do is get out of here. I want to be able to see daylight again. So I can't think about my Dad right now, if I do, I'll just be a wreck and that's not going to help anyone. I'll grieve him when we're safe. Wisp please get us out of here."

"I'll try. Alex are you, can you, I mean are you ready to…"

Alex grunted and wiped her face with her top. Without looking up she thrust the lighter towards Wisp and waited for it to be collected. Wisp took it carefully and started walking. The others fell into line and followed her down the twisting tunnels.

27

They had been walking for hours over loose rocks and up sharp inclines. Todd and Alex rubbed at their legs, trying to ease the tightening cramps sitting in their thighs. Jacob's feet were bruised and bleeding. The dirt had seeped into the wounds making them itchy and irritated. Wisp rubbed absently at her back, every step made it twinge.

"Can we stop for a bit please?" asked Alex

"If we keep stopping, we'll lose our advantage," said Wisp.

"I don't think my Dad being dead is an advantage."

"I'm sorry I didn't mean it like that. I just meant, while The Raven is regrouping we have an opportunity."

"Fine. How much longer?"

"I don't know. I've never made it this far out before. My markings stopped ages ago but we seem to be going up, that's got to be a good sign."

Wisp slowed as she turned the corner. Using the lighter she examined the stalactites and stalagmites littering the path ahead. To the left the path fell away revealing a dark chasm. Wisp wobbled as she looked down, Jacob grabbed her arm and pulled her back from the edge.

"Thanks. This is going to be a tight fit. Everyone reckon they'll be able to squeeze through?"

They replied with a tired, "yeah."

Wisp went first. She weaved in and out of the rocky icicles then dropped to her knees to crawl through a gap. The sound of loose gravel bouncing off the rocks below made her pulse quicken. She could hear each beat. Her palms felt sweaty. She kept crawling, resisting the temptation to look.

Making it through, she signalled to Alex to come next. She manoeuvred around the obstacles like a gymnast. Her petite frame made getting through the alcoves in the rocks easier to manage. Todd was next. He tentatively looked over the edge. The endless darkness made him feel small and looking at the path filled him with dread.

I'm not going to be able to get through there. Wisp had trouble and she's much smaller than me. I wonder how stable that path is. It's probably going to fall away as soon as I step on it. I don't have a choice though, it's not like I can go back.

Todd tentatively placed his foot, toes first on to the path. Slowly he added more weight until he was confident it wouldn't give way. He kept his head down, staring intently at the path and only glancing up intermittently to check what was coming ahead. Navigating through the shards he ducked to avoid the lower hanging stalactites.

"That's it. Keep going. You've nearly made it across," said Wisp.

Todd's chin rose and his shoulders fell. A proud smile passed across his face. As his head tilted up a stalactite jabbed into it, pushing him off balance. He wobbled awkwardly, flailing his arms in panic. He managed to grip hold of the rocky icicle, feeling the cold slime coat his palm. Twisting his feet away from the edge, he shuffled closer to the wall and managed to regain his balance.

"Shit that was close," he said panting.

"You okay?" called Wisp.

"Just about."

He ran his hand along the jagged rocks, using them for stability. The sharp, hard texture gave his mind something else to focus on. A row of stalagmites stood between him and the others. The formation reminded him of teeth, sharp and chomping. He kept his hand against the rocks and lifted his leg up, reaching over the spiky points. Planting his leg firmly on to stable ground, he swung his other leg over. His trousers caught and he screamed.

"It's okay, the material's caught. Stay still and I'll unhook it."

Wisp bent down and unwound the fabric. Todd felt the pull on his trousers release and stepped clear of the chasm, sighing with relief.

"Your turn Jacob," called Wisp.

Jacob scanned the area. The dusky light made it difficult for him to work out a safe path across. Each step started on tiptoes then slowly progressed until he could feel the gravel piercing into the soles of his feet.

A twitching cold crawled down his neck. He felt a warmth building on the back of his head and swung round, looking behind him into the darkness.

There's nothing there. This place is just getting to me.

He twisted round again and caught sight of Wisp smiling at him, egging him on. Stepping towards her, his head jerked awkwardly backwards. The collar of his shirt rubbed angrily around his neck.

Oh shit, The Raven's behind me. He's got me. This is it.

Panic rose with his eyebrows and Wisp stared at him puzzled. He ran his fingers along his collar, half expecting to feel smoke lapping at his skin. Instead they brushed against a cold slimy point.

"My t-shirt is snagged, that's all," he called out to them.

He looped the material free and crawled the final few metres towards the others. As he approached them, he stood and remembered to lift his legs high to clamber over the last set of stalagmites. Elated, Wisp, Todd and Jacob hugged each other. Alex stayed tucked in against the rocks, covering her face and replaying Michael's death. The sound of his flesh scraping against the gravel and the silence as he fell lingered in her mind. The distant thud of his body impacting with the rocks below boomed in her ears.

Why aren't they upset? They're acting like nothing happened. We killed Dad. I killed Mum. They're both dead because of me. I could have stopped it happening. I'm the reason they're dead. Jacob's gonna be next and that'll be my fault too. He would be better off if I was dead.

Jacob's eye was drawn to the pink fur lying on the rocks. Alex's jade necklace lay glinting around Fuzz's neck. He broke away from the hug and looked down the tunnel into the darkness.

"Where's she gone?" he cried out to the others.

Wisp and Todd looked on worried and searching as Jacob bent down and picked up Fuzz. The necklace fell down and hung loosely around his elbow. Retrieving it he adjusted the black thread and dropped it around his neck. Wisp took Fuzz and stuffed him into her back pocket.

They looked around them and barely kept up as Jacob took off in one direction. Footsteps echoed as they ran through the caves. Wisp had to shield the flame with her hand to keep it alight. They searched every nook, calling her name and listening for a reply.

"Maybe she went a different way," said Todd.

"There was no other way to go. It was this way or the chasm," Jacob replied angrily.

"Well, are we sure she didn't..."

"Don't finish that sentence Todd. We would have seen her. She went this way, she must have," said Wisp.

"Stop talking and keep looking," said Jacob.

He ran ahead. The darkness surrounded him and he felt the cold air cool his warm skin.

"Where are you Alex? I can't lose you," he muttered under his breath.

Goosebumps prickled across his arms and his hairs stood on end. His hands waved blindly in front of him searching for obstacles. Jacob stopped dead and listened. Sobs echoed from the distance. His footsteps became more controlled, quieter, following the sound. Behind him he could hear Wisp and Todd rushing to keep up, but unsure of which direction he had gone in.

If I call out to them I might scare Alex off. They have the lighter, they'll find me.

Alex sat wedged between two rocks. Her hands were clamped over her ears and she rocked back and forth, listening to the swooshing of her own heartbeat.

She muttered, "It's my fault," over and over.

Jacob stopped a few metres away. He ran his left hand over his right. Holding his breath, he took the last few steps towards her.

"Alex listen to me. It's not your fault."

He knelt down beside her and gently brushed his hand against her arm. She pulled away, tucking herself further into the alcove. Her hands wrapped around her knees, drawing them closer to her body.

"I'm here Alex and I'm not going anywhere. We can sit here forever if you want, but I'm not leaving you."

"No. No. No! It's my fault. You'll be next and it'll be my fault. I can't go with you. I can't."

"You can Alex because I'm not going to be next and neither are you. Jack killed Mum not you. The Raven killed Dad and it was The Raven who fell down into that cavern. It wasn't Dad. Please Alex, I can't lose you too."

Alex looked up at the single light inching closer.

"Go with them. Just leave me here."

"I'm not leaving you."

The flame threw up shadows on to the wall. Her eyes watched as two black outlines approached. They're bodies merging with the darkness around them.

Wisp pulled Fuzz from her back pocket and leant down to present him to Alex. She swiped him away, knocking him on to the floor. Wisp didn't speak as she bent down and picked him up, brushing him off and holding him out to her again.

"Why do you even want me to come? I just bring death."

"No you don't. You're my sister. I love you. You're strong and amazing and I don't want to face the rest of my life without you right here by my side," said Jacob.

"The Raven brings death, you don't. You built the rock pile, without you we would still be stuck. You're smart," said Wisp.

"I never would have got out of that hole. You saved me. You're strong," added Todd.

Alex looked up and surveyed the faces staring at her. Each one was dusty and dirty. Their features were hidden slightly but she could make out the lines on their foreheads, the worried looks in their eyes and the fast pace of their breathing.

Jacob pulled the thread of the necklace up over his head and held it out to her. She hesitated then bowed to receive it. It caught on her ear and she reached up to brush it off. Her hand wrapped around the pendant and she whispered to herself.

"Mum, I'm sorry. What should I do?"

Silence settled over them and no one wanted to move in case they actually heard a reply.

Alex sighed then took a deep breath.

"Okay, I'll go."

28

He pulled back the clasp of the notebook. The sweet musty smell rose to meet his nostrils and he inhaled the lingering scent. The yellowing pages fell open to the last entry. Picking up the pen, he started to write in long swirling strokes. Each letter formed perfectly until Michael's name sat opposite Jacob's. Two dates a few days apart were entered into the columns.

"Such a shame, but those few last seconds as he plunged towards the rocks, oh so exquisite. I could taste the bitterness. It bubbled and fizzed as it seeped from his bones. Absorbing all that disappointment, the years of despair, so much power."

He stood up from the desk and carefully pushed in the chair so it was aligned with the inkwell in the middle. A wisp of smoke curled around the journal and compressed the pages together. Another clicked the clasp into place. He ran his fingers over the cover, feeling the contours of the metallic bones under his fingertips. The leather began to unravel and twisted outwards, circling his arm. Curls of black smoke infiltrated it as it bound itself to his skin.

"Hmmm, they're close to the surface. That just won't do."

The Raven walked downstairs to the kitchen and opened the adjoining cupboard. The floorboards were still split and broken. He reached down and touched the wood. Flames of blue sparked from his fingertips and saturated the grains of dirt. He watched as they started to vibrate and pull together, rising up from the ground and circling around him. Energy surged through his body, dancing and sparking like a thousand electric shocks. It flowed through his fingertips pulsing and twitching through the air. He sculpted the dirt into three beasts each with four muscular legs, matted black fur, long sharp claws, a growling head, rows of razor sharp teeth and yellow burning eyes.

"Trap them then send them back into the tunnels. Play

with their minds and make them never want to leave."

The heads nodded in unison, accepting the request. The beasts circled The Raven one last time before plunging back into the ground. Flecks of dirt sprayed into the air as they pushed against the earth. Compacted dirt crumpled as they drilled deeper. The loose particles were drawn to the beasts like magnets sculpting around them and increasing their size.

Short bursts of sparks fizzled from The Raven's fingertips. They turned from blue to dark spluttering black as the last of his reserves dried up. His shoulders sagged and his body drooped. He stumbled from the cupboard and grasped the worktop to steady himself. Plumes of black smoke leaked from Jack's skin as the human crawled back in control of his body.

"You shouldn't have taken Michael."

"Shut up. They are so close to breaking. Once my beasts start poking around in their heads they won't know what's real anymore and after that, well they will be begging me to stay."

"Let's hope your plan works because they're close to the surface. If they get out, tracking them is going to require a lot of meals."

29

"Hey, stop a minute. It looks different up ahead," said Todd.

"Yeah, he's right. It looks brighter," said Jacob, "Close the lighter for a minute; I want to see if I'm right."

"Wisp snapped the lid closed and looked at the walls in the distance. Small cracks of light cast shadows on to the rocks. She ran over and mimicked the movement of the light with her fingertips. The others joined her and watched in awe as little glimpses of light crept through the rocks.

"We must be close to the surface," said Jacob excitedly.

"Daylight, I haven't seen daylight in over a year. It's so pretty." said Wisp.

Jacob pulled her close and hugged her.

"We're all gonna get out of here. You're going home Wisp."

"But some of us haven't got anywhere to go," said Alex.

Todd nodded in agreement, "I don't want to go back to the streets."

"You won't. The police will have to protect you. They'll have to protect all of us. We'll be safe again," said Jacob.

"They didn't protect me before."

"But we'll have information for them. We'll be able to lead them back here and they'll stop The Raven."

"Dreaming much?!"

"You'll see. Come on let's keep going. I can smell flowers on the breeze. We're so close."

Jacob's feet pounded into the dirt with a new sense of purpose. With every stride, more light filtered through the cracks. A single circle of light shone at the end of the shaft like a beacon in a computer game. Jacob reached it and tentatively placed his fingertips inside. Warmth coated his skin like a thick blanket on a winter's night. He immersed himself in it, staring upwards at the sky. His hand partially covered his eyes, giving them time to adjust. When he refocused he noticed jagged rocks protruding from the walls. The warm sun and soft floating clouds peeked over the edges.

"Come and look. It's amazing. I can see the sky and white fluffy clouds. It's beautiful. Hey, what's keeping you guys? You need to see this."

Jacob spun round and peered into the murky cave, momentarily blinded by the change in light. He saw their eyes, white and pleading. Their bodies pinned up against the rocks. Their chests rising and falling with a desperate uncertainty.

"The Raven," he muttered in terror.

Three beasts circled the others. Long dark legs led down to huge heavy paws. Wisps of dust jumped from the floor after every step. Rows of snarling teeth dripped with spit as they grinned at their victims. Their eyes glowed a fiery yellow. Wisp could feel hot foul breath against her skin. The stench overwhelmed her, bubbles of bile rose in her throat. Burning pain seared through her eyes, trapping her gaze. Her mouth fell open and the bile flowed freely over her tongue, clinging to her teeth before dripping slowly down her chin.

She felt the creature rifling through her mind like an excited child on Christmas morning. Snapshots of memories flashed and faded – her brothers playing, her Mum's birthday, walking with her Dad, going for a drive and finishing her technology project for school. She saw the same scenes again linked to other memories – Corey breaking his leg, an argument with her Mum, her Dad being rushed to hospital, the car crash and the first time she cut.

All those things were your fault. Your brother wouldn't have needed surgery to fix his broken leg if you had watched him closer on the trampoline. Your Mum only got cross because you wanted to check your phone. Your Dad collapsed because you made him walk those extra two miles to look at the birds. The car crashed because you were talking to the driver. You cut because you knew your work wasn't going to be good enough. You know you're not good enough. You just hurt everyone you love. You've thought they would be better off without you. You're right. They're glad you're gone. All you brought to their lives was misery.

She could feel prickly heat building in her nose and water welling in her eyes, but she couldn't blink. Her vision blurred. Tiny trickles of water ran down past her nostrils. In the distance she could make out Todd's silhouette pinned against the wall.

Todd's legs prickled with heat, heaviness filled his toes and clambered up his calves. His arms hung lifelessly by his side. Wide eyes stared reflecting the yellow glow from the beast. The gaze pried through his thoughts, delving deeper.

You pushed your parents to their limit. You stole from them to pay for drugs. They never came forward when the news reports came out. No one offered a reward for your return. People were glad it was you, rather than them. You'll always be unwanted. No one's missing you.

Alex's hands tremored. Flames danced in her dilated pupils as its paws pinned her to the wall. Its eyes flickered like water at sunset, probing her mind.

You didn't help your Mum when she needed you. You drove your father away. He left on the day you were born. It was your fault. Just looking at you reminded him of all the things he lost. That's why he could only bear seeing you a few times a year. You were a complete disappointment to him. He didn't even come and look after you when your Mum died. He wanted to look after Jacob but he knew he would get stuck with you too. He didn't want you. You killed your Mum. You killed your Dad. You're going to end up killing Jacob. You don't deserve to live.

Jacob's hand fell against his ribs, guarding the bruises and trying to slow the rise and fall of his chest. His eyes honed in on their faces, lips drawn and eyes wide. Black veins ran down from their ears. He studied their positions, working out how he could distract the beasts. Wisp's beast was closest and Jacob knew he wouldn't be able to get to the others. He scrambled around gathering stones and rocks, searching for the largest he could find. He grabbed one and heaved it on to his shoulder. The effort sent sharp stabbing pains through his chest. He breathed deeper, which only made the pain worse. Stepping forwards he flung the rock towards the beast. It landed a few metres away with a crash. He waited for a reaction but it didn't move.

The intermittent pain in his chest was now a constant throb. Every breath sent bolts of red hot lightning shooting through his body. He squatted to grab the next rock, hoisted it up and aimed.

The rock collided sending the beast's head snapping to the right. Its eyes momentarily broke from Wisp's. She coughed, spewing up the leftover bile on to the floor and desperately trying to clear the taste from her mouth.

"It wasn't true. They love you. Todd and Jacob both said they were looking for you. They love you. Run," she whispered.

The beast glared at Jacob. Its jaws gnashed angrily as it approached. Wisp ran to the left, staying close to the wall.

"It's their eyes. If I can distract them I can set the others free too. Here goes nothing."

She grabbed a handful of rocks and centred herself in the cave. Her feet shuffled in the dirt, feeling the gravel shift under foot. Her eyes darted between Alex and Todd, tracking the beast's movements. She couldn't make out where Jacob was, but she heard feet pacing behind her. The steady thud of chasing paws matched the footsteps, back and forth.

One rock flew and bounced off the matted wet fur. Venomous blood trickled from the wound, but the beast didn't move. The second went straight through the gap between their heads. Wisp saw Alex's hand jerk slightly to the left, but her eyes stayed focused on the beast. The third and fourth stones both missed completely. She took the last smooth rock, arched her arm back and threw.

"Yes bullseye."

Turning away, she scrambled to pick up another rock and got ready to hurl it at the second beast, but the first was on her. Its claws ripped at her back. Her muscles went into spasm. The initial pop echoed as the claws tore through the top layers of flesh. She could hear the sound of skin ripping in a series of squeaks and squishes. Forcing her hand into her mouth she bit down to taper her screams. Teeth pierced her skin and warm blood trickled over her knuckles and down her wrist. A heavy paw pounded into her head, forcing it into the dirt. Dust billowed around her face. She blinked wildly trying to clear the debris. Her throat tickled and scratched as she inhaled.

The other beast's head shook as the rock impacted. Its gaze was broken. The heavy pressure in Alex's head began to waver. She blinked the darkness away from the corners of her eyes. Shivers ran down her spine. Her stomach churned. She tried to shake the feeling, grabbing at her head and rubbing her eyes. Muffled screams reached her ears and she turned to find Wisp trapped on the floor. The beast had one paw squashed against her head and the other sunk deep into her back. Alex's eyes darted around the tunnels.

"Where are Jacob and Todd?"

She spotted Todd off to the right. His stocky frame trapped between two paws of the beast. It stared at him intently and Todd stood unmoving. A heavy grin left his face looking demented.

"Is that what I looked like?"

Running at the beast the full force of her body slammed into its side. It grunted and rolled over into the dirt. She felt its chest compress slightly. Her momentum carried her over and she landed sprawling in the dirt. A glimpse of Todd showed he was up and moving.

"Where's Jacob?"

Her eyes darted again searching the shadows. She couldn't see him. Wisp's cries were getting louder. A glint of metal shone against the flames dancing in its eyes.

Alex ran towards the beast, crouching down to grab the knife glinting in Wisp's back pocket. Leaping over the creature, her foot caught against its matted fur and she tumbled down scraping the side of her face against the rocks.

Brushing off the dirt, she sprung to her feet wielding the knife in her right hand.

"Get off her," she screamed plunging it into one of the beast's yellow eyes.

Black venom oozed from the wound and the creature gnashed and gnawed at the air searching for flesh. The knife slid out with ease dripping the beast's blood over Wisp. Her throat vibrated uncontrollably, loud and deathly cries tore across her vocal chords. Alex froze. Her fingers loosened as she watched Wisp's face contort. A dull clink was lost beneath the screams as the knife dropped to the floor.

The snarling beast yanked its long white claws from Wisp and pounced on Alex smashing her head into the hard floor with an audible crunch. The noise echoed along the twisting caverns.

"I can't see! It's all blurry."

Large matted paws thick with dust slammed down on either side of her face. Its head dropped into view inches from her nose, staring intently. Alex felt nothing. It tried again. Nothing. The long white claws scraped into the rocks, etching deep indentations millimetres from her cheeks.

What was that noise? Why isn't it in my head?

She drew her legs up to her chest, feeling the weight of the beast under the soles of her feet. Her hands splayed into the dirt as her legs slammed into the wet matted fur. It flew backwards. The ground shook as it collided with the rock. Alex rolled on to her side and clambered unsteadily to her feet. Her fingers slid through her hair. A sticky warmth sat beneath her nails. Her hand shot out in front of her face.

"Am I bleeding? I can't see."

Watery vomit spluttered from her throat.

"Watch out!" yelled Jacob.

His hand snatched hers, dragging her along the ground. She scrambled to her feet again, tripping over herself as she tried to pick up the rhythm of his run. Alex braced, throwing her arms out as she collided into the wall.

"Stay here," he whispered.

She could feel the tightness of the rocks as her breath clung to her lips. Jacob glanced around the cave. Wisp was lying face down. The blackened knife lay nearby shielded by the unconscious creature. Todd was huddled in the shadows with a snarling beast towering over him.

"Where's the third one?"

Jacob rushed towards Wisp, cringing with every step as gravel sunk further into his wounds.

He grabbed the knife and wrapped his fingers tentatively around the handle. His hand rested by his ear and he could hear the blackened metal sizzle. The shadows moved to his right. He turned his head in time to see its claws poised. It leapt. His right elbow jabbed and wedged into the beast's throat, staving off its attacks. Every breath hurt and Jacob could see the edges of black intruding on his vision. The beast's weight knocked him to the floor. Bubbling black spit hung from its fangs, looming over Jacob. He drew the knife up and hacked into the matted hairs, slicing and tearing through the dripping flesh.

"This isn't working."

He took another swing. The pupil ruptured as he plunged the blade deep into the socket. Blood poured and Jacob shielded his face with his right arm, whilst he aimed his left for the other eye. It popped upon impact. The beast hung weightless for a moment. Jacob peered through the gap. His mouth fell open as its black fur exploded sending dirt ripping through the cave and showering down on top of him.

"If they come at you, aim for the eyes."

His arms scooped under Wisp's neck and legs. He screamed taking her full weight against his chest. White flashes popped before his eyes and he stumbled into the rocks. Alex rushed from the alcove and grabbed his shoulder. Her other arm settled underneath Wisp's body and she helped Jacob carry her into the shadows.

"Look after her. I'll be back," said Jacob wincing from the pain.

Clutching the knife, he hobbled over in Todd's direction. He was huddled with his head pressed in against his knees. Jacob couldn't get any closer but he called out.

"Todd, you have to fight it."

"I can't. It's right, no one wants me. No one is missing me. What's the point?"

"We want you. Come on Todd, please."

Jacob launched the blade towards Todd. His head rose slightly at the sound of metal scraping across the ground. Instinctively he reached out and grabbed the handle with his good arm. His eyes rested on the beast's nose and mouth. He swung his foot out and smashed it into its muscular back legs. It crashed to the floor and Todd scrambled on top of it, stabbing and plunging the knife into its head. On the second deep stroke one eye ruptured the other exploded after the fifth, flinging mounds of dirt across the cave. Todd was blown backwards by the blast, gasping desperately as he crashed into the wall.

"Come on," said Jacob, offering his hand to Todd.

Todd grabbed it and they limped over to the girls.

"Is it over? asked Alex.

"We killed two of them. What happened to the third, did anyone see?" asked Jacob.

"I stabbed one of its eyes, but I didn't see what happened to it after I slammed it into the wall. I hit my head on the floor and everything was really blurry for a while. It's not as bad now," said Alex.

"Maybe it went back to The Raven," said Todd.

"I don't know, but I think we need to get out now

before it comes back. The shaft over there is only two maybe three metres tall. We should be able to climb up using the jagged rocks as hand holds."

"What about her?" Todd asked pointing to Wisp.

"We'll lift her up like we did at the hole. Use her belt as a harness or something."

"How's your head Alex, do you think you can climb up?" asked Jacob.

"Blurry, but I can try."

Alex grabbed Wisp's legs and each of the boys grabbed an arm. They part carried part dragged her across the floor to the opening of the shaft. Todd bent down and carefully pulled Wisp's belt free from the loops on her trousers.

"He wrapped it around Alex's neck. "Okay, we'll lift you up until you can grab hold. Ready?"

Jacob gave Alex a hug and linked his hand with Todd's. Jacob used his other arm to brace against her weight, as Alex pressed her foot down and sprung up towards the shaft. Her fingers scrambled to find a hold then steadied as they took her weight. Refusing to look down she scaled the rock face and pushed herself free.

"Grass! There's grass. It feels so soft," she called down to the others below.

Jacob and Todd looked at each other.

"You next," said Jacob.

"No, you'll need to help Alex pull Wisp up. You've got two working arms, I've only got one. You go next and I'll come up last."

"You sure?"

"Yeah, go on."

Todd held his crooked arm against the wall. Jacob used it as a foot hole and started to scale.

Looking at every possibility, he wedged his foot into a small gap and hoisted himself two thirds up the wall. Alex reached down from above, dangling the belt like a rope.

"Come on, you can do it. The belt's there if you need it."

Jacob scanned the remaining rock face, used his legs to

balance and reached up for the belt. She pulled, taking some of his weight and giving him the chance to use the last few foot holes to lever himself up high enough to crawl out of the shaft. He rolled out on to the grass, arms and legs splayed like a starfish. A gentle breeze stroked his cheek and he stared at the soft white clouds as he caught his breath.

After a few minutes, Alex called down to Todd, "we're ready."

Todd removed the knife from his back pocket and rested it on the ground. Then fiddled with the zipper on his trousers and let them fall around his ankles. He stood in his boxer shorts staring up at the bemused faces above.

"I'm making a harness."

After undoing his shoe laces he tugged at his shoes and pulled the trousers off over his toes. Winding the trouser legs around Wisp's back and over her thighs he made her an external pair of pants.

Alex lowered the belt down through the hole. Todd reached for it, but realised he wasn't tall enough to loop it through the harness.

"How are we going to get her up there? I can't reach it."

Alex and Jacob looked at each other. Her eyes rose skywards as she thought.

"Use me. I'll lower myself down. If you hold my ankles I'll be able to get the belt low enough so Todd can tie it on."

"That's kinda of what Wisp and Todd did for me when we were finding you. It'll work, but are you sure?"

"Yeah, I have to. We need to get them out. We don't know how long it'll be until The Raven is back. Come on, grab hold," she commanded as she slid her body into position.

With the belt looped around her wrist, Jacob lowered her back into the murky darkness. Todd manoeuvred Wisp on to his shoulder and used the adrenaline coursing through his veins to push up through the pain. He looped the belt through the trouser legs and twisted it round, pulling a knot into the leather. He signalled to the others to start pulling her up supporting her body weight the best he could.

Jacob hauled Alex backwards along the grass, leaving green stains streaking up her clothes. Alex tried to keep her arms locked and the belt straight. Even the slightest movement sent Wisp's body bashing against the rocks. The pocket snagged and ripped. Todd felt his heart jump into his throat.

"Be careful."

"We're trying."

"Jacob let go of my legs and help me. She's nearly at the top."

Wisp's head emerged through the hole and Alex grabbed at her shoulders pulling her upwards, whilst Jacob kept the strain on the belt. The tear in the pocket widened and the fabric ripped.

"Shit, it's tearing," said Alex.

The knotted belt came loose from the fabric. Jacob dived to grab Wisp's shoulders as Alex was dragged to the grass. Looping his arm under hers, he slowed her decent and gave Alex time to regain her grip. The two of them struggled and shuffled Wisp's body through the gap and on to the grass cushion.

"Well done," said Todd, "That was close."

"Your turn," called Jacob.

Todd reached up using his good arm and hooked his fingers into a hole. A sharp twinge shot between his shoulder blades causing his hand to spasm. He fought to keep his grip and used the foot holes to work his way up the shaft. Tilting his head back, he looked up at the sky, closed his eyes and breathed deeply, letting the fresh air circulate around his lungs.

"I'd forgotten what the breeze feels like," he called up to the faces above.

His blissful smile vanished.

His lungs filled with air and he expelled it violently as a

set of claws dug deep within his calf, ripping through his muscle with ease. An explosion of blistering white pain flashed before his eyes. A second paw smashed into his back, sending him thudding into the rocks, before dragging him back down to the cave floor.

"Todd!"

Adrenaline pumped through their bodies. Jacob scrambled back down the shaft with Alex watching anxiously from above. Her heart was pounding, the rush of blood pulsing through her ears drowning out the sounds around her. Todd was still in view. Blood poured from his fists as he gripped the jagged rocks and tore his palms open. His teeth sunk into his lip, trying to battle the pain.

"No, just go! Alex needs you," he screamed to the figure descending towards him.

Jacob looked down at Todd, blood oozed from his leg and down his wrists. Then he looked up at Alex, her eyes pleading for him to climb back up with heavy tears in her eyes.

"Use the knife," Jacob called down to Todd.

Todd's eyes searched through the plumes of dust. The metal glinted at him and his hand reached for the blade. His fingertips were mere millimetres away when a huge black paw slammed into his wrist, piercing his skin with its claws. Todd screamed, his fingers still searching for the metal. The claws slid out of his flesh like a rapier being removed from its sheath.

Jacob clambered back into the light whilst Alex's eyes stayed transfixed on Todd. All the fresh air was not enough, her lungs searched for more. They watched as Todd's body was dragged back into the cave. His eyes stared at the sky, keeping it in his sights until there was only darkness.

I forgot how beautiful the world can be.

30

"We need to go back for him," said Alex.

"We can't. Look at us. We need to go to hospital," said Jacob.

"But Todd."

"I know, but he told us to go. We can go and get help for him. Those things won't be able to withstand an army."

"No one is going to believe us. They're gonna lock us up and think we just ran away or something."

"We've gotta try."

"We need to leave a trail, something to help the police find their way back. I'll have a look around."

Jacob sat on the luscious green grass next to Wisp. His fingers stroked the stray hairs away from her eyes as he looked anxiously at her wounds. Congealed blood crusted over her shirt. She started to stir, her eyelids fluttered open.

"What happened? Where are Alex and Todd?

"We got attacked, but we managed to get out. Alex is looking for a way to leave a trail and Todd, erm, he didn't make it out."

She tried to sit up as uncontrollable sobs burst from her lungs forcing her shoulders to bounce with every new intake of breath. Jacob wrapped his arms around her and pulled her close. Peering over her shoulder, he spotted Alex walking towards them carrying some old broken logs and twigs. She placed them down in a heap and rummaged through them, choosing each one carefully.

"Eurgh, woodlice, get off, get off."

She managed to shake the small brown insects from her fingertips and sorted through the rotting wood. She lined up the discarded chunks of tree towards the shaft of the cave, making a giant arrow on the grass.

"I think it'll work. We need to get away from here, before The Raven comes looking for us," she said.

Wisp lumbered to her feet, leaning on Alex for support

whilst Jacob looked around for some sign of civilisation.

"I think there's a track down there, it might lead to a road or something."

They started walking down the hill towards the track. Jacob enjoyed the feeling of soft springy grass under his feet, leaving a trail of muddy blood ridden footprints glimmering on each trodden blade. The light breeze in the air carried the sweet scent of flowers.

"How far until we find someone do ya think? said Wisp, struggling with each step.

"When The Raven brought me here, he made me run. By the time we got here the lights had faded and it was just the night sky, so I reckon we are quite far out," said Jacob.

They reached the bottom of the hill. Muddy bike tracks had torn away the grass in both directions, leaving loose tufts scattered across the land.

"Which way?" asked Alex.

"I don't know. That way leads into the trees, this way is more open. It just looks like grasslands. What do ya reckon?" replied Jacob.

"Grasslands," they replied in unison.

"Okay."

Uneven terrain hampered the walk across the grasslands. Rabbit holes and old tree trunks littered their path. Alex and Jacob were vigilant with every step.

"Keep looking for obstacles, we can't afford to fall," said Jacob.

Swaying tall grass rustled in the wind and the gentle chirp of sparrows carried on the breeze. The track widened and split. One led to a broken rickety bridge, the other continued through the grasslands.

"Next decision," said Jacob.

Alex climbed up on to a rotting tree trunk and looked around her, considering each path.

She pointed to the left, "I think I can see a rooftop over there. There's just more grass that way," she said signalling to the right, "I hate to say it, but I say we take the bridge."

Jacob nodded in agreement and they set off.

"Those chains look strong enough, but the boards at the bottom have seen better days. The handrails don't look stable either."

"We'll have to go across one at a time then," said Wisp.

"But you can barely stand," replied Jacob.

"I'll manage. Bring me one of those branches and I'll use it as a crutch."

Jacob helped Wisp to the ground, whilst Alex went and grabbed a few branches from amongst the grass. They clunked together as she dropped them on to the ground and crouched down to examine the wood.

"This one looks okay."

She leant against the old branch and felt it give way a second before she heard it snap. Her arms instinctively shot out in front of her and protected her head as she crashed into the grass. Jacob and Wisp tried to stifle their laughter but the muffled chuckles and shuffling of their shoulders gave them away.

"Hey, stop laughing," Alex said whilst brushing herself down and clambering back to her feet.

With her feet evenly spaced apart she drove the next branch into the dirt. The wood creaked slightly as she applied more pressure to the flattened edge, but it held her weight. She gave the stick to Wisp then looped her arm under her armpit and hoisted her to her feet.

Jacob approached the bridge first. The frame was arched and the wooden slats were worn along the grain. The eroded edges gave Jacob his first view of the rushing river below. Jacob tried to hide his trepidation, but a gentle tremor was noticeable as his hands settled onto the rail.

"Take your time," called Alex.

The board swayed as Jacob tapped it with his foot. Metal clinked and the wood groaned as he tentatively made his way across. Green slimy algae from the rails coated his palms. The last board was missing and the one before it hung unevenly from the chains. The middle was splintered and arced towards the sky.

"This bit's tricky," he called to the others.

The cold wet wood felt rough under his feet. The individual grains left a grimy impression on his toes. Jacob took a deep breath, embracing the stabbing pain poking at his ribs and carefully placed his foot on the far left edge of the wood. The added weight made the bridge sway. Splintered remains and dark circular holes littered the right handrail. The left ran across the gap to the grassy bank. His nails gripped the sodden wood, leaving five tiny indentations scattered around the rail.

"Three, two, one, jump."

The girls clapped sarcastically and called out scores to mark his crossing.

"Four," said Wisp, "It was a clumsy dismount."

"Five," said Alex, "The one legged hop at the end got you an extra point."

"Hey, not fair," shouted Jacob, "If I had known you were scoring me I would have made it look much more stylish. Come on then, show me how it's done."

Wisp hobbled over to the bridge with her hand clamped tightly around the top of the walking stick. Her left hand grabbed the rail and she used the stick to test the wooden slats before she trusted them with her feet. Lumps of wood broke away as she bashed the walking stick into the fifth board. It plunged through the gap, sending her hurtling forwards. Her arms scrambled for something to grab. Jacob bound towards her, but she managed to regain her balance.

"Whoops, that wasn't my best idea. Do I get added marks for danger?"

"Stop mucking around and get across here already," said Jacob.

"Sorry, it wasn't intentional."

Wisp steadied herself, took a deep breath, placed both feet on the outer left rail and edged towards the bank. The old wooden structure grumbled under the added weight. Metal tangled around her legs impeding her movements. She worked her way around the hanging chains. Jacob reached out his hand. Wisp looked at it, then back at her own hands clinging to the rail. Her body was tired, every inch ached and she felt the now familiar sense of panic twitching in her stomach.

"I can't let go Jacob."

"You have to. Reach for me and I'll catch you."

Her right arm and leg worked in unison, swinging out towards Jacob in a stretching leaping combination.

Doof!

They collided and her momentum sent them both rolling through the grass down the bank.

"You both alright?" Alex shouted across to them.

"Yeah, I think so," Wisp replied as she giggled.

Alex approached the bridge and surveyed it from multiple angles.

"I reckon the right side is more stable but I'll have to jump further at the other end."

She settled her fingers around the wood, feeling the wet grain with her fingertips. In three graceful movements she was half way across.

"How did you do that?" said Jacob in awe.

"Elm Park Twister champion," she called back giggling.

"Where now? Broken boards, termite holes, splintered wood. Great!"

She placed her feet either side of a chain on the bottom rung and clung to the top rail with her arms twisted behind her.

This better work. Okay, spin, spin, spin, jump.

Wisp clapped loudly "Wow, truly amazing, you'll be representing Great Britain in the next Olympics with moves like that."

Feeling the blood rushing to her face, Alex curtsied.

"Right, let's find you another walking stick then get going. It's starting to get dark and I don't want to be out here when it does," she said.

31

Jacob rubbed at his forearms and the exposed flesh beneath his tattered pyjama bottoms. His head felt heavy and his muscles ached as though he had run a marathon.

"We need to find somewhere. It'll be dusk soon and we're already finding it difficult. We won't be able to manage in the dark," he said.

"If there are people in the house they aren't going to open their doors after curfew. We've got an hour at best," added Wisp.

"The roof we saw can't be much further. I'll make my way up the hill and have a look," said Alex.

"Okay, be careful."

Alex longed to be tucked up in a warm comfortable bed with a duvet wrapped around her. The long grass poked at her feet, irritating her cuts. Her arms hung loosely by her sides as she plodded slowly up the incline.

"I bet I can do it in twelve strides. Nah, maybe fifteen."

She overextended each stride, hoping her strategy would get her to the top faster. Rubbing at her eyes, she tried to stifle a yawn as it built within her jaw.

"Nine, ten, eleven, twelve, thirteen, fourteen."

Her knees buckled and a massive sigh left her lips. She lay with her eyes closed as the soft grass tickled her neck.

"Anything?" she heard from somewhere below her.

Rolling on to her side she forced her eyes open.

"Yeah, get up here quick," she replied.

A mixture of red and yellow bricks peered through the tree line. She could make out a silhouette in the upstairs window. Her eyes fixed on it, hoping the person would look out across the grasslands, spot her and rush down to help. Her eyelids started to close, until the sound of chattering and giggling floated on the breeze. Alex's eyes sprung open again, she glanced behind her, looking for Jacob and Wisp. They were stumbling silently up the incline.

"That's not them. It's other people!" she screamed as she sprung up into a sitting position.

Jacob and Wisp's heads bobbed into view.

"Did you say people?" asked Wisp.

"Shhhhhh, just listen," replied Alex.

"Oh my God, I can hear people too. There are people Jacob, real actual people!"

Jacob collapsed to his knees, his fingers pressed against either side of his nose, covering his mouth. He felt the comforting warm breath bounce off his hands and a trickle of tears run down the crevices of his skin.

Forcing their aching bodies back on to their feet, they walked the fifty metres to the tree line.

"There's a bloody fence in the way," said Wisp.

"Just shout. They might hear us," replied Alex.

"Help! Help! Help!"

Nothing.

"Help! Help! Help!"

Alex found a small hole in the fence and looked through. There was no one there, just a garden gnome and a small grey shed.

"Nothing," she said.

"Hello," said a voice, "Hello."

Alex pressed her eye back against the hole and jumped away in fright as a dazzling blue eye peered back at her.

A scurry of footsteps was replaced with muffled voices. The volume escalated as they drew closer to the fence.

"Who are you? What do you want?" said a man gruffly.

"We need an ambulance. Please help us," Alex replied.

Two voices argued, mumbling through the fence.

"They might try to rob us. How do we know they are telling the truth?"

"Look at them. No one would go to so much trouble for a rouse."

"But, but…"

"Well, I'm helping. Go lock yourself in the bathroom if you're worried."

"No need to be sarcastic Jasper."

"Go get the hammer."

A large hairy hand appeared at the top of the fence and yanked at the panel. A smaller more feminine hand, with a shiny silver wedding band grabbed the next panel. Jacob, Wisp and Alex sat on the floor and pressed their feet hard against the wood. Feeling it starting to give way, they pulled back and watched as two faces glared at them through the gap.

"Oh my, look at you. Jasper, go and call an ambulance. Quickly, tell them it's some of the missing children from the telly."

32

The electric lights hummed softly in the background against the beeps and alarms from the rooms nearby. Hurried footsteps raced up and down the corridor and snippets of conversations filtered through the walls into the ward. The ward itself was sparse with a large window at the far end. Two policemen were positioned at the door and a third stood staring out of the window. Dark blue curtains hung loosely around three hospital beds.

Jacob slowly opened his eyes; everything had a softened haze around the edges. A pleasurable warmth eased through his limbs. He noticed the bandages wrapped around his palm and wrist. His eyes glided upwards to the bag hanging on a large metal stand. A small wooden cabinet sat prominently next to his bed.

Where's Alex and Wisp? Are they okay? Why isn't anyone answering me? Oh, am I talking. I don't think I'm talking.

"Alex? Wisp?" he said.

His voice was gruff and his throat stung like a dozen needle pricks. A small cup sat on the tray positioned next to the cabinet. The bandages bumped against the plastic, knocking it over and sending it rolling off the tray and down the side of the cabinet. It bounced roughly off the floor and formed a small puddle beside his bed.

The curtain shuffled open briefly as a nurse rushed in and bent down to clean up the mess. She rose to her feet with the cup in her hands and smiled at Jacob.

"Hello, I'm Mia. You're in hospital. We've given you some painkillers to make you feel more comfortable. The police want to talk to you. They are just outside the curtain when you're ready. Do you want some water?"

"Yes please, sorry. Where are Alex and Wisp?"

She grabbed another cup from the cabinet and slowly poured a continuous stream of water into it from the jug. She held it to his mouth and his lips clamped tight around the straw.

"Here you go, take slow sips. They're both okay but they are still sleeping," Mia lifted the head of the bed upwards and the metal clicked into place, "Look."

The curtain hooks clattered together as she bunched them up, revealing the rest of the room. Jacob's eyes rested on to black metal and the freckled hands holding it. The arched handles sat below and a short barrel poked out from the rectangular frame.

He's got a gun.

"Gun?" said Jacob.

"It's alright Jacob he's here to protect you. Don't worry. Alex is in the bed opposite and Wisp is in the one next to her."

Jacob stared at the police officer for a few more seconds before he nodded his approval. His eyes sunk down to the cup and his mouth sucked at the water greedily.

"Todd? Is Todd here?"

"No Jacob. We only found the three of you," replied Mia.

His head fell back against the crisp white pillow and his eyes rolled upwards.

"Todd. Alex put a wooden arrow. Todd said no. Go."

"Okay Jacob, the police officer will let his colleagues know and they'll come and talk to you properly when your head is less fuzzy. You need to rest now."

"Fuzz? Alex needs Fuzz."

"The pink teddy?"

Jacob nodded.

"It's here. I stitched up its leg and gave it a bath. It's drying on her bedside cabinet."

Jacob smiled. His eyelids felt heavy again.

His head nuzzled down into the pillow. The soft folds of fabric brushed against his cheek. Voices rattled on around him and he caught snippets of conversations. His eyes opened occasionally to check he was still safe.

"Todd."

"In the caves."

"Yeah, a wooden arrow. I don't know the kid's out of it. Just let the search party know. Thanks."

When Jacob woke up again, dim lights shone near the door. The rest of the room was bathed in a dusky gloom. Cold folds of grey metal lined the windows, reflecting the dim glow on to the walls and ceiling. The freckled police officer had been replaced with a tall stocky man with huge hands, which made the gun look like a child's toy.

"No, no stay away. Don't hurt her. No, leave her alone," screamed Alex.

Jacob shot upright and swung his legs around to the side of the bed. A dull throb lingered across his chest. His bandaged feet landed on the floor unsteadily, throwing him off balance. The police officer rushed towards him, dropping his gun into one hand and scooping him up.

"You can't stand lad, your feet are all torn up."

"But Alex, she needs me."

"Hang on."

The policeman's huge thumb squashed the red call button into its casing. Hinges squeaked and a flash of light from the corridor illuminated the room.

"What's the matter?" asked a nurse.

"He tried to get out of bed. He wants to be next to his sister. She's having a nightmare. Can I wheel his bed over there without setting off any alarms?" replied the police officer.

The nurse reached across and blue cotton brushed past Jacob's head. Buttons clicked and metal clanked.

"There you go," she said.

Jerkily the bed lumbered across the floor and rumbled to a stop next to Alex's. Her legs were thrashing against the mattress and her head was bathed in sweat. Jacob reached across and softly stroked her hair.

"Hush now sleep and go to bed. Close your eyes and rest your head. It is time for you to dream, happy thoughts all agleam. Hush now sleep and don't you wake, until the morning light does break. Then you'll be ready again, to

164

make happy memories with your friends," sung Jacob.

Alex began to settle.

"What a nice song, where did you learn it?" asked the nurse.

"My Mum used to sing it to us when we had bad dreams. Can I stay next to her in case she wakes again?" whispered Jacob.

"Yeah, I'm sure that'll be okay. Try and get some rest."

33

Sunlight gently shimmered through the curtains. A soundtrack of giggling and quiet weeping filled the room. Jacob shuffled his bottom down into the mattress and gripped the handrail to prop himself up. The blue curtains were wrapped around Wisp's bed and he could hear her voice amongst a flurry of others.

"I love you so much. I thought we had lost you. We kept trying but we didn't know where you were," said Julie through the tears.

"I know Mum, Jacob and Todd told me about the appeals on the news. I love you too. I'm sorry," replied Wisp.

"You don't have anything to be sorry for. Look at you, you've changed so much. I'm just so glad to have you back," said Julie.

Her arms wrapped around Wisp like a strait jacket.

"Mum," Wisp said wincing as she patted her Mum on the back.

"I'm sorry darling it's just so good to have you back. I think I'm dreaming."

"You're not dreaming Mum. I'm here and look at you two. Wow, you've both got so big."

Corey and Liam clambered on to the end of Wisp's bed and crawled up beside her. Her hands rested on their shoulders and she pulled them both close to her as tears welled in her eyes.

"I missed you both so much," she whispered as she kissed their foreheads.

"Can I have a drink Mum? My mouth is dry," she asked.

"Yeah, I'll go and put some fresh water in the jug for you."

Julie pulled the curtains back and jumped slightly as Jacob stared at her.

"Erm, oh sorry, I just, erm, I didn't mean to make you

jump. Is Wisp okay?" he asked.

Julie looked at her daughter and noticed the light in her eyes and blissful smile creeping across her face at the sound of his voice. She stroked her arm and walked over to Jacob's bed.

"Yes she is and it's okay. I just didn't know you were awake. I hear you are to thank for getting her out of there," Julie said as she squeezed Jacob's arm.

Jacob shivered and felt large teardrops pour silently down his face.

"Oh my dear, I'm sorry. I didn't mean to make you cry."

"Sorry, it's just she saved me. If I hadn't met your daughter I would still be trapped in the darkness and so would my sister."

Julie plucked a tissue from the box and wiped it gently under his eyes and across his cheeks. His lip quivered and he bit it gently, smiling at the reminder of his Mum. He stroked Julie's hand and whispered, "thank you," as he looked into her big green eyes.

"Let me get you some water too," she said as she picked up his jug and pushed the door open with her bottom.

Jacob smiled, wiped his eyes one last time and turned to find Wisp smiling at him though her eyes were filled with sadness.

"What's wrong?" he asked.

"I just can't stop thinking about Todd."

"I know me too, but the police will find him."

"I hope so. I wouldn't be here without him."

"We'll ask the police officers if there's any news."

"Okay, how's Alex?"

"She had a nightmare last night. I haven't spoken to her yet."

Alex began to stir.

"Is this real?" she said as she rubbed her eyes and sat up in the bed.

"Yep," Jacob replied smiling.

Julie walked back into the room with Mia.

"Glad to see you are all awake. The police detectives are outside waiting to talk to you. Let me know when you feel ready," said Mia.

They looked at each other, sighed and nodded.

"We're ready," said Wisp.

34

The laptop announced its readiness with a series of chimes. The Raven poured some tea and settled down at the monitor. Stroking upwards, the cursor flicked onto the news bar. Headlines scrolled across the screen. One caught his eye and he clicked; sipping his tea as it loaded.

Bodies found as police search Scadhurst caves

Police released a statement earlier today confirming the discovery of five bodies after searching Scadhurst caves and the surrounding areas this morning. The search was initiated after three of the claimed victims escaped capture and were found in grasslands near the caves on Tuesday. Metropolitan Police Commissioner Clara Felks said "A team of specialist officers searched the Scadhurst caves at 8am this morning. During the search they found five bodies who are believed to be victims of The Raven. The families of four of the victims have been informed and it is with great sadness I can announce the deceased are:

Gabby Opel, 32
Hayden Phillips, 14
Joseph Stevens, 24
Michael Denby, 42

The fifth victim has yet to be named as police are still trying to identify him.

Speculation is now rife as to the reason why Michael Denby was taken and whether he had any involvement in the abductions. Denby, 42 is the father of two of the surviving victims Jacob and Alex Denby, who are said to be doing well in hospital. The third victim, Willow Matthews is also said to be making a steady recovery.

Police have released a description of a man they would like to talk to further their enquiries. The man is described as approximately 6ft 3in tall, thin, with square shoulders.

He is in his early to late 40's. He has sunken eyes and short brown hair which is cut into his neck. He is said to wear dark grey tailored suits and has deep calluses on his knuckles. Police believe he goes by the name of Jack and are asking anyone with information about his whereabouts to contact their local police station.

The Raven slammed down the lid of the laptop with his tea cup.

"So much potential wasted. I could have fed on those souls for months, maybe even years if I hadn't been so preoccupied. Instead I had to devour their lifelines in a few miserly hours and now I have to find a new place for the rest to mature."

He pushed the laptop across the table and slammed his hands into the wood. The table squeaked as he stood to wash the cup. As the last of the water gurgled down the plughole he placed the dried cup into cabinet and walked to the cupboard. The door opened with a click.

"Get comfortable, I'm going to get some new appetisers to build my strength. I'll be back for you soon. Be ready though, we don't want you to miss out on the main meal, especially after all the effort you put in."

The door swung shut and the wood slammed against the frame. The Raven shook the handle to check it was locked. He threw his head back and arms out, growing and twisting into smoke. It bellowed and danced towards the open window and poured out into the cold night sky.

35

Jacob clicked on the end call button and slid the phone back in his pocket.

"Is she coming over?" asked Alex.

"Yeah, she'll be over a bit," he replied.

"Okay, have you got the key?"

Jacob jangled the keys in front of her and flipped them round on his key chain until he found the right one. He slid it into the lock and took a deep breath.

"Ready?"

"No. but, just open it."

He turned the key and pushed against the door. It stuck and scrapped on the step. Popping it open released a strong musky odour of dust and mildew. Jacob covered his mouth and nose and took tiny breaths. Specks of dust floated in the air. Mottled light struggled through the heavy curtains and cobwebs hung from the corners of the room. White dust sheets covered the furniture. Jacob coughed heavily, inhaled too deeply and coughed again.

"It looks the same as the night she died. Why didn't Dad sell it?" asked Alex, gulping down the anguish rising in her eyes.

"The police said it was in his name and he was still paying off the mortgage each month, so even when they couldn't find him, their hands were tied. It just got locked up and left behind. The new keys were given to the children's home with a set of instruction that if Dad didn't turn up for us, I should receive them on my 16th birthday."

"Your birthday was fun; it reminded me of the parties Mum used to throw us. Wisp's family really tried to make it special. It's just a shame we were still in hospital."

"Yeah, I know. It was really nice of them. I just wish Mum, Dad and Todd had been there."

His face crumpled and water welled in his eyes. He dabbed around his cheeks as he looked around the room.

"I can't stay down here. Every time I look at the floor I

see her lying there. Let's go and check the boxes in the loft," he said.

As Alex glanced around the room, her mind flickered between the present and the devastating scenes The Raven had shown her. She saw her Mum reaching down to pick up Fuzz from beneath the red chair. Now, her eyes were drawn to shards of the red plastic visible from beneath the sofa. An empty spot on the floor signalled where Riley's favourite green chair once sat. Alex's mind pictured it splattered with blood. She screwed up her eyes and ran her hand down through her long brown hair, twirling the ends around her finger.

"Yeah, I can't take it either. Let's go upstairs."

The floorboards creaked under foot as they raced upstairs to escape the memories. On the landing Jacob tugged on the black cord hanging from the ceiling. A series of shudders and clicks echoed through the ceiling as the hatch opened and the metal ladder tumbled into view. Jacob grabbed a rung and pulled it towards the floor. It clattered into place.

He stared into the dark space above him and shivered. Pins and needles raced across his body bringing with it a wave of cold sweats.

It's too dark. I can't go up there.

He placed his hand on to a rung; his eyes paused and rested on the hundreds of tiny pink scars dispersed across his hands.

"The dark?" asked Alex.

"Yeah, I haven't been able to sleep without the light on since we got back."

"Me neither."

"I used to have a wind up torch, do you remember? It sounded like a pepper grinder. Do you reckon it's still in my room?" said Jacob.

"We can have a look."

Jacob walked around the ladder and stood next to a blue door covered in dinosaur stickers. Alex's hand slipped into his palm and he pressed down on the handle.

Inside, the room had the same musky scent as downstairs. Clothes littered the floor and piles of toys were stacked against the wardrobe. His duvet was heaped on the far side of the bed. The wind-up torch hid under some discarded tissues caked in dust. Behind it was a photo of Riley, Alex and Jacob smiling as they built a snowman in the back garden. Jacob swiped the tissues off of the torch and picked it up along with the photo. He slid the photo into his back pocket and proceeded to wind the handle of the crank shaft. The LEDs flickered.

"It still works," he said, "I better turn it off otherwise I'll waste the charge before I've used it."

Jacob's phone rang. He pulled it from his jeans, hit the answer button and swiped right. The corners of his mouth rose at the sound of her voice.

"Okay, I'll come let you in."

He hung up, slid the phone back into his pocket and thrust the torch towards Alex.

"Keep winding, I'm going to let Wisp in."

Alex sighed, "I get all the best jobs."

Jacob and Wisp took a few minutes to reappear. Alex didn't ask; she knew what they'd been doing.

"Hi Wisp, how are you? Here Jacob, your turn," she said, shoving the torch into his stomach.

"Good, the stitches come out in a few weeks. My family have been spending a lot of time at home with me. It's been nice to catch up on everything I missed. So where are we looking first?"

Jacob smiled, "We think it'll be in the loft, so let's go up there and start searching. It is a small black phone with a tattoo design on the back."

The LEDs shone brightly as he waved it through the hatch. Thick dust danced in the light and landed on the stacks of boxes scattered around the attic. He noticed the wooden boards Riley had placed over the beams after he had snuck into the loft and put his foot through the ceiling.

I'm getting sentimental over plywood. Come on, that's lame even for me. There's going to be loads of memories

173

in these boxes, you've got to pace yourself.

Jacob stooped, ducking under the old wooden rafters. The ends of his laces scratched and caught on the insulating foam. Black wire wove across the rafters and an old chain swayed in the breeze. He pulled on it and heard the mechanism click into place, illuminating the space.

"I forgot Mum put a light up here. I guess I'll start with this pile," he said putting the torch away.

Bubble wrap popped and brown paper rustled as they unwrapped each item carefully.

"Any luck?" asked Jacob after five minutes.

"No, but it's got it be here. You said the police returned it with the rest of your Mum's stuff, right?" said Wisp.

"That's what I was told when my social worker gave me the keys," he replied.

They continued looking, pulling out trinkets and photos, books and clothes. Wisp dug through a black bag and emerged holding a black leather jacket with racing patches sewn on to the arms.

"Was your Mum a biker?" she asked.

"Yeah, she rode a lot before she had us. She said it gave her time to think, but she stopped when I was born. I asked her why once and she wrapped her arms around me, kissed me on the head and said "because you're more important than any bike. I want to be around to see you both grow up," said Jacob, smearing dirt and tears across his cheeks.

Wisp was about to put the jacket back into the bag when Alex called across to her.

"Leave it out please. I'd like to keep it, if that's alright."

"Of course you can."

Alex avoided the boxes scattered across the floor as she clambered across to Wisp and took the jacket from her. She slipped her arms inside and pulled at the sleeves to reveal her hands poking out at the bottom.

"I think it's a bit big," she said.

"It's hanging awkwardly to one side. Let me fix you,"

174

said Wisp.

She adjusted the leather, shuffling it across Alex's shoulders and straightening the collar.

"It still doesn't look right. Is there anything in the pockets?"

Alex put her hand into the left pocket and fumbled around.

"This one's just got some receipts and stuff," she said, "The other one is heavier. It kinda feels like a phone but the zip is stuck on the lining. I can't pull it out."

Alex took her hand off of the pocket and jiggled the zip trying to free it. She yanked at the lining and jolted the zip up and down. It came loose and she wiggled the phone free.

"Try turning it on," suggested Jacob.

Alex searched around the phone and pressed any lumps of plastic resembling a button. Nothing happened.

"It's been in an attic for years. Do you reckon we can find the charger somewhere?" asked Wisp.

Jacob looked around the loft picking up boxes and slamming them down again. He pushed and shifted the boxes around searching for something.

"What are you looking for?" asked Alex.

"I saw a box marked electricals, but when I looked through it, it was just full of leads and stuff so I put it somewhere and just kept looking," he said.

Alex and Wisp hurried over to help him, turning all the boxes round and reading the labels. Eventually they had shifted most of them out of the way, leaving five boxes tucked in against the rafters. Jacob pulled each one out in turn and spun them round looking for the labels.

"Yes finally, electricals."

The cardboard was crushed on one side and wires hung through the gap in the bottom of the box. Jacob ripped the box down the middle. Plugs and wires spilled on to the floor.

"Right, anything that's definitely not a phone charger, throw back in the box. Anything that might be, give to

Alex. You can try the leads and hopefully we'll find one that fits."

Wisp and Jacob grabbed at the leads and sorted them into two piles. Alex tried them all.

"Found it. It's this one," she said triumphantly.

They jumped up and rushed to the ladder, taking the rungs two at a time. Their bodies piled into Jacob's bedroom and shoved the plug into the socket. A battery bar appeared on the screen and the trio cheered.

They sat and chatted, resisting the temptation to try and switch the phone on too early. After half an hour Jacob couldn't wait any longer.

The melody played and the phone vibrated into life. Company logos and catchy animations flashed across the screen. Jacob stretched and screwed up his fingers as his breathing became more manic.

"Calm down. It'll load in a minute," said Wisp as she slumped on to the floor next to him.

The home screen appeared. Jacob scrolled through the menu until he found the phonebook. He clicked on the button and held his breath, his thumb scrolled through the list of names.

A, B, C, D, F, G, H, I, Jack Holst, Jack R, Jack Ra, Jamie.

"There's three numbers with the name Jack. We need to do a search for them and see what comes up. One of these is the number for Uncle Jack. It might help us find out more about him and find out what happened to Mum."

He clicked back and went into messages. There were ten stored in the memory. Jacob clicked on Michael's name. A message popped up on to the screen.

I need to see you. J's out and when he can't find me, he might come after you and the kids. Stay safe. M x

36

Doric columns framed the white wooden door and ivy climbed across the yellow bricks. Four rows of windows scaled the building. Black wrought iron fences rested on top of the plinths forming a balcony. Jacob and Alex craned their necks to look at the exterior of the house.

"Wow, your house is amazing," said Alex.

"Dad inherited it from Granddad when he died. It's been in the family for over a hundred years," replied Wisp as she turned the key in the lock.

The door swung open to reveal a long cream hallway with a spiral staircase tucked to the left. The only other decoration was a vase of flowers. Oak doors led into the living room and Jacob's eye was drawn to a large portrait of Wisp and her brothers which sat proudly in the middle of the wall above a marble fireplace.

Voices neared and feet pattered against the wooden floors. Jacob's nerves twitched as the sound grew closer. His heart fluttered and his eyes darted to the door.

Corey and Liam burst into the room and high fived Wisp. They circled Jacob and Alex, jumping with excitement like puppies with a new toy.

"Calm down boys, you'll scare them away," said Julie from the doorway.

"Hi, it's okay. It's nice to be wanted," said Jacob.

"Mum, we need to use the laptop for a while. Is that okay?" asked Wisp.

"What do you want it for?" Julie asked trying to hide her concern.

"Jacob and I are going to set up new email addresses, the journalists have found out our old ones and we can't access them without having to delete fifty emails every time we log in. We thought this way things might get back to normal a bit quicker."

Julie nodded approvingly, "It's in the study."

Wisp led the others into the hallway and towards the

stairs. The metal chimed with every step. The doorway to the study had a combination lock blocking the way. Jacob and Alex averted their gaze as Wisp keyed in the number sequence. Inside, dark oak bookcases lined the walls. Some papers, a phone and a silver laptop rested on top of a circular desk. Jacob scanned the book shelves and ran his index finger along the rows of hardbacks.

"You've got a lot of books," said Jacob.

"Yeah, we all read a lot but most of the hardbacks belong to my Dad," Wisp replied as she sat down at the desk and hit the power button.

The gentle hum of the laptop whirred into life. Alex and Jacob piled around the desk and leant on Wisp's shoulders as she clicked on the keys. She went into the toolbar and selected the incognito option.

"What was the first number?" she asked.

Jacob read each digit slowly then repeated them for Wisp to check. His breath caught in his throat, hanging there as her finger hit enter. The screen filled with links and hundreds of numbers.

"That's no use to us. Try social media."

Wisp logged into her account and typed the number into the search bar. The name Jack Holst and a picture flashed on to the screen as soon as she clicked enter.

"A short balding man and three kids, it doesn't look like the Jack we're looking for to me," said Jacob.

"Nope, definitely not him. What's the next number?"

Wisp typed in the final 9 and clicked search. The name Jack_Roar appeared next to a photo of a sandy beach with crystal blue waters. The man featured in most of the posts was tall and thin, with long black hair and a wiry beard.

"It could be him I guess, maybe if he shaved," Alex said unconvinced.

"But it says he lives in Germany and is 33. That's too young for the Jack we're looking for. I reckon we try the other number and then decide which one is most likely," replied Jacob.

Jacob's nails dug into Wisp's shoulder. His elbow

locked and his full body weight forced Wisp's arm into the padded armrest. Alex shifted her weight, rocking between heel and toe. Her arms folded across her body squeezing tightly.

Wisp inputted the numbers, placed her finger on the enter key and turned away, pressing her face into Jacob's chest.

Click.

The whirr of the laptop was overpowered by firm deep breaths.

Alex slowly opened her eyes. Staring back at her were two tired sunken eyes and a few wrinkle lines across the bridge of the nose. The rest of the face was hidden. Her stomach churned and she felt an uneasy cold shiver down her arms.

"It's him. His eyes are blurred but I'm sure it's him. Well, I think it's him. Click on the link Wisp. I need to know," said Alex.

The page loaded.

"Hit the refresh button, it hasn't loaded properly," said Jacob.

"I think it has. There's just nothing really on it," replied Wisp.

No friends or details appeared down the side of the screen and a few sparse posts about football scores were listed in the most recent updates, but even those were from years ago.

"Scroll to the earlier posts at the bottom. There's got to be something else," said Alex.

"These posts are from 8 years ago," said Wisp as she read the last entry aloud.

'Just got out and can't wait to catch up with an old friend. I bet he's dying to see me. Four years without a visit is such a long time.'

"Do you reckon he's talking about Dad?" asked Alex.

Black spots flashed in front of Jacob's eyes. His breathing and pulse quickened and his head swam with thousands of thoughts. They piled on top of each other building, growing and tumbling down again. Pressure built in his forehead and the spots grew. Jacob's elbow gave way and he slipped towards the desk. Wisp reached out and caught him, holding him steady until he regained his balance.

"Yeah, but we saw him loads of times before Mum died. Why would she let him near her or us if Dad was so afraid of what he could do? I just don't get it," said Alex.

"Maybe she wasn't afraid of him. I remember hearing his name before you were born, when I burnt my hand. Maybe she actually thought he was her friend and when he couldn't find Dad he just decided to try and muscle in on his family instead. He knew seeing Mum playing happy families with someone else would wind Dad up. Maybe he was hoping it was enough to drag Dad out of the woodwork, but when it didn't work as fast as he wanted it to he tried to speed up the process," said Jacob.

"By killing her?" asked Alex.

"Maybe, he didn't mean to kill her. I don't know. Only Jack knows why he did what he did."

"I know what I saw though. He tried to rape her but when she fought back he got angry. Mum was the one who grabbed the knife. He had taken it from the kitchen and had it tucked in the belt of his trousers. Maybe he planned to kill her, or maybe he hoped Dad would come over and it was for him. I don't know."

Alex's knees buckled. She reached out to try and steady herself, but misjudged the distance. Her hand jolted into the papers and phone near the laptop, sending them hurtling towards the floor. Black plastic exploded from the phone casing with shards scattering around the room. The crash was followed by a loud bump as she crumbled onto the hard wooden floor.

Wisp jumped to her feet and hurried around the desk to gather up the papers. She fumbled them into a pile, whilst Jacob helped Alex up on to the chair. The metallic clank of feet on metal rang across the silence.

"Shit, my Mum's coming. Close the screen, quick."

Jacob repeatedly hit on the x. Working frantically, his fingers typed into the search bar then he clicked and started typing again.

Quickening footsteps were replaced with an out of breath, red faced woman.

"Is everyone okay? What on earth happened in here? Wisp, really, I thought you would know better. After everything, I don't need to hear a massive bang and then you didn't answer me when I called to you. I thought he was trying to take you again. Oh my goodness. I was so scared," said Julie panicked.

Wisp dropped the pieces of phone, stood up and flung her arms around her Mum.

"I'm sorry. We we're mucking around and I bumped into Alex. She lost her footing and landed on the floor but managed to knock everything from the desk in the process. I'm really sorry. We didn't mean to scare you," said Wisp.

Julie's shoulders softened, "I guess we can buy a new phone, it's not the end of the world. Alex are you alright? You look very pale."

"We're really sorry Mrs Matthews. I have some tape in my bag, maybe we can use it to fix the phone. I think Alex just needs some fresh air. Is it okay if I take her out into the garden?" said Jacob.

Julie nodded. Jacob crouched down in front of Alex, stared at her then flicked his eyes upwards. Alex pushed herself to her feet and kept her head down and her eyes low as she stumbled past Julie.

"You okay?" Jacob whispered as they reached the top of the stairs.

"Yeah, sorry as I was talking about it, the images kept replaying and I couldn't shake them. Every time I tried my mind just zoomed in closer."

"What do you mean?"

"Like the beads of sweat clinging to her brow or the dirt under his fingernails as he clutched the knife and twisted it into her neck. I see it every time I try to sleep. It never stops."

"I know but we've got to find out the truth, no matter how much it hurts. We owe Mum and Dad that."

"I'm not arguing with you. It's just hard. You've got Wisp to talk to. I've got the doctors who think I'm crazy and you, but I can't always talk to you. I don't want to have to explain all the messed up thoughts in my head. I have to constantly keep busy just to keep them at bay. It's exhausting and when I stop they leak in. I keep this mask on most of the time, but behind my eyes it's carnage. Then when I do smile, I feel guilty for being happy. I can't win."

Jacob looked at his sister, her eyes were red and bloodshot, her face was pale and her skin looked clammy. Indents from her teeth lay in little red dots along her bottom lip. Her fingers were twitching and scratching at her legs.

She's hurting so much and I don't know what to do.

"I can't take it away. I wish The Raven hadn't shown you what he did, but he did it to get into your head. It's not going to go away, but maybe with time it'll ease. I'm here and I'm listening. When you feel it's all too much, talk to me."

Alex didn't speak. Her head was tucked into her chest. It rose and fell with every breath. Prickles of heat built in her nose and she rubbed her eyes to stop the tears from forming. Jacob's arms wrapped around her and pulled her into to his chest.

"How are you feeling Alex?" Julie's voice cut through the moment startling them both.

Alex pulled away and rubbed the back of her hand across her eyes. A sad smile crossed her lips as she walked over to Julie.

"I'm okay, thank you. I just had a flashback and needed some time to clear my head, but I'm okay now."

Julie's eyebrows rose and she looked Alex up and down.

What did this poor soul see down there? Wisp won't tell me much about what happened, but it must have been bad, just look at her. She's a wreck. How is a 16 year old

182

supposed to be a parent to an 11 year old? They need someone to look after them.

"Okay, as long as you're sure," she said unconvinced, "lunch is ready, if you're hungry."

Alex smiled and Jacob's eyes grew in anticipation. Julie had brought lunch into the hospital a few times and it was always a delicious spread. They followed her inside as she led them into a large dining room with eight wooden chairs placed at equal distances around a long wooden table. Bowls of crisps, a plate of carrot sticks, hummus and a platter of sandwiches rested in the middle.

"Help yourselves," said Julie.

Alex and Jacob looked at each other, their eyebrows twitched happily as they reached for the sandwiches. Taking two sandwiches and a handful of crisps each, they watched as Corey and Liam piled four sandwiches on to their plates and double dipped endless carrot sticks into the hummus.

"Boys, we have guests. Where are your table manners?" said Julie.

Corey and Liam looked awkwardly at each other and shuffled back into their chairs.

Wisp spoke between mouthfuls of food, "Mum, we still need to do Jacob's email account, it won't take us much longer. Would you be able to give them a lift back to their foster parent's after? They need to be back well before curfew. It takes a while to do all the checks and stuff."

"Yes, fine love. We can set off as soon as you've finished but be carefully this time. No more mucking around."

They made their way back upstairs after lunch. Jacob wiggled his finger over the mouse pad and the screen jumped back into life. He finished the email application form he had hurriedly opened when Julie was coming then reopened Wisp's account. Scrolling down he clicked on the photos tab. He scrolled to the bottom of the page. A single photo waited under a date heading from twelve years ago.

"Click there," said Wisp.

"It's Jack, Mum and another bloke outside our house. Look at all the boxes in the background and the caption underneath – 'helping out on moving day,'" said Alex.

"Right, so it's definitely him and he was friends with them, so what happened for it all to go so drastically wrong? Remember Dad on the phone, he was adamant he hadn't stole something but someone else had. We need to find out what the phone call was about. Does it say who that other bloke is? Maybe he knows what happened," said Jacob.

He moved the cursor and hovered over the smiling faces on the screen. Two names instantly popped up - Jack Raves and Riley York. The third name flashed and disappeared.

"Shit, sorry I moved the cursor too quickly. Hold on. Stuart Connors. I don't remember anyone called Stuart, do you?"

"No."

"Check your Mum's phone. See if there's a Stuart in there," suggested Wisp.

Jacob pulled the phone from his back pocket, pressed the button and waited for it to load. He clicked and scrolled through the contacts until S appeared on the screen.

"Scott, Sean, Shaz, Stephen, Stu, Sue. There's no Stuart. Now what?" Jacob said defeated.

"There's no Stuart, but there is a Stu," Wisp said, "call it."

The dialling tone seemed to ring forever and Jacob could hear his own breath as he held the phone to his ear.

A grumpy deep voice answered with confusion, "Hello? How did you get this phone? The person who owned this number died years ago. How did you get it?"

Jacob took a deep breath and tried to explain who he was and why he was calling.

"Right, okay, so you're Riley's son and you want to talk to me about your Mum and Jack. Well, I'm at work at the moment but I can meet you tomorrow morning in Den's café on the corner. Let's say at 10."

Jacob smiled to the others and said a simple, "yes, that's great," to the voice at the other end before hanging up.

"We're meeting tomorrow morning at 10. Can we use your printer? I want to show him the picture, just to make sure we are talking about the same bloke. This might be it, tomorrow we might find out why Mum died and why Dad left," said Jacob.

"Have you finished yet?" called Julie.

"Yep, almost, we just need to print the confirmation and we'll be down. Thanks Mum," replied Wisp.

Jacob folded the photo over four times and slid it into his pocket before climbing into the back of the Audi and clicking his seatbelt into the holder. The journey to their foster home was full of banal chatter and awkward silences.

"Thanks Mrs Matthews. Wisp, I'll call you tomorrow," Jacob said as he clambered out of the backseat and closed the car door.

As Jacob and Alex walked up the path, his phone buzzed 'Get some sleep. Tomorrow we find out the truth. Wisp xxx.'

37

Water thundered on to the corrugated metal roof and the windows rattled against the frames. Steady drips and intermittent screams echoed through the abandoned corridors. Broken glass glinted from the floor, cemented into the concrete. Muffled voices sounded like whispers behind the heavy metal doors. Red lights blinked at either end of the corridor and across the warehouse floor. Smoke crept across the ceiling, seeping into every room simultaneously.

A single voice screamed louder than the rest, "Why am I here? What do you want?"The thick black smoke coiled around her ankles and wrists, slamming her body into the cold metal walls.

"You let the darkness in. I'm here to take it back, admittedly a bit ahead of schedule but I'm sure after a few weeks of being here you'll catch up," The Raven's voice vibrated through every particle, "I'm sorry for the accommodation, it's not up to my usual standard, but I didn't have much time to make it home. I've got plans for the place though. No, actually I don't want to give any secrets away. You'll find out soon enough."

The smoke loosened its grip and crawled back under the door. Bodies crumpled to the floor. Fingers pressed gently above the swollen blisters glimmering in the dim light. Each blister traced the crisp white scars upon their wrists. A single sound started off low and built as each new occupant was shown their fate. Deep and guttural, loud and sharp, tones merging and breaking, forming a continual depth of noise into one drawn out scream.

The corridor led into the main warehouse where three small enclosures were visible and set into the corners of the room. Each was no bigger than a port-aloo, with heavy chains screwed in tight against the walls. The boxes were made from steel, welded together and cemented into the floor. There were no windows just two tiny slits to allow smoke in and out and a small access hatch.

Darkness slowly crept into every corner as the low level lights switched off one by one. A door slammed, chains churned together as a single key turned in the heavy lock. The screams faded, trapped within the warehouse as the smoke was carried away on the howling wind.

38

Jacob sat on the hard bucket seat looking at the linoleum table top splattered with drops of ketchup. A short stocky bloke walked in wearing a flat cap and paint covered overalls. His hands engulfed Jacob's as he shook hello.

"So you're Riley's son. Nice to meet you. Sorry about your Mum and Dad. I've read a lot about you the last few weeks. What really happened?" said Stuart.

Jacob squirmed in his seat.

"Thanks. Erm, it's like you read in the papers. I don't really want to talk about it. Bad memories you know."

Stuart nodded like he had been trapped there too and asked, "So what do you want to know? I thought it was a bit odd to hear from one of Riley's kids after what happened and all."

"I need to know about my Mum and Dad and how they were connected to Jack. Can you tell me anything?"

"Which Jack? We hung around we three or four Jacks back in the day."

Jacob pulled the picture from his pocket, unfolded it and smoothed down the creases with his fingertips. He slid it across the table and pointed at the other man in the photo.

"This Jack," he said with conviction.

"Oh, I had hoped you meant Jack Holst, but I knew deep down it was probably that son of bitch you were talking about. He was the kind of bloke who went to the pub and scrounged off everyone else all night to buy him a pint. He only helped that day because he fancied your Mum and hoped if he hung around long enough your Dad would screw up and he could swoop in like a knight in shining armour to pick up the pieces," Stuart said with a deep East End twang.

"So you didn't get along then?"

"No. He was in with some shifty blokes who sold on stolen goods and stuff. He got done for burglary a few years before your Mum died, around the same time as I lost touch with your Dad actually. We used to call him Magpie Jack, if it wasn't screwed down he'd try to pinch it. Useless though, that's why he got caught."

"When he got out did he try to get in touch?"

"Nah, he didn't get in touch as such, though I saw him a few times when he got out. He had changed though, more precise, focussed. Every thought and action was planned out, almost like he was a different person. Before he was arrested he lived in tracksuits and only washed at the weekends. Afterwards though he wore smart jeans and shirts, always washed and clean apart from his fingernails. They always looked like they were clumped full of dirt, but they weren't. They were just a mottled shade of black. No reason for it. What's with all the questions? Has he done something stupid or what?"

Jacob responded cagily. "Nah, nothing like that, I just remember him spending time with me and my Mum and he always seemed alright. We were going through some of my Mum's stuff and with my Dad dying and all; we just wanted to find out more about them both. He seemed close to them both so I just want to find out a bit more about him."

"Huh, well he wasn't much fond of your Dad, I remember that. Got him involved in all the dodgy stuff from what I understand and then tried to throw him under the bus when the big bosses found out Jack had been swindling them. He blamed your Dad for his arrest. If you ask me, I reckon that's why your Dad took off. Jack wasn't the smartest bloke but he knew people, people you wouldn't want to meet in a dark alleyway, if you get my drift."

"Can you tell me anything else about him?"

"Not much really, he kept himself to himself after he got out. The last time I saw him he was wearing a crisp grey suit though, which I thought was a bit odd considering. His nails were totally black by then, looked disgusting. He told me he had a new job at a warehouse off new road, but the place shut down a few years ago, so I don't know what he is doing now."

Jacob nodded his thanks across the table.

"Is that all you wanted to know?"

"Yeah, thanks. If I think of anything else can I give you a ring?"

"Yeah mate anything for Riley's son. Your Mum was a gooden."

Jacob reached across for a handshake then got up and walked to the café door. A buzzer sounded as he pulled the latch, letting the cold air filter in.

"Thanks again. Oh, one more thing. What was his surname? I couldn't find it written on any of Mum's old pictures."

"Ah, that's an easy one. Ravenscroft. Jack Ravenscroft that was his name."

39

"It's got to be linked, seriously think about it. I'm sure the curfew started a few months after your Mum died and the names, the names alone are a link," said Wisp down the phone.

"I know. I just don't want to believe it," said Jacob as he walked down the bustling high street.

"I don't think my Mum will let us use the laptop again after last time. Meet me at the library we can search there."

"Okay, I'm almost at the bus stop so I'll see ya in half an hour or so."

Jacob hung up and pushed the phone back into his bag. He pulled a black hood up over his ears and kept his head down as he reached the bus stop. The red bench had random initials carved into the plastic and he settled down on top of 'VP 4ever'. Last week's newspapers lay around the base of a nearby bin. Jacob glimpsed the headline. He fiddled with his hoodie trying to cover more of his face and twisted his body round to stop passer-by's from spotting him.

It's not even a decent bloody photo. It's the one from the care home. I don't get why we're still in the papers. It's been over a month since we escaped. Why can't they just leave us alone?

"Shocking isn't it?" said a voice from behind him.

"Eh?" replied Jacob.

"All this business about people being claimed. I mean, those poor kids have been through enough they don't need everyone trawling it all up again."

Jacob kept his head down and shuffled his body round on the seat. Old black leather shoes, wrinkled tights and a pale lilac skirt came into view. Her voice sounded like an old record; there were deep gravel undertones with a lilt of whimsy.

"Yeah, you're right," he replied.

"I remember hearing about a creature when I lived in

Canada, they called it the obscurité. Awful business, just awful."

Jacob nodded in agreement and looked up to find a bus sitting at the lights. A warm slightly sweaty palm came to rest on Jacob's shoulder. Instinctively, Jacob's head turned sharply to find a small wrinkled face staring back at him. Locks of white hair curled on her forehead and light blue eyes widened as she recognised him.

"Oh sorry love, my feet aren't as steady as they used to be. You're that lad aren't you? The one from the news?"

The words caught in his throat so he nodded. He waited for her to steady herself before walking the two steps to the kerb to hail the bus.

She's still staring at me.

Jacob shuffled awkwardly to one side, trying to avoid eye contact as he spoke.

"After you," he said.

"Thanks love, good luck and don't let the bastards get you down," she said, winking at him and holding a finger to her lips.

A single chuckle rose from his diaphragm and crept over the corners of his mouth.

"Cheers," said Jacob as he climbed aboard and edged through the thrall of people crammed inches from the doorway. The tannoy announced 'please move down inside the bus. Seats are available on the upper deck'. Jacob managed to weave through the bodies and find a space, pressed between a buggy and a handrail. Feet clambered up the stairs drearily searching for one of the allusive seats they had been promised. Minutes passed. Finally the bus lurched forwards as it pulled away.

He turned towards the window and stared out at the street. People bustled along the pavements. A Mum was pushing a buggy with her older children racing ahead and a man dropped his shopping as they ran past. Jacob kept his hood up and his head down, counting the stops. He grabbed the handrail, his body jarred forwards and back.

The doors beeped as they opened. Sweaty bodies irked for space, elbowing through the crowd, desperately trying to feel the cool breeze against their red blotching skin. Jacob wriggled into a space as people piled out on to the street. The old lady from the bus stop smiled across at him and patted the seat next to her.

Jacob looked down at her and wondered whether he should sit there. He wasn't in the mood for lots of questions and that was all anyone ever wanted to ask him. She continued to stare at him, her eyes almost pleading for him to join her. Jacob took a step towards the seat and saw the dried in brown stains scattered across the fabric. He tried to hide his disgust behind his hand as he sat down.

"Hi again," she said.

"Hi," he replied.

"Bit more room over here."

"Yeah, it was a bit squashed but I've only got a few more stops. What about you?"

"I'm going to see my daughter. She lives at the shops up near the library. She used to live in Canada with me but when people started getting taken; she decided she wanted to move back to the UK and I came with her."

Jacob shuffled in his seat. His mouth opened and closed, exhaling a long sigh.

"What did people say about the creature in Canada?"

"I heard about it when I was a kid. It was a fairy tale to us, until the boy three doors away was taken then it all became real. He never came back. They said the creature took those in despair, but a few managed to fight back. I don't recall all the details, I'm afraid."

"Oh, I'm sorry about your neighbour," Jacob said staring at his hands, unsure of what to say next.

Stop after stop in silence. He twisted his watch around his wrist and willed the hands to tick by faster.

The bus pulled up and Jacob leapt off of the seat. He nodded at the lady as he jumped out of the doors and ran down the street. Cool air stroked across his cheeks and the awkward knots in his muscles began to subside. Wisp

193

waved in the distance and he picked up his pace.

He's been panicking. I can see it on his face. Do I say anything? No, just give him the chance to calm down.

"Hi," she said as casually as she could.

His shoulders fell and his hand reached for her, "hi."

"So, shall we go and see what we can find out?"

"Yeah, I'm hoping we find out a bit more about him. There has got to be info on where he is now or newspaper reports about when he went to prison or something. I reckon we go to the local history section and ask if we can view old newspapers. It might give us a head start to find out more about him."

"Sounds like a plan."

They walked up the marble steps and through the foyer. Rows of computers lined the back wall and a sign swayed below the air conditioning unit.

"It's that way, look," said Jacob.

An older gentleman with grey frizzy hair smiled at them as he looked up from his desk.

"Hello there. How can I help you today?"

"We were hoping to look at local newspaper cuttings from ten or eleven years ago," Wisp replied.

"Looking for anything specific? I've looked through a lot of them over the years. I might be able to narrow it down a bit for you."

"We're doing a project at school about crime and we're hoping to find out about local crimes in the area from the last ten years or so, burglaries and stuff like that."

"Hmmm, there was a spate of burglaries about ten years ago. A gang thing if I remember, some blokes got sent to prison for a few years after getting caught out. The papers speculated someone must have grassed on them. Here, I'll load them up for you and you can take a look."

He busied himself for a few minutes before moving away from the microfilm reader and exclaiming, "There you go. All set up for you. Call me if you need anything else."

"Thanks."

They both pulled up a chair and began to click through the images.

"This is going to take forever. You keep trying here and I'll go try the internet," Jacob said as he pushed his chair back and walked towards the back wall.

He wandered over to the computers and chose one hidden in the corner. Settling down, he typed in Jack's name and hit the search button. 366,500 results popped up. The first page was links to businesses and social media pages for Jack Ravenscroft's from around the world. Page two was much of the same. Jacob scrolled and clicked through pages of links until one caught his eye.

Wisp rested her head on her hand and absently clicked through reels of slides. Her hand dropped and her head shot upright as she noticed the headline from eleven years ago.

'Local man imprisoned for 3 years for a string of burglaries in the area.'

Jacob tapped her on the shoulder waving a piece of paper. She glanced in his direction and signalled for him to sit down as she continued to read. "Local man Jack Ravenscroft was sentenced to three years in prison at Drayton crown court today. He shouted at the gallery as he was taken away. Ravenscroft was the only member of the notorious Shelton gang who faced trial today.'

"I wonder what he was shouting?" he asked, excitedly.

"What's the paper for?" she said.

"I've managed to find where Jack was living. It's amazing what you can find if you don't mind paying a few quid for answers."

"Okay, so where are we heading next?"

"It's on the outskirts of town. Maybe twenty, twenty five minutes on the bus but I reckon we need a plan before we just go barging in. We need more information first."

"See what else you can find out and I'll go and see if there's anything on the Shelton gang it mentioned."

Wisp rested her hand around his back and kissed his cheek before Jacob walked away. He felt a bit unsure as he approached the librarian, tripping over his words as he started to speak, "Er, em, sorry, er, exc...excuse me, I was just wondering, we found a report mentioning the Shelton gang. Does that name mean anything to you?"

"Hmmm, the Shelton gang, yeah I remember them. They used to terrorise the streets round here, burglaries, robbing people at knife point that sort of thing. Finally got put away trying to rob the bank on the high street. I met one of them once down the pub. He seemed like a nice enough bloke to start with then someone looked at him wrong and well, I never knew one person could bleed so much so quickly. He popped his nose like a shaken soda can," the librarian shivered as he relived the memory.

"Do you know if they are all still in prison?" Jacob asked.

"Last I heard they were all still inside. Well actually I say that, but I saw one of them a few years ago. He was sent down for some burglaries, wasn't around when the bank robbery went wrong. Looked different though, smarter but I don't know, there was just something about him. I crossed over to the other side of the street. I'm not proud of it, but I just sensed a vibe from him that made me want to get away."

"Thanks for your help."

Jacob nodded, then turned and walked back towards Wisp. She stayed engrossed in the slides as he relayed the new information.

"Looks like the rest are in prison, but he said he had seen one of the gang a few years ago. It sounded like he was describing Jack, Raven Jack that is. Suited and booted with a twisted evil vibe."

"Yeah, it fits with what we've been told before. I haven't been able to dig up much else. Just a quote from when Jack was sent down. He made a comment about Mickey, 'I'll see you soon enough Mickey, don't get too comfortable.' Do you reckon Mickey is your Dad?"

She slid the chair under the desk and they started to walk back towards the automatic doors.

"Jeez, that's given me goose bumps," he rubbed at his arms trying to free them from the crawling feeling, "Yeah, I think he was giving my Dad a warning. We need to tell Alex what's going on, make a plan then visit Jack and put an end to all of this. I can't keep waiting for him to come back for us. Every night I sleep with the light on. Every creak and hum startles me. I'm permanently on amber alert, my whole body is fighting against the exhaustion. The doctor has given me sleeping pills but I won't take them, I'm afraid when I wake up I'll be back in those caves."

"I know. I'm the same. My parents wanted to move my bed into their room, so they can keep an eye on me and make sure I'm safe, but I'm 16 and I don't want to share a room with my parents forever. I'm terrified he'll let me live and I'll wake up one morning and they'll be lying in a pool of their own blood. Their throats cut and I'll have slept through it all. My head's always been a mess, a minefield of traps and triggers. I know I could have lived in those caves just carrying on the way I was. It wasn't being down there that got to me, it was the fact I didn't know what was happening to my family. I gave up caring about myself long before I was taken, but I kept going for them. Those nightmares he put in my head only tore so deep because I couldn't bear the thought of anything happening to them. They love me in spite of me. I can't be the reason they suffer."

"They're not going to suffer. We're going to put an end to this so we can get on with our lives."

Jacob's jaw was clenched shut but his eyes betrayed him. He used his sleeve to dab at his reddening eye lids.

"Next bus is in two minutes. Alex will be back from her counselling session by quarter past so we shouldn't have to wait long. I wonder how she's gonna take it when we tell her we have Jack's address?" he mumbled whilst wrapping his hood around his face.

"She stronger than we give her credit for but she's still trying to get a grip on everything. It's hard enough for a normal eleven year old, let alone one that's had all this to deal with. She'll be okay, she's got you," Wisp replied.

A spray of brown splattered over the kerb as thick rubber tyres crushed an opened can left in the road. Jacob jumped backwards to avoid the liquid.

"Eurgh! Yuck! Great now I'm covered in cola."

He reached into his pocket and fumbled for his Oyster card then boarded the bus with Wisp a few steps behind.

40

"So basically Dad got Jack sent down and he came back for revenge. Then at some point The Raven took control and here we are, so what do we do now?" Alex asked.

"This old lady on the bus said something about a creature like The Raven in Canada. I looked into it at the library and there have been hundreds of missing people in different countries over the years all linked to a creature like The Raven. There were stories of whole hospital wings vanishing in a single night, but one thing they all had in common was all the disappearances started with a murder," Jacob added.

"But how does that help us?" replied Wisp.

"I'm not sure, but there are stories of people managing to banish the creature, the how is a bit vague though."

"Great, that doesn't help then. It's not like we can just go and knock on Jack's front door say hi and then I don't even know."

Jacob slumped into the sofa and drew his legs up to his chest. Alex crumpled into the seat next to him and rested her head on to his shoulders.

"I've got an idea but it's a bit well erm…" mumbled Alex.

"Don't hold us in suspense; it can't be any worse than nothing," a sad smile crossed Jacob's face.

"The Raven feeds on depression right, despair, darkness and all things bad."

"Yeah, so?"

"Maybe we just have to overwhelm him with hope. Jack didn't go to Mum's that night to kill her. He had the knife, but it was Mum who pulled it from his jeans in the struggle. Maybe he only had it as a precaution and when she pulled it out in the heat of the moment he didn't know what else to do. Before The Raven showed me the night Mum died, Jack said he was sorry. I think he really was. I don't know because it all happened so fast but I'm sure he sounded genuine."

"So you are saying we just have to forgive him," Wisp said unconvinced.

"No, I'm not saying it would be that easy, but maybe if Jack knew we forgave him, he would be able to fight from the inside. I know it's bonkers, sorry," Alex twirled her hair, looking at the creases in her top.

"Before we even consider the possibility of it working we need to think about whether we can actually forgive him. We can say it but we're actually going to have to mean it and even then it only helps with Jack not The Raven," said Jacob.

Alex rubbed her temples and sat up. Wisp was pacing back and forth across the floor. The carpet was brushed down along the path. Her thumbs were shifting at speed and her eyes were fixed on the glass front of her phone. A series of beeps filled the silence. Jacob couldn't take it anymore, he jumped up from the sofa and walked back towards the kitchen. Alex could hear the clatter of metal and banging of plates colliding with the marble worktop.

"I need to get out of here for a bit. I'm going to walk round the block. I'll be back in a bit," Alex announced as she opened the front door.

"It's nearly curfew, just go upstairs or something if you need some space," Wisp replied but Alex had already slammed the door.

Jacob ran into the living room, "Where did she go?" he asked.

"For a walk," Wisp replied rolling her eyes, "I tried to stop her but she wasn't in the mood to listen."

"I should go after her," he muttered as he grabbed his coat.

Wisp moved and stood between Jacob and the door. Her hands gripped his shoulders and she squeezed gently.

"Give her some time," she said quietly.

"But...," he exclaimed.

"I know, but she just needs some space. Are you both staying here tonight? I can ask Mum to set up the sofa bed.

She should be home soon."

"Nah, we better go back to the foster carers they're already annoyed because I didn't phone about the library. We've got almost an hour to curfew, that'll be enough time to get back."

"Okay, if you're sure."

"I'm not sure about anything anymore. That's half of the problem."

41

Alex sighed and forced her hands into her pockets. The streets were bustling with people, all trying to get home before curfew. She dodged left and right to avoid them. Small pockets of calm were dispersed between the rabble. Houses towered above and cars lined the streets increasing the steady footfall on the pavements. Alex tucked her chin to her chest and weaved through the masses, trying to draw the least amount of attention as possible. She reached the crossroads and looked up towards the church, it was teeming with people.

"There's too many people everywhere. Hmmm, maybe if I go down this way, it looks quieter."

She wandered down past some old houses and noticed a few were boarded up. Heavy wooden planks were screwed into the window panes and aluminium panels were attached to the doors. Loose bricks and debris were scattered across the front gardens and black spray paint adorned the walls.

Her muscles tightened. Every stride was a little wider, every step a little faster. Alex felt her nerves twitching and the hairs on her arms stood on end. She turned around sharply and started walking back towards the main road. Her feet echoed on the pavement and with each step she thought she could hear a second pair of shoes just a beat behind her own.

Craning her neck, she looked around.

Nothing.

She stopped but the footsteps continued, steady and sure. Her eyes focused on the main road ahead, whilst her legs struck against the pavement, motoring round faster and faster. The thud of every footstep rang in her ears, matching every stride with a seconds delay. She tried to swallow down the panic, trapping it between her gasps for air.

A few more metres and I'll be back on the main road. I

can go back to Wisp's and apologise for leaving without letting Jacob know and then I'll laugh about thinking someone was following me.

She spun round again whilst her legs kept her moving towards the street. The overhead lights were beginning to glow in readiness for curfew. Specks of black were dotted amongst the beams of light. Alex watched as they started to flurry towards the ground, like ash from a volcano.

Run!

She turned her back on the particles settling behind her and sprinted towards the throng of people up ahead. A dusty shadow loomed over her, growing with every step.

"Help me, someone is following me!" she called towards a group waiting at the traffic lights.

A few people turned around to seek out the owner of the shouts. Others stayed staring straight ahead hoping if they didn't look they could avoid whatever was about to unfold. Alex desperately wanted to look behind her and see how far he was into his metamorphosis. The hand on her ankle and the pavement colliding with her face, answered her question. Smoke rapidly engulfed her, trapping her to the concrete. She wriggled and kicked out wildly with her other foot. His grip loosened just for a second.

She seized the chance, forcing her hands into the ground and propelling herself up and over the bumpy paving slabs near the crossing. Panicked screams echoed off of the buildings and the thrall of people separated, spilling over into the street. Tyres squealed and shrieked as bumpers collided with metal. Alex clambered to her feet and tried to run again. Bodies fell around her, tripping and cursing. This time she barely got to her feet before she felt smoke clawing at her skin, wrapping itself around her frame. It lifted her up towards the street lights. Below her, eyes lay aghast, watching a nightmare unfold above. Alex could just make out their slack jaws and raised eyebrows amongst the gentle glow of the street lights as she struggled against the curls of smoke covering her eyes.

With laboured breathing and pressure building across her rib cage, she felt the oxygen being pushed from her lungs. Her muscles burnt and cramped. Darkness ebbed into the corners of her eyes, creeping across them both. She screamed in panic as her eyes were engulfed in darkness. She could feel the rush of air against her skin, making her hairs stand on end from the cold. She tried to pull her limbs in tighter to retain her body heat. The smoke resisted making her body shudder, then the pace slowed.

We've landed somewhere.

Chains rattled and clunked. A key turned in a heavy lock and glass crunched underfoot. Pain pierced through every nerve in her body as it was forced and squeezed through the tiniest of vents. Then there was nothing. The noises faded as the grip loosened. She began to move. Her fingers searched, expecting to find layers of rock. There were none. In its place was cold metal, flat and solid. No rivets or bumps. Alex tried to shuffle round but her shoulders collided against the sides. She tried to squat but her knees bashed against the cold steel. A single sound reached her ears. Screams, hundreds of screams amalgamated into one intense pulse bombarding the steel through tiny speakers above her head. She wiggled her fingers up to cover her ears, whilst her teeth vibrated in her mouth. A gentle trickle dribbled from her nose, filling her lungs with the aroma of iron.

"Welcome back, I hope you enjoy your new home. Don't worry. The others will be here soon."

42

Pacing the floor, his nails were bitten down to the quick. His eyes darted around the room, focussing on the door every time he heard a noise from outside.

"It's been forty five minutes, where is she? Something's happened Wisp. She would have come back by now otherwise, wouldn't she?" worried Jacob.

"Ring her again!" Wisp replied.

Jacob pulled the phone out of his jeans and hit redial. A single flat tone blared from the speaker.

"Nothing! He's got her. I know it," he cried.

"Stay calm. Check in with your foster parents and see if she's gone there," Wisp said trying to keep a calm tone to her voice.

Jacob hit at the screen, his fingers slipping between the numbers. Deleting his first attempt he tried again. The phone began to dial and he silenced the speakerphone and steadied his breathing before anyone picked up.

"Hi, Yeah, I'm fine. Erm, I know I said I would be home but it's nearly curfew and the bus is delayed. I'm at Wisp's. Yeah, Alex is with me. Okay. Yeah, I'm sorry, we'll be home first thing tomorrow. Okay. Yep. Yep. I know. See you tomorrow."

Jacob clicked on the end call icon and held his phone loosely. His shoulders shook and he bit down hard on his tongue. Pain radiated from the spot and a subtle metallic taste slowly swirled across his taste buds.

"She's not there."

His fingers rested just above his knuckles. His nails grated back and forth against his skin. Small white flecks fell away over his jeans.

"Why did you lie to them? Is there anywhere else she'd go?" Wisp asked.

"I couldn't tell them the truth. No. There's nowhere else. Mum's place is too far. She wouldn't have gone there without me anyway, too many memories."

"Time for the police?"

"Yeah I guess, but they won't find her unless he wants them to."

Julie walked in as Wisp took the phone from his trembling hand and started to dial. She cancelled the call quickly and hid the phone behind her back.

"I'm guessing you are both staying here tonight then? Where's Alex?" Julie asked as she scanned the room.

Julie watched as their faces changed. Jacob's teeth ran over his lips leaving groves in his skin. Wisp's hands shuffled the phone behind her back and into her pocket.

"What's going on? Is everything okay?" Julie asked with an increasingly worried tone.

"She got annoyed with us and went out and she's been gone for ages and we don't know where she is. It's nearly curfew and she's not at her foster parents. Jacob can't think of anywhere else she'd have gone and we're worried, really worried. We think The Raven's got her. We're going to call the police but we need to find her," Wisp blurted out.

Julie staggered backwards and reached out for the nearest chair.

"Not again, please not again. If he's taken her, he'll be after both of you next. Why did you let her go out alone? Okay, don't answer that. It doesn't matter. Jacob, look at me, it's going to be alright. We will get her back. We just need to find her.

Right, I'll call the police and then we'll ring your foster parents and let them know what's going on. We don't want them finding out with a knock on their door, or worse on the bloody news. Wisp go and make Jacob a tea with loads of sugar. My Mum always said it was good for shock. Erm, er, stay away from the windows though and stay together, just in case," Julie rambled.

She made the necessary phone calls and sat next to them on the sofa. Her hand rested on top of Jacob's. He squeezed her fingers and tried to raise a smile whilst they waited for news.

"The police are investigating but they said they won't send anyone until the morning because of the curfew. Your foster parents are beside themselves with worry too. They asked why you lied to them. I told them you were in shock. There's nothing else we can do tonight and it's nearly curfew so…"

"So they just expect me to go to sleep?" he said, slamming his fists into his knees.

"I know love, but there's nothing we can do. I've given them the name and address you mentioned and they said they would look into it. Really love, there's nothing else we can do tonight. You need to try and get some sleep for tomorrow. They said they'll be here as soon as the curfew is lifted in the morning to interview you," Julie placated.

"I'm not going to be able to sleep though. Who knows what he's doing to her."

Julie reached inside her bag and pulled out a small vial of pills. She slid them into Jacob's hand and grabbed a glass of water from the coffee table.

"Take two of these. You'll be asleep soon enough and won't wake up until morning. I know you want to go and find her, but you'll be no use to her if he gets you too."

Wisp stayed silent throughout the exchange, running scenarios through her head. Each one ended the same way, with Jacob and Alex gone. In some she went with them, in others The Raven focused only on them. Each made cold prickles cascade down her back and along her arms.

Jacob looked down at the pill bottle. Brown tinted glass mottled his fingertips. A few years ago he had held a similar bottle and tipped the contents into his palm. A fine white dust had coated his skin and his fingers had played with the small white tablets, pushing them into a regimented line. He remembered counting each one slowly, methodically. His breathing had slowed and he felt an odd sense of calm ripple across his body. He recalled the sharp jarring pain as one had stuck in his throat and the desperate gulps and swallows to clear the path for the next, the instant regret at his decision and the panicked voices of those around him. His recollection after that was sparse, just his throat on fire and the unforgettable taste of active charcoal.

He grasped the bottle and covered the label with his fingertips, thrusting it back towards Julie and muttering.

"I can't take these. I don't take tablets anymore."

Julie didn't ask, "Okay love, you don't need to take them, but you do need to try and get some sleep. I've made up the bed in the spare room. Just go and lie down. You might manage a few hours at least."

I should argue, storm out of the house and slam the door. I should be searching through the night to find Alex and fighting to bring her home safely in the morning just to prove to Julie, Wisp and the police that The Raven is not in control.

If you leave here you'll be no use to Alex. The Raven has your scent. He probably knows where you are right now. You just need to bide your time and wait until morning then you'll have the upper hand.

The room danced and see sawed as Jacob stood up. He snatched at the nearest stable object, trying to maintain his balance.

"Here, hold me," whispered Wisp from next to him.

He clung on to her arm and she ushered him out the door and up the spiral staircase to the spare room. His body sunk into the foam mattress as Wisp pulled at his trainers, trying to free his feet from within.

"Don't take them off. I sleep with them on now," he grunted.

Wisp sighed and lay down beside him gently stroking his soft brown hair. Jacob could feel his body giving into sleep and he tried to fight it but his eyelids settled and his breathing slowed. Wisp edged herself off of the bed and tiptoed towards the door.

"Sleep tight," she whispered as her hand hovered over the light switch.

She thought about turning the soft glow of the lightbulb off, but thought better of it. The door rested ajar and she walked back down the stairs towards her own room.

Her hand rested on the light switch and flicked it down just as a voice whispered, "Don't call out if you want your family to live. Let's make this as calm as we can, shall we. After all you knew I would be coming for you soon."

The room flickered back to black and an eerie silence settled over the house.

43

Screams shattered the peaceful sleep Jacob had managed to settle into. His eyelids flickered open just as the door flung open. Julie and the boys piled into the room, all of them shouting. The words got lost twisting on top of each other. Jacob managed to pick out a few.

"Wisp"

"The Raven"

"Why?"

Each word was accentuated with anguished cries and stinging tears. Jacob sat bolt upright and rubbed wildly at his eyes, forcing the sleep away.

"Wait, slow down, what's happened?" he asked with trepidation.

"He took her. My baby's gone again. I didn't think I could feel more pain than when I lost her the first time but my heart has been ripped out. She came back to me so fleetingly. I can't lose her," Julie wailed and crumbled on to the mattress, her body rocked with huge powerful sobs.

Jacob felt the familiar rise of panic. His hands shook and a cold clamminess crept down his back. His lips went dry and his nose began to flare.

This isn't happening. I can't lose both of them.

"I'll get her back somehow Julie," Jacob announced trying to speak with conviction.

"How?" she screamed with bitterness, "The police are waiting for you downstairs. They want to talk to you."

The boys stared at their mother, taken back by the rawness of her grief. They ran out of the room and downstairs into the comforting arms of their heartbroken father who was talking to the case detectives.

Jacob stared at Julie's quivering frame and stroked her shoulder, trying to ease her pain. She pulled away, repelled by his touch. Jacob sighed. He pushed himself to his feet and steadied himself on the headboard. Closing his eyes he took three deep breaths before making his way downstairs.

The boys were huddled into their father's chest. Jacob noticed the expression on the detectives faces. He had met them before but then they had been jubilant now their eyes were downcast. Deep worry lines sat across their foreheads.

"Hello Jacob, do you remember us? We met at the hospital."

"Yes, I remember," he replied blankly as the realisation began to sink in.

The detectives asked about Alex and Wisp. Endless questions about their states of mind, where Alex was going, how long she had been gone for before they realised there was anything wrong, what Wisp had said to him before he had gone to sleep and had he heard anything when she was taken. Jacob answered all of them as fully as he could. He occasionally glanced across at Wisp's Dad who was motionless in the chair.

"We've been to Jack's house and we've got teams positioned throughout the caves but he hasn't taken them there. Do you know anything else that could help us find them?"

Jacob paused and thought, deciding whether to tell them about the warehouse. He hoped they hadn't noticed but a sideways glance indicated to him they had.

"Erm, I don't know if this will help. We were trying to find out more about my Mum's death and we came across a photo of Jack. We were going to phone you and let you know once we had some more information but I met a bloke who knew my Mum. He said Jack had had a job at a warehouse off new road but that's all I know."

The detectives shared a glance and muttered their thanks. A PC was left in residence and the house emptied again. Jacob looked across at the Matthew's family. Julie had managed to navigate the stairs and had come to join her husband and sons. They huddled together trapped in their grief. Jacob watched them for a few minutes and realised he wasn't wanted or needed here. He grabbed his jacket from the peg and slipped out of the door whilst the PC was in the kitchen making tea for everyone.

44

Huge wrought iron gates circled the perimeter. Thick metal chains were woven through the bars and secured with a heavy lock. Jacob followed the gates around the building searching for a way inside.

"This is ridiculous. The first two were still working factories. This one looks derelict. I'm just gonna have to climb the gates, but how the hell am I going to do that?"

He looked around trying to find anything he could use to give himself a boost over the fencing. A pile of old broken pallets lay just outside the gates. His hands pulled at the branches that interlocked between the gaps in the wood. Single green leaves fluttered down into the undergrowth as he snapped and twisted the branches free. Broken splinters of wood dug beneath his fingernails as he heaved the pallets into position. Jacob grabbed some discarded bricks from deep within the dirt. Sludge slid free as he flipped them over and planted them against the bottom rungs of the fence. The wood shook when he lifted it into place and rested it against the metal poles.

"That should do it."

Grunting and struggling, he pulled his body up on to the bars whilst his feet clambered up the makeshift tower. Ten feet up, his hands reached a horizontal rail connecting all the bars together. Individual spikes protruded from the rail and Jacob steadied himself. His hands clasped the bars and he lowered himself down, dangling his feet towards the ground. His muscles began to tremor under the strain. He lined his feet up within the bars and used them as guidance for his decent. Shuffling his hands down he loosened his grip slightly and slid towards the concrete.

Overgrown grass tangled around his legs and jabbed into his jeans. His toes hit against the rail at the bottom of the gates. Springy green blades settled underneath his feet and he crouched down within them and surveyed the area. Rows of brick casted heavy shadows on to the grass and metal shutters rattled in the wind. Jacob watched and waited for any movement. No one came in or out of the building. He scuttled closer through the grass, keeping low to the ground. His heart was pounding in his chest and his eyes darted around the wasteland searching for any signs of life. Sunlight refracted from shards of glass scattered on the ground from the windows above. Placing his hands carefully amongst them he managed to weave towards the outer shell of the warehouse.

He reached the heavy metal doors and examined the chains woven between the handles. Jacob pulled out his phone and took a photo of the markings on the lock. It buzzed quietly as he hit send. The chains clanked metal on metal as he shook the door. He managed to pry his fingers in through the gap and used his phone as a torch, shining light through the crack. In the haze he could just make out a concrete floor and dust dancing in the sunlight.

Retreating from the door, he crept round the side of the building to find another way inside. An old broken ladder rested against the red brick wall. Jacob looked up at the building and saw the flimsy panes of glass rattling in the breeze. Some of the higher panes were cracked in the corners. He reached down and scooped up a stone, wound his arm back and lined up ready to throw. The stone ricocheted off of the wooden window pane and plummeted back down towards him. He ducked and rolled out of the way.

The smooth edges of the rock rubbed against his fingertips. He felt the weight of it, throwing it into the air a few times and catching it, before stepping back and lining up. It tumbled over itself as it hurtled towards the pane. Crashing through, shattered glass rained down on to the concrete floor inside. Jacob shuffled the ladder into place and tested the bottom rungs with his foot. It took his weight and he started to climb. Beads of sweat rolled down his nose and hung to the tip like a diver afraid to jump. Splinters of wood jabbed into his palms as he ascended up the wooden rungs. He paused as he reached the top and rifled through his bag until he found his jumper. Wiggling it free from his bag, he wrapped it around his fist and smashed the remaining glass into the warehouse. He hoisted himself up through the open window and sat on the edge, looking down to assess the drop.

A large metal casket stood a few feet below him. Jacob pushed himself away from the window sill and landed with a thud on to the metal frame. The glass crunched under foot, grinding slowly into his trainers. Dangling his feet down, he twisted his body round and lowered himself towards the floor. His feet hit the ground and he heard a low unmistakable tone.

"Hello Jacob, I've been waiting for you," heckled The Raven.

Jacob edged around the room, keeping his back to the wall. His eyes searched the shadows for the owner of the voice, whilst his feet kept him moving, heading towards the door. Reaching for the handle he felt cool metal in his grip. He pulled it slowly, testing whether it was locked. The heavy chains rattled on the other side.

"Did you really think it would suddenly be open?" laughed The Raven.

Jacob swallowed hard and adjusted his gaze to meet The Raven's eyes. His hand dropped down from the handle and settled on to the bulge in his pocket. He counted the buttons and pressed gently against the keys for reassurance.

"Where's Alex and Wisp?" Jacob asked trying to keep the tremor out of his voice.

"They'll be joining us soon," The Raven replied calmly.

Two distance voices carried across the empty warehouse. Jacob tried to make out what they were saying, straining his ears. His eyes searched around the vast open space. He noticed the metal girders suspended high above him. In the distance, grey concrete shimmered in the light. Jacob blinked and stared more closely. His eyes focused on the shards of glass protruding through the cement, sharp and jagged. Spots of red clung along the edges and drops of red scarred the floor. Three large metal pillars stood in the corners of the room. Jacob's eyes were drawn to the blackened slits just visible along the tops of each of them. He didn't need to see inside, the realisation of their purpose was apparent. His skin turned cold and his shoulder blades hugged his ears. Every nerve tingled and pulsed, his lungs burnt against the extra weight of breaths and thousands of thoughts bombarded his mind.

"In case you are wondering that one's yours. Would you like a tour of your new accommodation?"

"No, I won't need one, I'm not staying and neither is my sister or Wisp."

"So sure of yourself, that's interesting because I can hear every beat of your heart and right now it sounds like a freight train."

Jacob felt a shiver run down his spine. His eyes stayed fixed on The Raven's until sunlight streamed through the far window shimmering off of one of the metal boxes. A small indent lay in a rectangle along the top. He stared more closely at the small circle of steel protruding from the frame.

I think that's a lock.

"Well if you won't go in willingly…"

Black smoke snaked across the concrete towards Jacob's ankles. He darted right, leaping over the shards of glass and dashing towards the metal casket at the far end.

"There's no point running. There's nowhere to go."

Jacob's palm slammed into the steel. His chest heaved as he circled the box.

"Jacob, help me!" Wisp called from within.

He caught a glimpse of his reflection, his eyes were wide, trapped within dark circles. Glistening sweat clung to his face and his cheeks glowed red. He wiped his brow with his shirt as his eyes searched the warehouse for anything he could use.

"There's a hatch near the top. That's your only way out, but it needs a key."

"He's right Wisp, but unfortunately, I'm the key. I know, I'll help you out," the voice came from above.

Jacob's eyes shot up towards the heavy rafters. A cloud of black smoke descended upon him. His eyes stung, water welled and rolled down his cheeks. A gentle click, followed by a scream. Jacob rubbed at his face, blinking against the residual smoke. The cold steel mirrored his movements. Four tired eyes glared back at him. Two were yellow framed with glass. His jaw went slack and he spun round to find Wisp's vacant eyes staring.

"Wisp? Wisp! What have you done to her?"

"You wanted to see me, here I am," she replied.

Her head tilted to the right and her glasses sat awkwardly balancing on her nose. Dark circles wrapped around her fixed stare, whilst chapped lips blended with her paling complexion.

"Leave her alone!"

"No! Thanks to you I need to find a new home. Let's see what she can do."

Wisp lunged at Jacob, her fingers clawed at his cheeks. He ducked and weaved out of the way, noticing the mottled spots of black climbing her nails like damp on a wall.

"Hmmm, she's trying to fight me. Don't do that because now I have to break you."

Her right hand wrapped around her little finger on the left and wretched it back towards her wrist. The yellow flames dancing in her eyes receded. Her jaw dropped open and her head flung backwards. The bone cracked and her scream echoed throughout the empty space. Jacob covered his ears from the noise but couldn't pull his eyes away from her face. Her head lurched forwards again. Her eyes pleaded with Jacob until yellow filtered across the whites and a malevolent grin settled on her lips.

Jacob's shoulders slumped and his head fell against his chest. He carefully edged away. Wisp followed.

"Where are you going?"

"Please, leave her alone. Let them both go, you can

have me."

"Nice idea, but that ship has sailed. If you want them to be free; you'll have to earn it."

"How?"

"Wisp knows what I want you to do."

"I won't fight her."

"We'll see."

Her fist swung again narrowly missing his ear. Instinctively, his arms rose to protect his face. The second blow landed in his stomach and the third smashed into his side. Jacob winced. Flashes of white jumped before his eyes. His hand gripped his ribs and he panted through the pain. Glimpses of Wisp peered through the yellow veil. Jacob read her look, his lips fell.

"I'm sorry," he said, swinging his left fist.

His knuckles crunched into her chin, sending her head flying. It sprung back sharply. His right collided with her hip, whilst his foot clipped the back of her knees. She tumbled forwards and started clapping, slow and steady.

"That was a quick turnaround."

"I…"

"You don't need to explain yourself."

"Fight him Wisp. Think of your family and fight him. You are strong, you can beat him."

Wisp's mind struggled. Images of Corey and Liam flashed into view, black singed the edges. She fought against it, pushing the enclosing darkness away. The Raven squirmed. Traces of black withdrew from her veins. Her eyes scrunched up. Jacob, her Mum, her Dad, Alex and Todd fired up in quick succession.

"That's it. Keep focussing on them. You can do this," called Jacob from a few metres away.

She looked up. He could see her green eyes clearly. Yellow tinged the edges. Her legs and arms started to twitch. Glass jabbed into her skin. Wisp felt it and clenched her teeth together, fighting against the pain. Jacob desperately wanted to run to her, but he pressed his feet into the floor and tensed his calves, making his body feel heavier. Unsteadily, she rose to her feet and limped towards the second metal box. Her arm reached for the hatch. Twists of black smoke circled her fingers, clicking and crunching as it twisted in the lock.

Her body thudded on to the ground. Black smoke licked from her lips, clawing at the concrete, desperate to escape. It poured and twisted across the floor, heading for the third metal box. Jacob darted across the warehouse and crouched next to her. A lump of glistening red shone on her chin. Her eyes were closed. His hands rocked against her shoulders but she lay still and unconscious.

The hatch grated against the rungs and a voice called out.

"Jacob, help me out."

Jacob sprung to his feet and reached up towards the hatch. A hand then an elbow clambered into view. He gripped the wrist and pulled. Alex's head poked through the gap and she tumbled out into his arms.

"What happened?"

"He possessed Wisp. She fought him though, I don't know how, but she managed to make him open the lock."

"Is he still inside her?"

"No, the smoke went towards the box over there. Are you okay?"

"Yeah, I think so. I'm sorry for walking out, I just needed some space. I didn't think."

"Well this reunion is heart-warming but I've got to say I think I like being back in my old skin," said The Raven as Jack walked into view.

Smoke danced from his fingertips and flickers of blue crackled over his skin. He navigated the floor and stood before them. Heavy panting crept up from behind. Alex glanced over her shoulder and clung to Jacob. Hot breath lapped at their necks, whilst stained fangs dripped with yellow spit. It sizzled and popped as it burnt through the floor.

Alex saw the handle of a knife in Jacob's pocket. She pulled it free and flicked it into position. Jack lunged at her; his nails sunk into her arm and tore at her skin. She yanked it away and cradled it against her chest. Spots of blood dribbled through her fingers. She stepped back as Jacob lashed out at him. The blue flames singed the hairs on his hand, turning the flesh on his knuckles a smoky shade of black. Jack threw his head back, deep guttural laughter blared out. Jacob reached for the knife and sliced at Jack who jumped back, out of the way. His shoulders bashed against the powerful legs of the beast. Its paws pounded against Jacob's back, sending him hurtling across the warehouse. He landed with a thud and rolled on to his back. The world spun, dizziness caused everything to shake. The beast galloped towards him, chasing him down like a dog bringing a ball back to its master.

The shards of glass dug into Jacob's shoulder blades. He tried to wiggle free, but it nipped and pulled at his skin. His own breath rushed and jarred in his throat. Gasping for air, his lungs burnt. He knew instantly his ribs had cracked again. White and red lights shot through his vision. His hand clamped to his side. He tried to roll on to his front, but the ripples of pain exploded and he collapsed back on to the concrete.

The beast's head towered above him, moving closer, the jaws scratched at his neck. Drips of acidic spit splashed on his cheek. Instinctively, Jacob tried to wipe it away with his hand. His flesh bubbled and popped. White pustules grew causing his cheek to sizzle and the smell of burning flesh to fill his nostrils. He brushed his tongue along the inside of his mouth and swallowed, drawing air in through a gaping hole in his cheek.

Its jaws were on him again, running down his skin and nudging at his ribs. Jacob pulled his legs up and kicked at its neck. The wet matted fur fired off balls of dust, covering Jacob like an ash cloud. Spluttering, he lifted the knife up and swung at its head. His first blow missed sending him rolling to his right. Sparks of pain raced through his nerves. His eyes closed and he swung again. Fur sliced away, turning to dust. The knife sat high above his head. He stabbed at the air, forcing the blade towards the beast.

It saw the attack and raised its paw trying to block the sharpened metal. Jacob countered, swerving and striking the blade between its eyes. The heavy paw slammed into his head. Over and over, pressure and release. Jacob's head felt heavy, the rafters looked like they were falling towards him. Flecks of grey flickered across his vision. He held the handle of the blade, keeping the beast's snapping jaws at arm's length and jerked it down towards its eyes. Ripping flesh, sent dust and dirt into the air. Its paw crashed into his skull one last time before a subtle snap followed by a huge explosion rang in his ears. The dirt forced his head back into the concrete and everything faded to black.

Alex stood watching the action unfold, unable to move. Flashes of memories clumped and collided as The Raven poked through her head. One kept repeating; her Mum's death. Alex focused on the knife, how her Mum had grabbed it first. The Raven tried to twist the memory but Alex kept replaying it, never giving him the chance. Her eyelids slammed shut, blinking wildly. When they reopened fully, she saw Jacob lying in the distance and Jack standing inches away from her face.

"Why did you have the knife?"

"To kill her," The Raven replied.

"I wasn't asking you. I want to speak to Jack. Why did you have the knife?"

"Jack can't talk now."

"Yes he can. Why did you have the knife? I'm going to keep asking until you let him speak. You're keeping me here anyway. I want to know."

Synapses fired. Jack felt a tiny spark and a single memory flashed through the darkness. His eyes scrunched closed, gripping tightly to the thought. His arm jerked and the flames dancing in his eyes began to subside. Spluttering over his words, his lips felt funny and it took a few attempts to create the right sounds.

"I had it to scare her. I didn't mean for her to die. It all happened so fast. She grabbed it and I had to, otherwise it would have been me."

Alex paused and took a breath, watching his eyes and the ticks in his hands. She knew he was telling the truth.

"I believe you. I saw Mum grabbing the knife. I couldn't see your face at first, but I believe you. I know you didn't mean for her to die. You loved her and it killed you when she didn't want you, that was why you tried to frame my Dad, wasn't it?"

"He wasn't good enough for her. She couldn't see it. I was always just the friend. When I got sent down, I decided, no more. I was going to be in charge. I'm sorry. Now I know it was stupid, but this is my penance."

Alex swallowed, the lump in her throat hung in her neck. She saw the water clinging to his eyes and dripping over his cheeks. The yellow flames edged across the whites of his vision. He blinked and they retreated.

"You knew we were upstairs. You knew we would find her, but you still took her away from us."

"I was scared, the blood, the spray, the gentle thud of footsteps from upstairs. I knew what I had done. I thought Michael would come round. It was his night to visit. He would find her and…. I didn't think you and Jacob would have to see her. I didn't know her death would lead to all of this."

"I don't know if I can forgive you for her death, but I'm willing to try, but you need to end this. Stop him from hurting anyone else."

"How?"

His muscles snapped and twisted, spasms sent his limbs jerking in different directions. The yellow flames sprung back across his eyes and his hands pulled at the edges of his suit smoothing the fabric.

"Good try, but Jack can't talk anymore."

"He can't but I can. Jack, Wisp managed it. I don't know how but she fought him. You need to do the same. Think of something he can't manipulate. A happy

222

memory, a sad memory, anything he can't get his claws into. Think of it. Over and over, push him down and take back control."

Alex watched Jack's head twitch. His hands clawed at the callouses on his knuckles. Blood trickled at first then flowed down his fingers. Small particles of skin flaked to the floor. Jack's mind fought against the enclosing darkness, the tiniest memory grew and expanded, filling his mind and pushing the yellow away from his eyes, leaving Jack's sad sunken glare. He stared at Alex for a moment before he took a step towards her. She flinched, waiting for The Raven's smoke to settle on her skin. It didn't come, in its place a few mumbled words uttered with urgency.

"You have to seal the vents. Hurry, I can't keep him out for long."

Alex dropped to her knees and scrambled for Jacob's bag. Her hands raked through and threw items out over her shoulder.

"Please be in here, please come on."

The pile around her grew bigger. Her arm reached further into the bag, trawling the bottom. The tape felt smooth to the touch. She pulled it free and ripped at the material, tearing off long strips. Jack wedged them over the vents adding more and more in different directions and covering the keyhole. He grabbed the bottom of the hatch and pulled himself up into the metal box. His legs kicked against the sides.

"Quickly, he's fighting back. Shut the hatch as soon as I'm inside."

"I can't lock it though."

"There's a second lock on the side. It's a lever you need to pull it down. Ready?"

His body tumbled into the steel. She heard the clangs of bones on metal and a call from within.

"Shut it now."

She pulled Jacob's bag over to the casing and jumped on it, reaching for the hatch. It slid closed, as her fingers glided across the metal. Grasping the lever she pulled it towards the floor. It grinded and clicked into place then a voice muttered through the steel.

"Todd's in one of the rooms at the back."

Alex felt her heart flutter. She let go of the latch and turned towards the distance corridors. Jack let the memory slip momentarily and a tiny wisp of smoke licked at the tape and dispersed into the air. A cold shiver traced the outline of her spine. She turned briefly and checked behind her, before reaching up and smoothing the tape over the vents, sealing them shut. Alex shook the feeling off and hurried across the concrete, negotiating the glass and leaping through the sharp maze. She weaved through the corridors calling out Todd's name. Her calls were initially met with silence until a distant voice replied.

Inside, Jack regained the memory and pushed back against The Raven's attempts to twist its form. Smoke clawed at his lips and he gulped down the air, dragging it back down into the bowels of his gut. His stomach muscles tensed, whilst his mind clung onto the memory of Riley's death. He replayed it over and over, focusing on the knife, the spray of blood, her last breath. Tiny droplets of pain littered his cheeks but he kept his focus, knowing he needed to buy Alex and the others time.

She followed the voice down along the corridor. Huge metal doors on runners lined one side. She pulled the levers on each one. The doors rumbled open. Bleary eyed and tear stained, people emerged. Burns and deep wounds lined their arms and legs. Their faces were drawn, unsure of where they were or what was real. Alex tried to placate them and directed them up the corridor into the vast space beyond, whilst still searching. The final handle crunched as she pulled it. She yanked it down, using her body weight to click it into place. The door rolled slowly open.

A face stared back at her. It was pale, with dark circles resting under its eyes. Her nose tingled and burnt slightly. She felt tiny drops trickle down her face and her arms flung open, engulfing Todd's frame.

"Ow!" he called.

"Sorry, but we thought you were dead."

"He thought about it. I saw it in his eyes, but he decided to trap me here instead."

"I'm so glad to see you."

"Where are the others? Why are you here? What's happened?"

"The others are down there unconscious. The Raven took Wisp and I, then Jacob came looking for us. Jack helped us trap him. The Raven's locked in one of the metal boxes down there. We sealed up the vents."

"Where's Jack?"

"He's trapped in the box too."

"But how is he breathing?"

"Oh shit, we didn't think of that. Can you walk? Watch out for the glass, it's cemented into the concrete."

Todd rushed after Alex down the corridor. His footsteps matched hers. People milled about, shuffling around the walls, trying to find a way out.

Calls and shouts from outside, drowned out the noise from within. A bustle of bodies, then panic as the chains were cut and the doors flung open. Police ushered people out into the daylight. Todd grabbed Alex's hand, trying not to be carried away by the throng of bodies. Reaching the metal casket, she banged on the wall. A gentle rat-a-tat-tat came in reply.

"He's still alive. The Raven won't let him die. He needs him to live."

"You go to Jacob. I'll stay here and make sure nothing escapes. Send the police in my direction. I'm going to stay with The Raven. I'm going to make sure he never hurts anyone again."

Alex saw the look in his eyes and swallowed down her arguments. She leant in and hugged him, then walked away back towards Jacob.

"It's okay, it's over. Open your eyes Jacob please."

He began to stir, his eyes opened and he looked up at Alex.

"Has he gone?"

"I think so. Todd's going to make sure he doesn't come back. The police are here. I saw them take Wisp outside."

"The police? Todd? They must have traced my call. I hoped they would."

She dragged him to his feet and rested her arm around his back as he limped towards the large metal doors. Sunlight took over from the shadows and they walked into its gentle warmth.

45

Drips fell from the ceiling and landed on Alex's head. She wiped them away from her brow using the back of her hand, sighing heavily. Jacob looked down from the ladder and giggled.

"Sorry, I guess I put too much on the roller."

He clambered down the steps. Alex dipped her own brush into the paint and bent back the bristles using her finger. She counted quietly to herself waiting for Jacob to face her. As soon as he turned she let go of the tensioned hairs. Paint splattered across his t-shirt and over his face.

"No fair, I did it by accident," he laughed.

"So did I," she sniggered.

"What's going on in here?" Wisp and Julie asked in unison as they stood in the doorway.

"Nothing," Alex chuckled as she sprayed them with paint.

"That's it. It's war," Wisp giggled, grabbing a roller from the tray.

Paint splattered the walls as Wisp spun the roller between her palms. As Alex ducked for cover, Wisp seized her moment, grabbed the handle and painted a long white line down Alex's forehead and across her overalls. Alex spluttered as the paint coated her lips. Jacob jumped to her aid and used his roller to coat Wisp in a shiny white sheen.

"Cease! Cease!" Julie called from behind a cupboard.

Everyone paused to look at her. She saw the glints in their eyes and ran downstairs with the three of them in fast pursuit. Paint dripped on the floorboards and over the rug. Julie's eyes darted around the room. She backed up towards the door. Wisp was to her right, Alex was in the middle and Jacob was to the left.

"No, no, no no no!" she screamed and flung the door open.

She stumbled backwards on to the step and out into the cool night air. The others followed her outside and sprayed her with little droplets of paint.

Jacob's roller dropped to his side as the others continues to scuffle. His head tipped back and he sighed contently. The dark night sky hung above him. He watched the stars twinkle against the blackness and felt a single tear of joy roll down his cheek. Wiping it away he left a white streak under his eye. Wisp stopped, looked at him and ushered the others into silence. They all stood and followed his gaze to the stars.

"I never thought I'd be outside watching the stars again. It's almost 11 but the air's refreshing, it's not as cold as I remember," Jacob mumbled lost in his own thoughts.

"It's still such a strange feeling. I know it's been six months since the curfew, but this still feels as good as the first night we stood here," Wisp replied as Alex and Julie nodded.

"Come on, shall we finish this painting? Curfew might be over, but we still need to sleep," Julie suggested, ushering Alex back inside.

"Yeah, we'll be in in a minute," Wisp called after them.

"The house is looking good. I think a few more coats of paint and the bedrooms will be finished. Have you decided what you're going to do with your Mum's room yet?"

"Alex and I talked about it. We've decided for now we're going to leave it as it is. We know she's not here, but it makes us feel closer to her somehow. I know we're doing the house up but I think we all need some time to adjust, so I'm kinda glad I'm staying on with our foster parents until I'm 18. Everything might feel less raw by then," said Jacob.

"I think it's the right choice," Wisp replied.

"I suppose we better go back in and get this painting finished, but first…"

Jacob reached across and rested his hand on the back of her neck. His other hand brushed gently across her cheek, smearing the paint across her nose. He chuckled as she reached up and wiped the paint from her face on to his.

They bundled back inside and closed the door. The gentle click of the latch could be heard through the wood by the single black raven sitting high upon the street lights watching the stars.

Epilogue

Todd looked and saw the time passing like a clock lost in a Dali painting. He knew time was against him and nothing seemed to make sense anymore. The hands on the clock ticked by, the noise melted away and vanished around his body. He took one final look around and decided now was the time to leave.

Jack didn't flinch as he got up. Todd watched the rise and fall of his chest, slow and calculated. In his peripheral vision he noticed the whites of Jack's eyes had vanished completely amidst the spreading yellow. It had been weeks since Jack had moved but The Raven had remained silent in his cell. The guards outside had fallen silent too and Todd's stomach churned with nervous anticipation.

Jack didn't move as Todd walked past his cage, but as Todd reached to open the door, cackles of laughter rippled through the air, sending shivers down his spine. Shaking slightly his fingers stretched for the keypad and punched in the numbers. The weight of Todd's body pressed down on the handle and it sunk with a satisfying click. A spark of adrenaline raced through his body.

I can do this. He's been trapped here for months, he's in his cage and he's weak. I just need to check they're okay and then I'll be back.

He faltered one final time as the sunlight filtered through the strengthened panes of glass. It was just a second, but it was all The Raven needed. He had spent months preparing and now smoke slowly, quietly, seeped through the seals. Todd's eyes were fixed on the clock, watching the hands tick by. Forty seconds passed. Todd checked the cage. Black shadows and smoke danced around Jack's body. Despite the fear bubbling up inside, Todd tried to calm himself and momentarily turned back to the door.

Claws of smoke wrapped across Todd's knuckles. Pain ripped through his fingers, intense and pure. The Raven's thoughts poured into his brain. He clamped his arms around his head, trying to block the penetrating thoughts out with brute force. His nails dug into his scalp tearing at the flesh. Clumps of hair embedded themselves beneath his cuticles. Jack's lips curled into a momentary grin before drifting back into nothingness.

The intensity subsided and Todd was back in control.

"A passing gift to remember me by," heckled The Raven.

Todd stared at Jack and refused to move.

The seconds were still counting down and neither of them had changed position, then it all happened so quickly. Todd's hand freed itself from his head and snapped down on to the handle. He ran, his legs pounding hard into the sterilised corridor.

How did I get out? I can't think straight.

One thought played over and over.

Just run!

Bodies littered the facility, their eyes were closed and their limbs still. Their uniforms hung from their withered frames. Arms and legs were strewed across the floor. Guns rested in blood soaked palms but there were no bullet holes. Todd tried to stop and help but his legs refused to listen, leaping over the bodies with a strength and determination his mind was unsure of. His hand thumped into the exit bar and bright sunshine shone down heavily on to the tarmacked streets. The heat burnt through the soles of his trainers as he turned down street after street.

A group of kids were giggling and playfully arguing over a football. Ten pairs of eyes widened in unison as Todd approached. The screams grated harshly against his ears, he could sense the terror in their voices. Tiny feet scattered through open doorways, others were banging heavily on doors pleading to be let inside. Todd wiped at his face.

Why are they running? Is he following me?

He swung his head back and forth wildly trying to check over his shoulder, searching for the source of their screams. There was no one behind him and people were still scattering as he approached. A right turn led into the main high street. Sunlight glared off of the shop fronts. Todd caught his reflection in the glass, bloodshot eyes sunken and tired, exuding pain, whilst yellow flames danced from the eyes above him, piercing back into his mind. The wisps of smoke lapped at his skin, skirting around his neck. As the blackened nails slowly scored across Todd's cheek, he realised.

He needed me to leave. Shit, I carried him out. I've brought him back into the world. Whatever happens next is my fault. Please no not again.

The nails dug deeper searching through blood and bone for the very essence of Todd. He stumbled and dropped to his knees and The Raven began to tune into his brain, turning on all the forgotten memories, all the mistakes, all the wrong choices, the horrible words, the anger, the violence, every part of himself that he had tried to block out. The twisted notions of The Raven weaved into Todd's memories flooding forwards in a barrage on his senses. The darkness oozed from his skin, dripping like sweat from every pore.

Todd tried to fight, remembering happy memories, ones he had held onto deep within the chasms of his mind. Ones The Raven hadn't been able to change despite months of constant torture in the caves.

Instantly the urge to fight stopped. Darkness flooded in coating the memories like crude oil. Everything faded to black. No memories. No thoughts. The world vanished momentarily. Todd's eyes were open but there was nothing there. A cold wet trickle ran down his face. He reached up and wiped it away. A clammy stickiness resided and he brought his fingers down to his nose. The unmistakable smell of blood filled his nostrils.

Snap!

White light shone. Todd's body convulsed in agony as

The Raven sunk deeper, taking over every cell within his body, writhing like a snake to get comfortable in his new skin.

I'm so hungry. It's been so long. I need to feed.

Todd could hear voices and screams then the sound of footsteps quickening as they past him. One set after another, pounding against the cobbled streets, desperate to find solace from the twisting terror unfolding before them. He saw his arm stretching out across the cobbles and the sensation of hot and soft filtered through his brain, but he couldn't hold on to the thoughts. They bypassed his own mind and settled into The Raven's black void.

Todd's fingers sunk into a hairy sweaty leg. Its owner tried to pull away, but Todd felt his grip tightening, stronger and stronger until the bone shattered against his palm. A piercing scream danced through his ears. Todd wanted to let go but The Raven revelled in the orchestration.

It's screaming. It won't stop. Wait, no not it, he. He! It's a man not an it. It's a human being just like me. He probably has a family at home, friends. Real! Alive! Not an it.

Todd heard the screams subside and a wavering quiver he recognised as his own voice left his lips, "Not an it! Not an it!"

Despite the circumstances the sound of his own voice brought him some comfort, it was familiar, a part of himself The Raven couldn't take away. He felt his hand loosen its grip and he pushed himself up off of the ground.

"Please, please don't. I have a family, 3 kids and a dog. They are having a party for me, it's my birth…"

The gargle of blood weighed against his last syllables, trapping them and expelling them through the sudden rush of air and bright red that exploded from his throat. Todd looked down and saw his own hand, his fingers outstretched. His nails now a midnight black. He saw them protruding from a flap of flesh that hung just right of the man's jugular. His nails drew away from the neck and

Todd licked at them, lapping up the taste of pain, desperation and fear. It tasted like bitter chocolate and old rusty coins, but as the warm droplets rested on his tongue, it started to feel good.

Todd's fingers dug deep into the man's face. This man whose name he never knew, was now lying dead in front of him. His fingers prodded at his flesh, searching. A gooey heat oozed from his eye sockets. Internally, Todd recoiled as his nails squelched. He held the slimy spheres within his palms and crushed them slowly. Memories flooded into the void. Images of his first day at school, his first kiss, his wedding and the births of his children were all discarded and replaced with darkness. A single name, John, hit Todd like a flash of lightening. It dispersed as quickly as it had appeared, displaced with anger, John's anger. Every last drop flowed through Todd's veins.

What's happening?

His muscles locked and tightened, absorbing the anger into the sinews. The Raven grew stronger. Todd was just a passenger now. His eyes glazed to black, before the flickers of yellow appeared and faded making the world visible again. His last thought fixed in his mind.

I've got to get a message to them.

Acknowledgements

This book would not have been possible without the support of a lot of special people.

Thank you to my Mum and Dad for everything. For bearing with me through the stresses that go hand in hand with life. Thank you for all the other ways you've supported me over the years. The hours of unwavering support and love that has made writing this novel possible. You've helped me through all the ups and downs and there are not enough words to say thank you for all that you have done.

Special thanks to Lee for responding to my messages in the early hours of the morning, for letting me rant about the book, the characters and my inability to find the words I wanted to write. You have provided me with continual support and encouragement. You have been a sounding board for all my random ideas and have made me stop and reassess. You've laughed with me and been a shoulder to cry on when I thought I would never finish. Your words of wisdom really made the difference when I was ready to give up, so thank you.

Thank you to all of my friends who offered words of support and encouragement throughout the process and special thanks to Emma for your unwavering enthusiasm and continual encouragement. Your endless excitement gave me hope when balancing work and writing seemed like a never ending struggle.

Thank you to Keith and Lesley and all my friends at university that helped me find my feet when I started out on the journey of becoming a writer.

A big thank you to all the staff at Pen to Print who have given me the opportunity to write this story. Jaqueline, thank you for being my mentor throughout the manic process of writing and editing, for driving for hours to meet me and guiding me through the writing process.

Finally, I would like to say thank you to everyone who has picked this book up to look at the cover, to those who have flicked through the pages or read it intently in one sitting. Thank you for looking. Thank you for reading.

Lightning Source UK Ltd.
Milton Keynes UK
UKHW041044281118
333073UK00001B/74/P